⬦—⬥ PRAISE FOR ⬥—⬦
THE PERFECT PLACE TO DIE

"Fans of true-crime murder mysteries won't want to miss this one."
· *BOOKLIST*, STARRED REVIEW ·

"[This] novel will appeal to readers excited about an account of gruesome historical events steered by an intrepid young woman."
· *KIRKUS REVIEWS* ·

"[An] entertaining thriller…Moore deftly captures the bustle of 1890s Chicago, as well as the near-claustrophobic feel of the Castle."
· *PUBLISHERS WEEKLY* ·

"True crime buffs will appreciate the passages at the beginning of each chapter, which are excerpts from serial killer H.H. Holmes' published confession."
· *SCHOOL LIBRARY JOURNAL* ·

"Zuretta's gumption makes the heroine easy to root for, as she faces off with a murderer and also confronts the powerful men who don't see missing working class girls as a problem."
· *THE BULLETIN OF THE CENTER FOR CHILDREN'S BOOKS* ·

"An entertaining blend of historical fiction, thriller and an earnest look at how tough it was for women to get ahead in this era. Zuretta cracks it in the end though. Go girl!"

"Bryce Moore does a fantastic job at delivering suspense, mystery, and both lovable and horrific characters."

◇—❈ ALSO BY BRYCE MOORE ❈—◇

The Perfect Place to Die

DON'T GO TO SLEEP

BRYCE MOORE

sourcebooks
fire

Copyright © 2022 by Bryce Moore
Cover and internal design © 2022 by Sourcebooks
Cover design by Amanda Hudson/Faceout Studio
Cover images © VikaValter/Getty, Eduardo Morcillo/
Getty, MirageC/Getty, Renphoto/Getty
Internal design by Danielle McNaughton/Sourcebooks

Sourcebooks and the colophon are registered trademarks of Sourcebooks.

The characters and events portrayed in this book are fictitious or are used
fictitiously. Apart from well-known historical figures, any similarity to real
persons, living or dead, is purely coincidental and not intended by the author.

Published by Sourcebooks Fire, an imprint of Sourcebooks
P.O. Box 4410, Naperville, Illinois 60567-4410
(630) 961-3900
sourcebooks.com

Cataloging-in-Publication Data is on file with the Library of Congress.

Printed and bound in Canada.
MBP 10 9 8 7 6 5 4 3

For Daniela,
a most excellent daughter

PROLOGUE

In all cases both husband and wife were assaulted while they slept.

―――――――――――

W<small>HEN YOU HAVE THE SAME</small> nightmare two or three times a week for six years, you might think you'd get used to it. Even after all this time, as soon as it started to play out in my sleep, my stomach sank, and I wanted to throw up. It doesn't matter how many times you see your parents get chopped into by an axe. It never stops horrifying you.

I was back in my bed, ten years old, listening to my parents sleep while strange sounds came from somewhere else in the house. A steady scraping, like a woodworker planing a board. I hadn't woken my parents up back then, and I couldn't do it during the nightmare, either. I was forced to relive it, right down to the last drop of blood.

So instead of running to Papa and screaming for him to get our own axe or call for help, I rolled onto my stomach and tried to go back to sleep. Five minutes later, the scraping stopped.

And the footsteps began.

Nothing loud or steady enough for me to recognize, of course. Only enough to echo in my memory ever since. Enough to keep me up at night, wondering what would have happened if I'd only called out in fright. Mama and Papa would have been awake when the door burst open. Papa could have gotten an arm up to stop the first blow. My entire life might have been different.

But, that night, I only wanted to go back to sleep, and the Axeman flung open the door without any warning. I didn't see any of it, of course. My parents had the curtain up across our room to give them privacy. But I heard it *all*. My mother's shriek of terror, the wet *thunk* that sounded like someone chopping into a ripe melon, the crash of the lamp as it fell to the floor, scattering glass everywhere.

I stayed in my bed, a frightened little mouse, wishing for the sounds to stop and praying this was just a dream. Three more blows came in quick succession, and Mama howled in pain before her voice cut off after a final hit.

More footsteps as the Axeman ran out of the room, and only then was I brave enough to get out of bed. I inched the curtain aside. "Mama? Papa?" No answer came, only ragged breaths and a low moan. I padded over the floor to the light switch, stepping through something warm and wet and dreading what came next.

Why had I turned on the light instead of running after the monster? A single glance at that room had burrowed into my memory, haunting me ever since. Each of my parents lay in a pool of scarlet. Papa in the middle of the floor, blood pumping out of a wound in his neck that had laid bare the bone. Mama slumped on the bed, red flowing from a gash on her chin, trickling down her cheek and into her hair before it dripped to the floor. Blood splattered across their dresser and the wall, a spray of drops to match each blow.

The sight ripped the breath from my throat like I'd been punched in the gut. My ten-year-old mind couldn't grasp it, but I'd had plenty of time to relive it after each nightmare. It would fade to black now, and I'd—

The blood on the wall began to move, trickling left and right, up and down, defying gravity. I stared at it, confused. The nightmare never deviated. Not since the Axeman's string of attacks stopped seven years ago. I'd had variations back then, right after it happened. Enzo and I had thought I'd made some sort of psychic link with the villain that night. We'd tried to use those nightmares to guess where the Axeman might strike next.

Ten-year-olds can't help thinking of themselves as the hero of any story around them.

But, after those first few months, the nightmares had settled into a single routine. A song that never changed.

Until now.

The blood began to trace out words on the wall, coming together letter by letter to spell out a single message: *I'm coming.*

The nightmare swirled, and, when it stopped, *I* was the one standing before a door, holding an axe. *I* was the one who kicked it in and started chopping into people left and right. And, instead of horror at my actions, I felt…excited.

I woke breathless, my pulse racing and my heart pounding in my ears. After having relived the same nightmare for so long, this change made me sick to my stomach. *I'm coming*, the message had read. I tried to tell myself it was just another dream. That it made sense that the same nightmare couldn't continue unchanged, year after year. It had to vary eventually.

But I couldn't forget the feel of that axe in my hand, or the words written in blood on my bedroom wall.

I'm coming.

CHAPTER ONE

In the Crutti case, as well as in the Rissetto case, both of
which occurred within the present year, all the victims were
Italians.

———————

ENZO WAS MAD AT ME when I showed up to meet him. It was
never hard to tell. His shoulders got stiffer, and he shoved his
hands in his pockets like a thundercloud. He might as well have
been carrying a sign that said, "Gianna, you're late. Again." I held
up my hands in surrender.

"I know. I know. I'm a terrible person. I made you wait a whole
ten minutes, and now we're only going to be fifty minutes early
instead of an hour."

Some of the edge left his face as he fought back a smile, which
was a relief. I leaned up to him and brushed my lips against each of
his cheeks. Just because I'd told him I didn't want our relationship
to get any more serious didn't mean we had to treat each other like
strangers. This was the boy I'd practically grown up with, even if

it did look like he should have shaved again before coming out tonight.

"It's not the concert I'm worried about missing," Enzo said. His voice had gotten lower in the last year, and the rest of him had filled out even more. All that exercise, wishing he could be in the army, and now he was practically twice my size. "We haven't talked in two weeks, and you come by out of the blue asking me to meet you for this. I thought it would be good to talk first."

"Of course," I said, hoping my voice sounded as light as I wanted it to be. After the last nightmare, I'd needed someone to talk to about it. Enzo had been my rock years before. I'd thought and thought about bringing it up then. In the end, I'd just asked him to meet me tonight. But it was one thing to know you should do something, and something totally different to actually do it. Talking about the nightmare would make it *real*.

I looked around the street, unable to meet his eyes for too long at a stretch. We stood on the corner of Canal and St. Charles, 6:10 on a Saturday afternoon. New Orleans was gearing up for another wild weekend. Neon lights shone against the purple sunset, and people people people, filling the area with the noise of chatter mixing into the whir of the electric trolley and the clatter of automobiles and horses. The air was just cold enough to make you happy you'd worn long sleeves. Perfect. "Lighten up, Vincenzo Rissetto. We live in a wonderful city, and we're going to see Sidney Bechet, un clarinettista who could play for the gods."

He cocked an eyebrow skeptically. Enzo didn't view music the same way I did, and he wasn't too keen on taking God lightly, either. Was it any wonder we didn't always get along perfectly? Still, he hooked his arm into mine just like he used to, and I found myself blinking back tears. *This was all going to be better with Enzo on my side,* I told myself. I just had to somehow force myself to go through with it.

Better to get my mind off that as fast as I could. I hung my head and slouched my shoulders and said, "You're right. I'm late, and I shouldn't have been. There was this sassofonista I'd never heard on the corner of Bourbon and Toulouse, though. He was good, and I stopped to talk to him. He's straight from Chicago, and he wants to play with some of the groups here. I gave him a few tips, and I lost track of time."

"You haven't eaten yet either, have you?" he said.

"I'll eat on the way," I replied, then pulled him north along Canal. My ankle flared up with pain for a moment, and I stumbled, leaning on Enzo before I caught my balance.

"Are you okay?"

I waved off his concern. "You know me. I'm always tripping or bumping into something or other. I must have twisted my ankle earlier today—it's been bothering me all evening. Have you read the news? How are things in Europe?"

"They're starting another push after Saint Mihiel," Enzo said, glancing at my ankle once before diving into a discussion about the Great War, military tactics, and a whole bunch of other things I didn't really understand. I let him talk, though. That had always been our understanding. I did my best to follow his obsession with the war, and he tried to develop a love for jazz. Never mind that one of those was a much bigger favor than the other.

"I should never have let you talk me out of enlisting last year," Enzo said.

"Thousands of Americans died just two weeks ago, and you're sad you missed out on it?"

"They need more troops. I could make a difference."

"There are over a million American soldiers there. And, besides, you were sixteen when you wanted to enlist, and you looked like you were fourteen. If you'd have shown up, they'd have laughed you out of the room. And what about your parents? What sort of son lets his disabled parents run a store by themselves while he's off trying to get killed in Europe? If the war is still going next year when you're eighteen, you can go and do your duty then. Let's stop here. I'll have a…how do you say it in English? Ananas?"

"Pineapple."

"Pine apple. I always forget that silly word for it. It isn't made of pine, and it tastes nothing like an apple." I dragged him along to a nearby grocer. "I would like a pine apple for dinner. Would you buy it for me, though? I'll give you the money, but Signora Caravaggio said I need to be especially careful about strangers and disease for the next month."

"You make fun of me for being worried about time, but you're much worse about your superstitions."

The smile left my face. "Fate will kill you, Enzo. Being late won't. And who can put a price on knowing what the future holds? The influenza is everywhere. It will be here in New Orleans soon enough, and I'll be ready."

He closed his eyes and tilted his head to the side, his way of saying "I think you're silly but I'm going to humor you," which he did because he knew, if he said it out loud, I'd have more to say about it. I let it slide. I had been ten minutes late, after all.

But, when he bought the pineapple and the grocer sliced into it, my mind flashed back on the nightmare. *The axe arcing down, plunging into his head with a moist* thunk, *blood welling up around the edges as I watched, enraptured.*

I blinked my eyes and shook my head slightly. *Think happy thoughts, Gianna. Sidney Bechet. Crisp, cool air. Time well-spent with your best friend.* The grocer gave him the pineapple, now neatly cut into seven long pieces, like a yellow watermelon. He had the knife tucked into his off hand, the glint sending me for a moment back to that room. To the screams…

"You want the whole thing?" Enzo asked as we resumed walking. He stared at me for a moment, and I wondered if my expression had given me away.

"Do I want to eat an entire pine apple by myself? Do I look like I'm two people hiding in one coat? The other half is for you. You probably have to eat twenty times a day to keep all those muscles happy."

"You've been speaking less English the last few months. Your accent is getting stronger."

"Non mi va," I said. "I speak it well enough when I need to, and I only need to when I'm out and about with you doing all of this. There are enough Italians in this city to let us ignore all the rest the same way they ignore us, no? Signora Caravaggio says I will marry a good Italian man."

Enzo blanched.

"No," I told him. "Not tonight. We're not going over that again. Tonight is for Sidney Bechet and *pineapple*." I tried to say the word with as strong of an American accent as I could manage to show him I was getting it down right. I could *think* the language just fine, but, when it came out of my mouth, it tended to get a little muddled.

"Business is good?" he asked me in what I'm sure he thought was a casual tone.

"What?" I looked up at him over the slice, juice running down the corner of my mouth. "Why are you doing this? We are out for a walk and jazz and the night air, not to talk about why I spend too much money and how my family and your family are so different even though they are the same. Have some pine apple. You'll talk less."

I chided myself. He'd made a stray comment, and I'd overreacted.

I'd told myself I wouldn't do that when I sent him the letter asking him to come with me to this performance. Papa had told me I'd have to keep my tongue in check. "You're wonderful with strangers, Gia," he'd said. "Now you need to work on treating your friends and family the same way." Mama had only rolled her eyes.

Enzo and I continued down Canal Street, heading for the Orpheum Theater. It was still being built, but it was finished enough to have some events. Since they closed Storyville, all the excitement had to move somewhere. While that somewhere was being figured out, they used places like the Orpheum to keep things going. Tonight's concert was just for those in the know, but I made it my business to stay on top of anything connected to music in New Orleans.

We paused when we got to the theater, only nine blocks or so from where we'd met. Enzo wanted to go in, but I insisted we finish the pineapple first. "That's all I need. For us to get kicked out because we couldn't eat the fruit ahead of time."

"Do you think you'll play in there one day?" he asked, looking up at the stone theater. It was made from granite blocks. A smooth gray front broken up in sections by carved panels of vines and urns, with a straight overhang protecting the main entrance from rain.

I finished the last bite of my slice and shook my head. "An Italian girl, playing on a big stage? I'd have to practice more to get there, and when am I going to have time to practice? I already have the pastor mad enough as it is. He doesn't like anything but

Bach being played on his piano. Bach was a good guy, but *these* hands were not made for Bach." I held up my juice-covered fingers, shrugged, and licked them clean.

When I finished, Enzo was staring at me. For once, I couldn't read the gaze. I thought I'd been masking the feeling in the pit of my stomach well enough, but it might have been peeking out the edges.

"Enzo!" I said, snapping him out of his reverie. "What is it? Pine apple on my cheek?" I rubbed at my face.

"It's gone now," he said.

I turned and looked at the rest of the street. "Ah!" I cried out, seeing my friend and waving to the jovial-looking Black man standing just around the corner. "Harry!"

He paused and squinted in our direction. I laughed and pulled Enzo along. "What's the matter, Harry? Do your glasses make you ugly?"

As we got closer, the man broke out into a smile. "Gianna! What are you doing waiting out here? You think they're just going to open the doors and let you in?"

"People open doors for me wherever I go," I said. "But I was not done with my snack just yet. Unless the Orpheum would like to taste some pine apple as well? I could have dropped it all over the seats and the carpet."

Harry grimaced. "The Orpheum owners don't exactly know about Bechet playing here for an audience. It's more of a…rehearsal. Some of the fellows working on the place have keys, and they knew it was going to be empty tonight. Shame to let a stage sit lonely when it could be put to good use. So, yeah, maybe your pineapple was better left outside."

We followed him down an alley to an innocent back door that led to a tangle of corridors and rooms lined with covered boxes, ropes, tools, and sawdust. I chatted with Harry about the concert and who else might be there, and Enzo followed in our wake. Then Harry opened a door, and we moved from a construction zone into the middle of a palace.

The main auditorium was cavernous. Blood-red velvet seats for well over a thousand lined the main floor and the three balconies. A crystal chandelier five times as big as me hung from the ceiling, and the walls were covered in ornate blue and gold decorations. The stage was to my right, framed by a drawn red curtain with gold trim. A group of men stood there already, chatting and tuning their instruments, playing licks of songs, riffs, and arpeggios. The sound echoed more than it did in a club. Less crisp, but much larger. It wasn't quite right for jazz, but it was different, and you never knew how a change would make you see parts of the music you didn't catch before.

Harry waved goodbye to us and went to join some of his other friends: the main floor already had around a hundred people there, though that still left the vast majority of the seats empty. I let him go, turning to Enzo. "È incredibile, vero? Come on. I want to see what it's like from the balconies."

A man sat next to a table with an upturned hat in the middle of it, filled with coins. He cocked an eyebrow at us, and I laughed, digging into my purse as Enzo reached into his pocket. "I can pay for both of us," he said, but I shook my head.

"I've been saving up." If he paid for me, then he'd think of this as a date. If he thought of it as a date, things might get messed up between us again. Better to have firm boundaries, and anyway, what was another dollar? It wouldn't be enough to keep my parent's store open longer. I dropped the four quarters into the hat and put the worries behind me.

The man nodded his thanks, and Enzo and I padded off down the aisle, only getting lost once as we looked for the way upstairs. The railings were smooth brass, the carpet soft and new. "Are you sure we should even be here?" Enzo asked, unable to keep from looking over his shoulder. "This is trespassing."

I shook my head. "Sometimes you're a mouse, Enzo. A tiny little mouse. It's Saturday night. Take a break from your worrying and have a good time. The police aren't going to barge in here and arrest you. You worry about rules too much."

We came to the balcony, and I went straight for the front center seats, sitting down and putting my feet up on the railing, throwing my arms wide and smiling again. "This is the place for me. Like a queen, right in the middle of the theater. Best seat in the house."

"Don't you want to be closer to the music?"

"We can move around when we want, but it won't start for a while. We can enjoy the view here for now."

Enzo stared down at the stage, not meeting my eyes. "Can you tell me what's going on?"

I froze, hoping the grin on my face hadn't dropped at all. "What do you mean?"

"Gianna. You used to talk about how easy it was for you to read me like your fortune-teller reads a pack of cards, but sometimes *you're* just as easy. You've gone quiet three times this evening, your eyes going distant. You jump at loud noises. What happened? Is it the store again? Your parents? Two weeks ago you told me you thought we should be apart for a month, and then you change your mind halfway through and ask to go out again? Don't get me wrong—I'm glad you did, and I hope we can iron things out. But something is wrong, and don't tell me it isn't."

The axe plunged into his skull. I had to jerk on it to get it unstuck, and when it came free, blood arced into the air, warm and wet.

I nodded. "The store. Papa's health is off and on, and times are tough. The neighborhood isn't like it was seven years ago, with the rent going up and the kinds of people changing. Not as many Italians now."

Enzo stared at me, his lips turned down in slight disappointment. "You think I'm an idiot, don't you? It's the nightmare again. I can't think of anything else you'd be trying to avoid this hard."

I leaned back in the seat. "When you have un incubo, it's better not to think about it. Thinking about it makes it more real. Talking about it to someone else makes you remember it even more. This one, I don't want to remember."

"But you've had it for years. What's changed?" He stared at me a moment longer before his eyes widened. "You had another one like the ones back then."

For Enzo and me, there was only one thing that "back then" ever meant. Seven years ago, when we first met. Some people had lovely stories about how they met their friends. New in school. Or at the playground. My parents were attacked in the middle of the night by a man who broke into our house with an axe. Two months later, the same man broke into Enzo's house to do the same thing. It was a miracle no one had died. Was it any wonder I'd started having bad dreams about it? Though, because we were ten, we somehow thought the nightmares were connected to the Axeman. That I was seeing into his head.

"Who can remember how bad they were?" I said, still trying to keep a light tone to my voice. "But they're more often now than they have been since then, and this last one was more…specific."

"Specific how?"

"I don't know," I snapped, folding my arms and taking my feet down from the railing. "I don't *want* to know. I don't want to think about them or remember them or talk about them. I want to sit here with my friend and listen to jazz music and forget."

He chewed on the inside of his cheek for a moment, thinking it through. If he knew what I knew, he wouldn't have hesitated.

If it were just a bloody nightmare, I could have dismissed it. I'd had a traumatic experience when I was ten. It made sense I would have nightmares about it years later. Memories of the attack itself, or the blood in the room after he'd left. My mother gasping for air as blood poured from the wound in her neck, my father still as a corpse, his head wound pulsing.

When I'd asked Enzo out this morning, I'd intended on spilling everything to him, but, now that he was here, I couldn't force myself to go through with it. We'd made that promise all those years ago. But it was easy to promise something when you didn't really believe it could ever be possible, and the world looked different at seventeen than it had at ten.

"You'll tell me if it gets worse?" he asked at last.

"Of course I will," I said. "I'll tell you before I tell anyone else, cross my heart."

Whether it was my expression or my words, Enzo let the matter drop. It was better that way, I told myself, even if part of me hated myself for being such a fraidy-cat. All I wanted was to listen to jazz. When a band was playing, I stopped being in the past or the future. I could just live in the music. The pastor might like Bach, but there was no life in Bach. It was all rules and order, as if someone had planned everything out in advance. Classical music had all the excitement of a bowl of oatmeal.

Jazz? Jazz was different each time you heard it. Even the same song could be totally new with a different set of players or instruments. The drums and piano would lay down the field, and then you'd have the bass tie those together, letting the clarinet roll around wherever it wanted, while the trombone slid in between. It was a conversation through music. There could be funny parts or sad parts. When someone played jazz, you could connect with their soul in a way like nothing else.

And it was *new*. New composers. New techniques. New rhythms. Sometimes I would look around at other people in New Orleans and wonder if they had any idea how lucky we were to be here. I couldn't imagine living anywhere else—any*when* else.

So for that evening, I let the jazz music carry me away. Enzo and I listened to the first few numbers up in the balcony, and then I dragged him down to be closer to the stage. We joined the rest of the audience, crowding up to the front, standing and dancing in the aisles and in our seats. Applauding the solos. Calling for more.

Sidney Bechet was a dream. Twenty years old. Strong and handsome in a dark suit and white hat. His fingers flew across the keys of his clarinet, diving and soaring with the melody like a bird. The group hadn't played together too often: you could tell by the way the musicians took turns more than normal. It was just like a party. Any time you got a few new people together, it took a while before they really became themselves. Until that happened, people would be more respectful and restrained, letting someone else finish completely before they dared add something to the conversation.

When a jazz group knew each other well enough, their music became something bigger than a series of individual solos. Each line twisted and surrounded the others. But I was willing to forgive

DON'T GO TO SLEEP

the players falling short of that peak. Bechet's performance alone was worth ten times what I'd paid, and the trombonist was almost as good as Frankie Dusen. I'd want to watch him as well if only Armstrong could have made it.

By the time the concert was over, I felt light as a cloud. My ankle was hurting more than it had been, but there were some songs you just had to dance to, injured or not. Enzo and I talked to a few more of the audience members, and then we followed Harry back out through the twists and turns of the backstage to get into the open air again.

"That was incredible. Assolutamente incredibile!"

Enzo smiled back, but it was the same sort of smile I gave him when he told me about an American victory in Europe. It took a bit of the edge off my feeling, but I didn't hold it against him. He'd come around eventually.

The air had turned colder while we were in the Orpheum. Thin clouds peppered the sky, hiding the moon behind a silver veil. I rubbed my arms and wished I'd brought a jacket. It had to be in the low sixties, at least.

"We should get back," Enzo said, noticing my movement.

I forced my arms down. "Nonsense. It's only 10:30. We should go for a walk. Get the blood moving. Harry was saying there might be another concert across town at midnight. Do you want to come?"

"Church is still going to be at nine tomorrow," he said, glancing up at the sky.

I laughed. "You can sleep through church better than I can. Your mother will drag you there half awake, and then you won't have to worry about anything until she prods you when it's over."

"Fine. We'll walk some and see if you can put up with the cold."

"How about we stop by my house and pick up a jacket? It'll be on the way."

We headed back into the Vieux Carré. Bourbon Street was in full swing still, of course, but all of it was just normal to me. The sights and sounds. People calling out to each other. The noise from bars spilling out into the streets. I'd grown up with it. Maybe that was why I noticed the small differences. The way people stood a bit stiffer. The laughter felt more forced. Was it nerves about the Great War, or about the stories of influenza heading this way?

The more we walked, the more things seemed off to me. There was more liquor, for one thing. People seemed set on getting drunk to forget themselves. More anger. We passed two fights before we even made it to Conti Street. Not just yelling: punches and kicks. We crossed the street and kept walking. A grown man—an Italian—stood in the middle of Toulouse, sobbing. The crowds parted around him, no one wanting to approach him.

Twenty yards farther down the street, a man stood in a sandwich board that read DEATH COMES FOR US ALL. He wore some sort of mask over his mouth, almost as if he were in a hospital. The fabric was frayed and stained. When he made eye contact with me, I broke the gaze as quickly as I could. When I glanced back—after we were well past him—he was still staring at me.

My stomach churned like I was going to be sick. For a moment, I stopped and leaned against one of the pillars holding up the balconies that ran the length of the streets.

"Are you okay?" Enzo asked.

I nodded, focusing on keeping my mouth closed and my food down. If I'd eaten recently, I wasn't sure I would have been able to hold it back. "It feels wrong," I said once I had myself under control.

Enzo looked around, confused. "What does?"

"Everything. The city. Like it's…sick."

"We need to get you home."

I closed my eyes, taking some deep breaths. When I opened my eyes, a newsstand across the street caught my attention. As soon as I noticed its papers behind the counter, I knew what I had to do. I straightened and crossed over to the stand. It was late, but they were still open, selling cigarettes to the people out on the town.

"I need a paper," I told the man running the place.

"Sunday's isn't out yet."

"*The Times-Picayune*," I said, fishing into my purse for a few pennies to cover the cost. "Today's."

He plucked one off a pile and handed it to me. "Free," he said. "Viva l'Italia."

I thanked him, forcing a smile. There were advantages, being Italian in a city where so many people disliked Italians. I took the paper and went to stand underneath a gas light, wishing it were turned up brighter.

"What are you doing?" Enzo asked me.

"There's something in here I need to read."

"Did you hear about something that happened?"

I ignored the question, flipping through paper and scanning the headlines. Someone had actually died of the influenza yesterday. I hadn't realized it had gotten that far along. Last I'd heard, there were just a couple of ships in the harbor that were under quarantine, coming over to New Orleans from Panama. The news was bad, but it wasn't what I was looking for.

There was another battle gearing up in France, this time around a place called the St. Quentin Canal. That was serious, but why would that have sparked with me? I kept flipping, sifting through the news about upcoming dances and new construction projects. Nothing clicked, but something drove me to keep searching, though I didn't know why.

I reached the end, and I went back a second time. Maybe it was a fever, and I wasn't thinking straight, or I might—

BROTHER'S RAZOR INVOLVES HIM IN DOUBLE KILLING.

It was right on the front page, but I'd dismissed it the first time through. When I came across it now, a passage immediately leapt out at me: "Early investigation indicated the victims had been hacked to death by an axe. Careful examination of the bodies several hours later, however, showed the murderer had cut the throats of Maggio and his wife with a keen instrument, then had beaten their heads with the axe to cover traces of the real death weapon."

I read the whole article. An Italian couple—the Maggios—had been attacked in the middle of the night while they were sleeping in their home, just off their attached grocery store. The assailant had run off into the night, leaving the couple bleeding from multiple axe wounds.

"Santo cielo!" I stared up at Enzo, pushing the paper to him and jabbing my finger down on the article.

He snatched it out of my hands and read it quickly. "It's close to what happened before, but—"

"Not close," I said. "No. It *is*. I can feel it, Enzo. Feel it in my soul."

"This says it was Maggio's brother. The Axeman went away," he said, shaking his head. But he said it like a parent would tell their child there were no monsters under the bed. "We're safe. There's nothing to worry about." Seeing Enzo—big, muscled Enzo— with that expression made me feel a little less guilty about the fear gnawing at my gut.

And, when I realized that—when I put a name to the feeling that was overwhelming me—old habits kicked in. Ever since the attack, I'd forced myself to be outgoing. Outspoken. I didn't want anyone to think I might be the same frightened girl I'd been that night, no matter how I might feel inside.

"Worry?" I forced my eyebrows up, and I stepped forward to place my hands on his shoulders, staring at him. "Who's worried?" I asked, swallowing the pit in my stomach and putting on a brave face. I'd made a promise to myself years ago, and those are the promises you keep. No matter what.

He drew back a few inches, examining my face. "You're not making any sense."

I dropped my voice down low enough so that only he would be able to hear me. "When my parents were attacked when I was ten, it ruined my world. My mother still checks the doors and windows three times each night, making sure they're all locked. My father doesn't laugh the way he used to, and his foot drags when he walks. Never mind that scar over half his face. I thought my life was over when I saw them there, screaming and covered in blood. But I met you, and you helped me through it. You'd had the same thing happen. You didn't treat me like some sort of doll that should be put on a shelf because it might get broken.

"The Axeman stole our childhood. Our innocence. And he got away. The police didn't catch him. The police didn't care enough. You and I tried, thinking my nightmares were clues, but we were ten. How were we going to do anything real? He got away, and I've had to live with that for seven years. I accepted it. But we promised ourselves back then, Enzo. *Promised.* He got away, but, if we caught his trail again, we'd put an end to him."

"You're saying we should go to the police?" he burst in.

I wanted to throw up. Run and find a bed to hide under. But wasn't that why I'd reached out to Enzo again? With no one else around, I didn't have to do anything, but with him there, I knew it would force my hand. "The police? Damn the police. They were worthless then, and they'll be worthless now. No, God gave me these nightmares for a reason. You think I'll be able to go to a police station and tell them I'm having visions of the Axeman's attacks? What did your parents say when we tried to tell them seven years ago? They thought we were insane. The police will think so, too, or else they'll think I'm the Axeman myself. We won't go to the police."

I pressed my forehead against his, forcing excitement I didn't feel into my eyes and my voice. "You and me, we're going to catch that demon ourselves."

CHAPTER TWO

Police...uncovered clews which they declare point to Andrew Maggio, a barber, as the slayer of his brother and sister-in-law, Joseph Maggio and wife, in their bedroom... at Magnolia and Upperline streets, where they conducted a barroom and grocery.

———

S AY ONE THING FOR ENZO: when he knew what he wanted, he went after it immediately. True, sometimes it could take him time to figure out what that was, but, as soon as I'd told him what I wanted, he didn't try to talk me out of it. Didn't question me or say we needed to think this through some more. He got to work figuring out the next steps.

And wasn't this what I'd wanted? Why I'd gone to Enzo again even after how our friendship blew up two weeks ago? Mama had told me once of one of her uncles, a sailor who'd dealt with mood swings his whole life. One night, he'd taken a cannonball and tied it to his leg before jumping off his ship. That's what going to Enzo had felt like now. You made the commitment to what you wanted, and you took away any chances you might have of reconsidering afterward. Enzo had made the same promise I had, seven years ago. Backing out now would disappoint him in a way I wasn't ready to handle.

But what had Mama's uncle felt like once he'd hit the water? Had he had the same sort of nausea and regret? Or had he even had time to think much of it before he was swallowing seawater?

Meanwhile, Enzo was barreling forward with plans for tomorrow. We'd meet up after church and go over to Freret, where the attack had taken place.

"Gia," he said as we walked up to my house, the windows dark, the streets empty. "I was happy to get your letter. After last time, I'd thought...I don't know what I'd thought. But, when I saw your handwriting, it was...nice. And maybe you just reached out to me because of your nightmares, but I'm still glad you reached out. I should have done it myself, but..."

He trailed off and waved his hand in front of his face in dismissal. "I don't know what I'm saying. Never mind. I'll see you tomorrow, okay?"

I stared off at him as he left, wondering how I could have such a mixture of feelings all at once, and wishing things could just be like they'd been even three weeks ago. But thinking about Enzo that way was exactly the wrong thing to do right now. If we could make it past the Axeman, there'd be time to figure the rest of it out later.

It was a long night, filled with restless sleep and nightmares I couldn't remember when I woke. My eyes drooped enough during church that I thought Mama would kill me with her glares. But Papa leaned over to her and whispered something that quieted her down. By the time the service ended, my roiling stomach was enough to wake me back up.

My family went to Saint Augustine's. Enzo's went to the Saint Louis Cathedral. Our families were separated by a twenty-minute walk through the city, but that twenty minutes made the difference between social classes. The cathedral was right in the middle of everything, beautiful and white and proud, with three steeples pointing to God and a congregation as white as the steeples. His family passed three other Catholic churches to attend this one each Sunday, just so they could be seen by the other people who went there. To show they were accepted. Respected. It was an exclusive club, and Enzo's parents could keep it.

Enzo was in his suit, brown and stiff, scratching at his collar when he thought no one was looking at him. I waved to him. "Salve, come va?"

He smiled back, though he waited until he was closer to answer. "How was church?"

"Boring as always. Whoever thought all that Latin was a good idea had to have been hit in the head one too many times, and may God strike me dead if I'm lying."

Enzo grinned, though his eyes widened just enough for me to know I'd shocked him. I'd missed that expression.

I jerked my head to the left. "Come. We'll walk to the streetcar. If we hurry, we can be home in time for supper, and my parents won't start getting the wrong ideas." Though better they thought I was off seeing Enzo than that they knew what else we were getting up to.

"You're not having second thoughts?"

"No," I lied, even though the thought of going to that crime scene was enough to make me light-headed. "What's the worst that happens? We get on the streetcar, we go for a ride, and we come back. We're out the price of a fare, and that's all. Let's walk. Enjoy the sun."

Nature had delivered a day in the low 80s for the last day of September. Fluffy clouds and a nice breeze. In the summer, an unseasonably warm temperature made you want to die. In September? It made you love the city, smells and all.

There were a few street musicians on different corners we passed. An accordion player, a trombonist, and a violin, each of them playing solos to the world, their music fading in and out as we continued on our way. Normally I loved the way the musicians of the city made it seem like a never-ending song, but there was a space between the violin and the trombonist that the tunes came together like a funereal dirge, discordant and unsettling. As much as I wanted to seem like I wasn't worried about what was coming, I knew that was a lie.

The thought of going to where the family had actually been

attacked made my knees weak. Seven years ago, I'd been so frightened when the Axeman struck us in the middle of the night. I'd done nothing. Gone still as a board and watched as my parents were mutilated. After that, I'd promised myself never to do nothing again. No more using fear as an excuse.

I'd just never thought I'd had a chance to really follow through on that promise. The pit of fear that had burrowed into my stomach was disappointing, but also undeniable. Part of me hoped by going to the scene of the crime, something would stand out to prove this wasn't from the Axeman. A bigger part roared in frustration that I would even think such a thing. Had I just pretended to be fearless for so long I'd fooled myself into believing it?

"Did you have another nightmare?" Enzo asked me.

"No," I answered, dodging around a couple of tourists standing in the middle of the sidewalk, consulting a map.

"Did you try?"

I spread my hands. "To force myself to have a nightmare? We went over this last night. You tell me how to try to do something like that, and I'll give it a shot. It's not something I can force. It just happens."

"You dream about what you think about before you go to sleep. Everyone knows that."

"Then everyone's wrong," I said. "I haven't stopped thinking about the nightmare since I had it, but, last night, I didn't dream at all."

"Did you drink the warm milk, like I told you to?"

"Mannaggia! Nothing happened. I tried."

"Maybe it will get easier with practice."

I didn't respond to that one. The truth was, I didn't *want* to have another dream or nightmare. I didn't want any kind of connection to the man who'd attacked my family, Enzo's parents, and three other families. Just thinking about it made my head pound, the sun going from cheerful to glaring. I wasn't even sure this was all going to work. We didn't know the nightmares had anything to do with the Axeman, other than what we'd guessed at when we were ten. All I knew is they were getting worse, they might be connected, and I wanted them to stop. When you were desperate, you tried anything you could think of. I might use the nightmares to catch that demon, but that didn't mean it made me happy to use them.

After a few deep breaths, I said, "Thank you."

Enzo glanced back. "For what?"

"For coming with me. For caring. For believing me."

"I want him caught as much as you do," he said.

"I know." It was easy sometimes to think Enzo didn't care about things as much as I did, just because he wasn't as loud about them. But he thought more about things. Considered them out in his head. When he decided to do something, he was smarter about what he did.

"Come," I said. "The car will be here in five minutes, and, if we miss this one, we might as well walk, for how long we'd have to wait for the next. I am not getting to the scene of the crime breathless and sweating like a pig."

We hustled ahead, focusing on navigating the crowd to get to Canal Street, where we'd pick up the streetcar that should get us within a couple of blocks. The Maggio store and barroom was across town, in Freret, on the corner of Magnolia and Upperline. It would take around fifteen minutes by streetcar.

It wasn't nearly as busy as it was during the week, but the nice weather had inspired many people to go out for casual strolls, and we earned our share of nasty looks as we kept dodging between people who seemed set on walking as slowly as possible. On the second story of the buildings we passed, others were standing on their balconies, smoking or talking or just watching the city go by. I should have been one of those people. Enjoying the day instead of morbidly going to see where a woman died.

Maybe, if I did things right this time, that was the sort of future that was possible. One where I didn't always have to wonder if the Axeman were out there somewhere. Waiting for me. I reached into my pocket and felt the silver coin in there to avoid jinxing myself. It wasn't iron, but it's what I'd used ever since that night seven years ago. I always had it with me as a ward against evil. It felt…right.

The streetcar squealed to a halt in front of us, and we got on with about fifteen people who had been waiting. It was more crowded than usual, with people practically standing on top of each other. Hadn't Signora Caravaggio warned me to be extra careful around germs for the next month? That streetcar was practically swarming with them. I swallowed my hesitation and barreled forward. Enzo and I went straight to the back, where the cool air sometimes liked to gather. Today, the windows were all shut.

"I swear," I murmured to Enzo once we'd staked out a postage stamp of space next to the back stairwell. "Something happens to a person once they turn forty. They stop wanting to enjoy the fresh air and they start worrying about drafts. As if air from a streetcar going by is going to be worse for you than the breeze outside."

Hopefully my voice sounded more sure of itself than I did. A woman next to me had sharp elbows, and that better have been the man on my right's briefcase.

Five minutes into the ride, a man walked on dressed for surgery. He had a white cloth mask over his mouth and nose, like the man with the sign from yesterday, only cleaner. He didn't look deranged. Everyone stared at him as he strode to the middle of the car, space magically appearing wherever he stepped. Was he with the city somehow? It was hard to tell what his expression was, with his mouth covered. I wondered if he was some kind of cross between a doctor and a bandit, but, in the end, he just stood there without speaking to anyone, as if he weren't doing anything out of the ordinary.

"That seems a bit extreme, doesn't it?" Enzo said to me.

I was still staring at the man, wondering if he were indeed sick. Why else would he be wearing a mask? I wasn't the only person to make the connection. An older lady got up and moved away from him, and several other people were murmuring to each other.

"Are you sick?" I called out to him, because what was the point in thinking something when you could answer it so easily?

He didn't seem to hear me, so I jostled forward to get closer. But not too close. "You in the mask! Are you ill?"

The man looked up and frowned at me. You could tell by the way his forehead creased and his eyes narrowed. "I'm not, but *you* might be."

I stared at him, caught completely flat-footed. I almost always had something to say, but it was if he'd punched me in the gut with that short sentence. I glanced around me at the other people on the car, then slunk back to stand next to Enzo.

Since we didn't have seats, we had to hold on to keep our balance as the car teetered back and forth along the track. It felt like everything had gotten louder. The brash ring of the bell, the clatter of the road beneath us, and the hum of electricity overhead.

By the time we rolled up to the Freret district, both of us were sweating and more than ready to be free of the streetcar. The doors at the back squealed open one last time, and Enzo and I stepped down back into the open. I took a few deep breaths of clean air and fought back the urge to shudder. *Everything is fine, Gianna. Focus on what needs doing next.*

The streets here were a far cry from the houses just a mile to the south. That part of New Orleans was filled with mansions and tree-lined views. Spanish moss and wrought iron fences. If the attack had happened down there, Enzo and I would have stood out like a red flag. Instead, we fit right in. The streets in Freret were full of squat houses, some falling apart, but most simple and sensible. Walls. A window here or there. A covered porch to keep out the afternoon sun.

"What are we going to do if the police are there?" I asked in a low voice as we took our bearings and headed over to Upperline.

"I'll distract them," Enzo said, unconcerned. "It shouldn't be hard to buy you a minute to slip inside without them seeing."

"But what if—"

"Why so worried, Gianna? Is there something you're not telling me? I thought I was the one who did all the worrying between the two of us."

I scratched the back of my waist, my blouse damp with sweat. "I just want to make sure we don't miss our chance is all."

He smiled at me. "A smart girl once told me something I haven't forgotten. 'Worrying does nothing, and doing nothing just because it feels like something is only a waste of doing.' Did I get that right?"

Using my own words against me was a low blow. I forced a smile, however. "That sounds like something a genius would say. She was right. Let's keep going."

I wasn't sure which I was more worried about: that I'd get there and nothing would be familiar at all, or that I'd get there and have some sort of connection. Spark a memory. Remind me of something from my nightmares. All I really wanted was to have nothing more to do with the Axeman ever again, but, as long as these nightmares kept happening, that wasn't a choice. If I did nothing, and the Axeman attacked again, how would I feel? Just like I had seven years ago, when I didn't understand where the nightmares were coming from.

We reached the Maggios' store five minutes later. If I hadn't known the address from checking the phone book, I would have still been able to guess just from the crowd of children gathered on the sidewalk outside. None of them could have been older than ten, and they stared at the house as if it were about to shriek. Across the street, a tall woman with long dark hair sat on her front porch, folding laundry and watching the children with half an eye.

Enzo and I walked up behind them. "So this is where it happened," I said, loud enough to startle a few of the kids in the group.

One of them—a boy with dark brown hair and a chin that jutted out too far—nodded. "Right in there. Mrs. Maggio got hit so hard, her head came off, I heard."

"Really?" Enzo asked. "I heard it was only the husband who was attacked."

"Shows what you know," the boy said, standing straighter. "My brother was here when they were taking the bodies out. They took Mr. Maggio to the hospital, but the other one had a cloth over her whole body. She's dead dead dead."

"Your brother was here?" I said, making sure to sound extra impressed. "What else did he see?"

"The cops think his brother did it. Smashed his head in with an axe, and then used a razor to cut her throat to the bone. Blood everywhere. I heard there was so much the killer had to change clothes, just so he could walk home without everybody knowing he'd done it."

Another boy piped up. "It's true. I heard that, too." He was followed by a chorus of agreement.

None of that was ringing any bells with my nightmare, but my memory of it all was still just foggy. Images here and there that didn't really connect. "Do the cops know who did it?" I asked.

The first boy sneered. "The cops? Please. My dad said they didn't find this guy seven years ago, and he's back now to keep on killing."

"It's true," the boy next to him said again. "I heard that, too." Once again, the rest of them chimed in agreement.

"Where are the police now?" Enzo asked.

"They took Mr. Maggio's brother to the station. He's a barber. They think he did it. But he didn't. It was the Axeman."

"The Axeman," the others echoed.

I stared at Enzo until he looked back at me, and then I tilted my head to the right, impatient. Worrying about the cops being here was one thing, but wasting time with some eight-year-olds was entirely different.

"Oh," Enzo said, then turned the group. "Uh. Could you show me around some?"

The crowd of boys couldn't have agreed faster if he'd offered them free ice cream. In no time they were dragging him down the street, gabbing on about where they were when they heard about the attack, and how it had happened. Where the Axeman might have come from, and where he might have vanished.

I held back, letting them disappear around the corner of the house before I glanced up and down the street. The woman on the porch across from us had disappeared for the moment, maybe going to put her folded laundry away. Without giving myself more time to think, I stepped forward onto the Maggios' front porch. The door was locked, but the Axeman had always been one for going in through the back. I hurried around the building in the opposite way the rest of the group had gone. There was a fence there, but it was open. The backyard was a little plot of land with a shed and garden. The door to the house was closed, but an entire panel had been pried out, leaving a gaping hole in the lower left part of the door.

I got down on my hands and knees and crawled through the opening.

A memory hit me so hard I got dizzy. The view of the store I had as I entered. Neat rows of cans and bags. A counter and a cash register. Like my family's grocery, but not as fully stocked.

Had I had seen this before?

I stood and brushed myself off, the feeling of connection

subsiding. It was just a regular store, and I was all alone. Something smelled wrong. Like meat that had spoiled. My stomach flipped, and I swallowed the urge to heave. Voices came from outside: Enzo and the gang of boys, continuing their tour of the crime scene. No time to waste.

There were two doors on my right, both closed. I went into the second one.

The stench grew even heavier, and the cause became clear. It looked like someone had taken a gallon of rust-colored paint and thrown it around the room. Splashed it onto the walls almost to the ceiling, let large pools of it stand on the floor. The bed was covered in it, the mosquito netting a sodden pile of trash and debris. Someone had ripped open the dresser and strewn clothes all over, and they were covered in blood, too.

A wave of emotion swept through me: excitement and anger and—worst of all—glee. Seeing those bloodstains was like Christmas morning. I wanted to run to them. I forgot who I was for a moment, stepping into the room and smiling. It had been marvelous. The screams. The feel of the axe striking home, hitting his head as if it had belonged there. Everything had been so *right*.

Just like I'd imagined it.

And then, after the husband, the wife. I could remember the cool touch of the razor's handle, the way her neck parted as it passed over her skin, offering almost no resistance at all. I had been like a god. The way her shriek bubbled into a liquid gurgle. How the razor dripped her blood, splattering it on the walls with each stroke in the same way as I might add a flourish to my signature.

That was too much. With a gasp, I was back out of whatever sort of trance I'd been thrust into. The blood, the reek, the moist air—all of it now assaulted my emotions. I couldn't be in there for a second longer. I turned and ran from the room, darting for the back door and racing through it as if I were running from death. I didn't care who saw me or heard me. I had to be free. Now.

I collapsed on the back porch in a heap, fighting back sobs as I gulped down air and reminded myself I was safe. Those hadn't been my emotions. I wasn't a bad person. I hadn't killed anyone, even if I remembered what it felt like. The blood warm on my skin and face and—

No! I forced my eyes open, searching for anything common. Trying to see the neighborhood as just another set of houses. Take in the daylight. The fluffy clouds. The way the leaves on a sapling in the backyard rippled in the breeze.

After a moment, I began to feel other senses. The rough wood of the boards where I sat. The voices coming from the far side of the house. Enzo. The boys. I couldn't let anyone find me looking like this. I checked the windows of the neighboring houses, sure I was going to find someone staring at me in shock.

They were all empty.

I stood and brushed myself, my knees weak as I tottered off the back porch and returned to the street. Enzo was still talking to the

DON'T GO TO SLEEP

boys, telling them some story about a past murder in New Orleans. The kids hung on his every word, but, when he glanced at me, he dropped the whole group, leaving them staring off at him as he came to join me.

"You saw something?" he murmured, taking me lightly by the arm.

"Nothing specific. Nothing useful. The connection was stronger, though. I…"

I stared back at the house I'd left, feeling those emotions wash over me again. The nightmares *were* connected to him somehow. Maybe it was some kind of psychic link that became stronger when he killed. Maybe they were just his fantasies, and, somehow, I picked up on them. I straightened my shoulders and focused back on Enzo, trying to will the determination back into my voice. "We have to stop him. Whatever it takes. I can't last through many more of these attacks without coming unstrung."

CHAPTER THREE

*Assembling this mass of information, the police find certain
similarity of circumstances which seems to support the
one-man theory of burglary and murder alike—one man,
a moral degenerate operating along fixed lines.*

———————

THE AXEMAN WOULD STRIKE AGAIN. Enzo knew it. I knew it. Our parents constantly worried about it. I could tell in the way my mother's shoulders hunched forward at the counter while she waited on customers. In the edge my father's voice had to it when he yelled at the kids playing ball in the street outside our store.

To most of the city, news of the murder was disturbing, but nothing to lose sleep over. But Italians viewed it differently. After all, seven years ago, it was our people who had been attacked. The Axeman went after Italian grocery stores, though no one knew why.

To have another murder in an Italian grocery, with an axe? It didn't take any imagination to connect the attack to those earlier ones. I still remembered men sitting on their porches in the middle of the night, loaded shotguns in their laps as they kept watch, protecting their families and their livelihoods. It had taken weeks of no more attacks seven years ago before things edged closer to normal.

It didn't mean life didn't keep moving forward, however. The store still needed to be run, and there were the countless little jobs that went into making something like that happen. Part of me wanted to tell Papa I couldn't help him repair the shutters on the front windows. Who cared about shutters when a madman lay in wait, planning to kill someone? But it was Papa, and who could say no to him? If I didn't help him, then he'd be up on the ladder by himself, and never mind the fact that he couldn't raise his right arm higher than his shoulder.

"What's so important you keep checking the time?" Papa asked me while I held the ladder for him.

"Niente di speciale," I said. "Enzo and I were talking about maybe meeting up later, is all." Technically true, though we hadn't set a real time yet.

Papa smiled down at me. "I'm glad you're back together again. He's a good boy, even if his parents have a bit too much money."

A pang of guilt shot through me. My parents had been crushed when I'd told them I'd ended things with Enzo. I didn't want them getting the wrong idea now, even if it would have been more convenient for me if they did. "It's not like that," I said. "We're still just friends. I was very clear with him."

Papa peered at the lower hinge and began tightening the screws. "Gia, you're seventeen. Your mother and I were already engaged when she was just a year older than you. I don't know why you have such an issue with Enzo."

"You and Mama were different. For Enzo and me…six years we went through life, doing everything together. Growing up. And then I was supposed to put that all on the line for love, and us only just seventeen? I'm not ready, but Enzo had it in his mind that we had to move forward. Think ahead. You know how he is. I haven't even kissed him yet."

"And why not?" Papa asked. He took the offending hinge off and fished the new one out of his pocket.

"Papa, when you kiss somebody, it messes everything up. Changing things with Enzo would have been like going into one of the gambling halls in Storyville and betting all my money on red. Yes, it might pay off and make me very happy, but it might just as easily make me indigente. When you take a risk like that, you need better odds."

"So, instead, you decided to end it with him and ruin a friendship," Papa said. "I had no idea I was raising such a wise young daughter."

"We had one fight," I snapped back. "That was all. I tried to explain it to him, and he got angry, and then I got angry, and…by the end of it, I said it was better if we spent some time apart."

Papa nodded, screwing the new hinge into place. "'Some time' can cover a lot of ground. Sure, it could be a month, but what if that turned into two, or six, or a year? And all because both of you are too stubborn to admit you were wrong. I know how that can happen. I'm just glad you're talking again is all." He moved the hinge back and forth, the shutter swinging freely now. "Do you think you can get the one on the other side? It's too high for my shoulder."

He came down, and we switched places, working in silence for a moment. Some of the other Italian families made such a big deal over their sons. Daughters were good for nothing more than laundry and cooking. Papa had raised me with every bit of attention he would have given me if I'd been a boy. He'd tutored me in math, shown me how to use tools, and even shown me how to make a fist and where to aim if I got in a fight. We had done so many jobs around the store together, we probably could have worked together with our eyes closed.

Papa was a king, and I would stand up to anyone who said otherwise.

He also had connections throughout the Italian American community. And so what if changing the subject moved it away from Enzo and over to something that might actually help us all? "What do you hear about the Axeman?" I asked, my eyes focused on the screwdriver in my hand. Papa was always more likely to answer your questions when you were showing proper respect for work.

"What's to hear?" he said, trying to sound casual but unable to keep that edge from his voice. "The Fazzios almost shot a late customer yesterday. They thought he was trying to break into their house. The Salvaggios swear they've had someone lurking around after-hours for weeks. But, when something like this happens, everyone starts paying attention to things they've ignored for months. None of it means anything."

"Do you think it's him?"

"The police seem to, though don't let your mother know I told you that." He glanced around, as if worried she might be hiding somewhere on the street. There were a few people out and about, but we were in the lull that usually came just before lunch. Mama was inside working on bread. She had very firm ideas about the police, and she didn't like anyone saying anything about them in our house.

"Why do you say that?" I asked.

"They've been asking around at the other stores. No one's telling them anything, of course. And all they keep asking about is the Black Hand, in any case. Whenever Italians are in trouble, the cops always assume it comes down to crime families. Idioti. But don't worry about that devil. We paid our price years ago. There are what—one or two hundred Italian groceries in this city? He won't be back to ours." He held his hand out to me, a gesture we both knew from the time I was four.

I took his hand, and he squeezed it three times in quick succession. It was a silent way of saying "I love you." I squeezed his hand back four times: code for "I love you too."

From there I let Papa move the conversation elsewhere. What he'd said just confirmed what Enzo and I had heard as well. And, besides, it was Tuesday. I had the afternoon off to go help Signora Caravaggio. We'd been trying all the normal sources of information.

What could it hurt to try a little of the paranormal?

If Enzo caught wind of my plan, he'd say something about how we had to keep this between us, and how we couldn't trust her, and never mind that she had been watching me since I was four years old. If you can't trust the woman who helped raise you, then you might as well give up all your other hopes. We had time to talk to strangers, so we had time to talk to confidants as well.

And did a part of me hope she'd tell me what I was doing was foolish? Yes, and that same part hoped the reading would give me some other choice. Some easier option. There was only one way to find out, and I had to try it.

Back when I'd been growing up, she'd been our next-door neighbor. She'd long since moved across the river to Algiers, and it took a whole afternoon to get there and back. The neighbors in the Vieux Carré had stopped looking as kindly on her assortment of animals, and they'd brought complaints to the police. Imagine an old woman being forced to choose between moving her house and giving up her pets.

Getting to Algiers meant catching the ferry, but that was no great burden on another beautiful fall day, and Mama liked that I went once a week to go help an old friend. The time by myself helped clear my head. What did I want to get out of a reading? Some direction. Maybe clues to the Axeman's identity, or what he might be planning. An idea about where he lived or what he looked like.

If the wind was right, you could smell her house before you saw it: a mixture of earth and blood and decay. You couldn't have so much life in one spot without a fair bit of death, after all. Though I didn't remember it being quite so pungent when she was our neighbor. At least the added space she'd gained in the move had let her spread out more.

Then again, the story that had gone around our neighborhood said the plantation had been the abandoned after the owner killed his wife and five children in the house, then slit his throat. My neighbors would believe the worst of anyone, if it made their own lives more bearable.

They looked at Signora Caravaggio, and they saw someone different, just as people had assumed of old spinsters for years. So she lived by herself with a few cats and other animals. So she grew herbs and made medicine for people. Did that make her a witch?

Not that she made it any easier on herself. She made some money off fortune-telling, and people paid more for the theatrics. So the front of the house seemed to be crumbling around her. The manor's thick white walls were now a dusty gray, with plaster peeling off the interior, and brickwork peeking out in multiple places on the exterior. Moss grew on the roof, and she'd let a tree actually burst through the clay tiles, spreading its branches into the air and casting its roots through the floorboards of the second story to drape down through the ceiling of her parlor. It dripped nonstop when it rained, but most of that stayed isolated to that one spot.

"I'm an old woman," she'd told me when I'd expressed concern about her health in that environment. "I don't need the whole house, and no one's going to inherit this after I crawl into a sepulcher. Besides, the snakes like the moisture, and so does Henry."

Her home was practically a zoo, though one without any real planning behind the exhibits. Cats ran around everywhere, naturally, but she also had more exotic pets. Parakeets, a trained ferret, a bearded lizard, an owl, chameleons, several types of snakes, three tarantulas, a bat, and a crocodile named Henry. And that wasn't counting all the other animals she kept around to act as food for the others. Rats and mice and moths. She had an entire glass cage that was nothing but a writhing mass of crickets.

Signora Caravaggio was in the wide covered porch on the first floor, just cutting the head off a chicken as I approached. It twitched in her hands, its wings spasming as she tied the feet together and strung the carcass up to drain. She waved to me absently as she studied the blood spatter on the floor, and I didn't interrupt her. She might have been doing a reading for someone. The chicken's head was still blinking, eyes moving around as it sat on the floor like a forgotten ball.

At last Signora Caravaggio looked up at me and smiled,

throwing her arms open for a hug, though she kept her hands outstretched to keep any blood from getting on me. "Is it Tuesday already?" she asked me in Italian. I was only too happy to keep the conversation in the same language.

"Seven days after the last one."

"Thank goodness. I could use the help. Come to the back."

The window shades were all open, but it still felt like I'd gone from midday to dusk within ten steps. If you went further into the house—beyond the trailing roots and hazy windows and peeling plaster—then you got to a part that was much better taken care of. I ought to know: I came to take care of it every week.

So many people who came looking for a fortune-teller wanted one like they read about in stories, so Signora Caravaggio made sure they got what they expected. That didn't mean she wanted to live in squalor, however. The back section of the house—the side no one saw—had electricity and plumbing and all the comforts of home. If it weren't for all her pets, it would have stayed much cleaner.

Today she put me to work washing the windows while she changed out of her dirty clothes. I didn't mind the task. She always visited with me while I worked, asking after Mama and Papa and some of the others in the neighborhood she still knew. In return, she gave me a free reading before I left. Today that kept running through my head, so much that I missed Signora's questions a little too often.

"You're back together with that Rissetto boy," she said. It wasn't a question.

"We're not 'together.' We're just—"

"The cards were very clear, Gianna. I checked them three times just to be sure. He will bring you heartache."

One of the main reasons Enzo had no faith in the supernatural is that Signora Caravaggio was convinced he was going to ruin my life. "I don't have any choice," I said. "I need help for what's coming."

"What's coming? When I checked last week, everything was focused on the influenza. Have you been avoiding germs like I told you to?"

It all poured out of me. The nightmares. My worries about the Axeman's return. My hopes to catch him and get some vengeance. If there was one person I could trust in this entire city other than Enzo or my family, it was Signora Caravaggio. She never judged me. Never made me feel guilty or foolish. She just listened and then offered her best advice, treating me like an equal and not someone to be bossed into obedience.

As I spoke, she sat completely still, all of her attention on me. When I was finished, she took a moment to think things through. "That's quite a lot for one person to handle," she said at last. "We'll need to do a new reading, yes? But which one?"

"Whichever one you think best," I said after she was clearly waiting for an answer.

"This isn't a reading for me. It's for you. What feels right?"

"I can have anything?" She normally insisted I stay to the more common tools. Tarot and tea leaves were her favorite.

"For this?" she asked. "Anything."

I didn't have to even consider the question. "I want the crystal ball, then."

She laughed. "You've been wanting that ball since you first came over to my house thirteen years ago. Are you sure you want a real ball reading? Once we use it, it can take us into darkness much faster than anything in my house."

Signora Caravaggio had so many different ways of peering into the future. For her paying clients, she would use the method they suggested. She always said what they were attracted to said as much about what she would find out as whatever tool she used. She had six different Tarot decks, a Ouija board, and astrology books. I'd heard her talk about reading palms, tea leaves, wax drippings, and even entrails. She'd held seances with groups of up to ten. But the crystal ball had always been my favorite.

"I'm sure," I said.

"Then go to my office and light the candles," she said. "The matches are in the right-hand drawer of the hutch. The one with the scorpion jar. I just have a few more things to do before I'm ready."

I practically ran to the room, so excited for this chance. If I were really lucky, the ball would tell me to avoid this whole mess completely. In my heart of hearts, I wanted nothing more than a solid excuse to put the Axeman behind me once and for all. This was my last chance.

The room was filled with an assortment of bizarre items: animal cages, bookshelves, paint cans, chess sets, tools, jars filled with everything from beetles to flour, a battle axe, a stuffed iguana, and more. The flickering light of the candles cast an uncertain orange glow on the scene, and my neck itched as if I were being watched, though, of course, that was nonsense.

No one came to Signora Caravaggio's unannounced.

Then again, what if it were a spirit, come to converse with her later on? So much could be solved if we just had a stronger connection to the afterlife. I could ask the victims of the Axeman what he looked like. Who he was. If the connection today were strong enough, maybe I'd have that chance.

I spent a full minute staring at the crystal ball in the middle of the room, moving my hands around behind it and wondering how it worked for her. Did pictures appear in it, or did it spark thoughts in her head as she focused on the ball? The thing was almost a foot wide, completely clear, and a perfect sphere. It rested on a mahogany stand that had been carved to look like a coiled dragon.

When she came in, she didn't go to the huge ball in the middle of her table, however. Signora Caravaggio walked to the bookcase on the far side of the room, leafing through the tomes until she took out a particularly wide one. She opened it, revealing a hollow space on the inside where the pages had been carved out. A small brown and black striped ball of stone rested inside it. She put on a white glove and picked it up. It was about the size of a baseball.

"If we're going to do this, we'll do it right," she said, then laughed when she noticed my expression. "Disappointed it's not the big one? That's for show. People come to me, they expect certain things. If they're foolish enough, I'll even pretend to use it. But I wouldn't do that to you. This ball here has done much more for me over the years. If you really want to know what's coming, this will do the trick. Come over here."

She led me to the corner of the room farthest from the candles. A couple of wicker chairs sat facing each other. Once we were seated, she handed the ball to me, smiling again when I hesitated to touch it. "I only use the gloves because it works better for the person doing the reading to have the most contact with it. It won't hurt you. Don't be afraid."

It was heavier than I expected, sitting in my palm like a smooth brick. My neck tingled as soon as I touched it, though that might have been my imagination taking over. "How does it work?" I asked.

"You'll hold it with both your hands in front of you. I'll take your wrists, and together we'll look at the ball. You'll tell me what you see, and I'll interpret if necessary."

"*I* will tell you?"

"This is about you, is it not?"

"But you're the one with the gift."

She took my wrists and forced my hands together, the orb between my palms. "I may know how to read, but, without a book, what use is that? You'll be my book for this. Trust me, Gianna."

It wasn't what I had expected when I'd asked to use the crystal, but I'd always believed her before. I pressed my lips together and gripped onto the ball with both hands.

"Not so tightly!" Signora Caravaggio told me. "The future isn't something you can force into being. You coax it toward you. Tempt it."

I loosened my grip and clenched my eyes closed, trying to rid myself of all my doubts and worries. When I opened them again, I stared at the striped orb. It was a rock. A smooth ball and nothing more.

"Stop thinking about thinking about it," she told me. "Just look at the ball and let your mind take you where it wants to go. This will focus your thoughts. Trust the process."

Let my mind go where it wanted to? As I stared at the ball, small flecks that I hadn't seen at first glinted against the candlelight. Hints of gold and silver and even colors. Red and green when the light caught the angle just right. In fact, the more I studied the ball, the more I realized it was more colorful than the simple brown and black stripes that had first struck me. If I moved the ball back and forth in my palms, the colors blended together more quickly, almost presenting the hints of a picture.

I leaned closer and tried to speed it up. Back one way and then forward the other, over and over, trying to have the glints move fast enough that they'd piece themselves together. But, no matter how quickly I did it, the focus didn't come. Finally I closed my eyes, trying to remember the positions of those glints and put them together in my imagination.

Signora Caravaggio's hands tightened on my wrists. "That's it," she said. "Focus. What do you see? What words come into your head?"

"A quilt," I said, not knowing why, though it felt right as soon as I did. "Tattered and dirty."

"Sickness," she answered. "Bad. Is there anything else you see about it?"

The glints of red. "Blood," I said. "Stains around the edges and underneath it. It's covering a large bloodstain."

"There will be death, and not just from illness." Her voice wasn't as sure of itself know. "I think you should stop there, Gianna."

But my hands wouldn't let the ball go. More images came to me, one after the other. "A broken Victrola, a ruined church filled with treasure in a dark swamp, a park at night, a freshly dug grave, cans of sardines." They were coming too fast for me to even hope to say them all. Glimpses and moments, some of them too fast for me to even recognize. A thin woman with long dark hair and a scar on her face shook her head at me, her face a mask of disappointment.

In the distance, I heard a voice: "Gianna. Put it down now." But my entire body had frozen, my hands clenching the ball, my teeth grinding. Someone grabbed hold of the orb and pushed me backward. A searing pain shot through my temples, and I blacked out.

The next thing I knew I was opening my eyes, trying to focus on the room around me, though it took some time before it was anything more than a blur. A faint screech whined at the edge of hearing. Signora Caravaggio sat slumped in her chair, the stone ball clutched in her ungloved right hand. Her eyes were closed, and she was breathing rapidly.

I tried to get to my feet, but my muscles didn't want to work, as if I'd forgotten how to use my body. On the fifth try, I managed to get to my knees, and I shuffled over to my friend. I shook her gently, but she didn't respond, her hand gripping the ball showing the whites of her knuckles. I picked up the dropped handkerchief Signora Caravaggio had used to handle the ball, then used it to shield my own hand as I struggled to wrench it free from her grip.

On the second pull, her eyes snapped open, and she released the ball, sending me tumbling backward again.

She looked around, blinking rapidly, and then her breathing slowed as she made eye contact with me again. Usually this would be where she cracked a smile and made some sort of a wry comment about what we'd just gone through. I'd heard her talk about real foretellings, but I'd never thought they'd be this...*violent*.

Her face remained serious, however. "That was bad, Gia. Very bad."

It was sobering to hear her tell me the same thing I'd been thinking. "It's a mistake," I said. "Me pushing forward with this."

"A mistake?" she asked, standing and coming over to me to offer me a hand up before she snatched the stone ball from the floor, using her gloves once again. "No. Not a mistake. There will only be one way out of this for you, I'm afraid, and that's to move forward."

I couldn't believe what I was hearing. "Did you interpret something different from that than what I did?" I asked. "There was so much death. Nothing but evil omens."

Signora Caravaggio nodded. "Yes, and it tears my heart to know what's coming for you. But it's coming for you whether you want it or not. That much was clear to me as well. Your future is dark, no matter what you do. And, if you want a hope of some light in it, it's going to be up to you."

"Did it say what I was supposed to do? Any hints about what actions I should take?"

She placed the ball back in the book and returned it to the shelf before turning to me and responding. "Sometimes the best the future can offer us is a warning not to look too deeply. This was a warning to you and to me. If we try looking again, it will only make things worse. I wish I were someone else, Gia. Someone stronger or with better connections. Someone who could help you. But, in this, I am just an old woman."

"You have to look again," I stammered out. "I need some help. Something. Anything."

"All I can say is that the answer is within you. That much was clear to me, and nothing more. To try to look again would risk hurting both of us, and I won't add to your troubles by doing that."

Her words echoed in my ears. I'd come here hoping to gain insight on what Enzo and I should do to beat this fiend, and I would be leaving with nothing but more questions. If I'd thought this might show me another path, I'd been wrong. I swallowed my fear and held my head high as I made my way back to the Vieux Carré. If I was going to have to face the Axeman, I was going to make him rue the day he ever attacked my family.

I could do this.

CHAPTER FOUR

The child was killed outright, the father was in a dying condition Sunday night in the Charity Hospital, and the mother, unconscious and piteously crying, "Mary, Mary," the name of her murdered child, was fighting for her life with five wounds in her head and a depressed fracture of the skull just over the left ear in a ward nearby.

M Y EYES SPRANG OPEN, MY breathing coming in gasps as my heart raced from the nightmare I'd just had. I'd been in another bedroom, hadn't I? The smooth heft of an axe handle in my palms, the weight of it going up and over my head before I brought it smashing down.

I shuddered, trying to put the memory behind me. I was at home in my bed, and, judging from the little amount of light wafting in through the shutters, it had to be hours yet before I was supposed to be up. Now wasn't the time to be losing sleep. I'd need all the rest I could get, if Signora Caravaggio's reading was right.

Lie back. Close my eyes. Clear my head. If I could calm down, I'd go back to sleep.

But little noises kept wriggling their way into my head. My parents' breathing from across the room. A horse clopping past outside. A dog barking a few houses down. And, each time one of those sounds came, it was followed by another image from that nightmare. The blood dripping from the axe's edge. The screams of the woman. The feeling of that little body soaring through the—

My eyes sprang open again. Little body? What little body? I didn't remember much of the nightmare. It had been the same as all the others, hadn't it? And yet, somehow, that single feeling— striking a child with an axe—was clear as sunlight in my head. It hadn't been one of the images that came to me when I was with Signora Caravaggio, was it?

Not possible. I would have remembered something like that.

I shifted in bed, my right shoulder protesting in pain at the move. I winced and rolled the joint some, surprised at just how much it hurt. Had I wrenched it during the day yesterday, or tried to—

Papa groaned in exasperation, then said, "Stai scherzando? Gia, if you're going to make such a racket, at least leave the bedroom to do it, sì? It's four-thirty in the morning."

"Sorry," I said, rolling out of bed and throwing on my robe as best I could in the dark. Trying to fall back asleep wasn't going to happen. I'd be better served getting up and doing something other than brooding over my problems. I pushed aside the curtain that separated my corner of the bedroom from the rest of it, and I only tripped over one pair of shoes as I made my way to the door. Papa grumbled again, and Mama murmured something to him in response.

Outside, the main room of our house—the grocery store itself— was also shrouded in darkness. I padded over to the windows and cracked open a few shades, letting in more of the streetlights from outside. My shoulder hurt as if I'd just pulled it. Had I been thrashing in my sleep? It wouldn't have been the first time, and it might explain why Papa had gotten so frustrated so quickly.

I sat down in the barber seat over in the far corner. Our store looked like many Italian grocers: a hodgepodge of different offerings jammed together in a central room, with our living areas all connecting to it. The doors to the kitchen, bathroom, and our bedroom were behind the main counter, so it wasn't as if just anyone could go marching in, but you tried to take care of your personal business when the store wasn't open.

The main room looked like it would explode if we tried to pack one more can into it. Baskets and smoked meats hanging from the rafters, brooms and tools in the corners, canned food and bags of sugar and flour along the walls and underneath the counter, and alcohol in bottles just like in a saloon. The newspapers were kept back there as well. Not as many as most newsstands, but enough if someone came in and asked for one. We had huge barrels for nuts and grains, smaller tubs for the penny candy, and we brought in the fruit and vegetable stands each evening to make sure they didn't walk away or get vandalized. Then there was the barber seat where Papa could give customers a shave or a haircut.

A cash register lorded over the entire room, with a metal spindle next to it for keeping track of receipts, notes for credit, and all the other stray bits of paper our store accumulated. Just take the note and slam it down on the spindle, which was nothing more than a metal rod sticking up in the air. The rod pierced the paper, the paper stayed in place. It was nothing like the one Enzo's parents had—all silver and sharp, like Apollo's arrow. Papa said having something like that be so sharp was just asking to get your hand stabbed. I thought it had more style.

The store was neat and orderly—it had to be, to fit it all in—but you needed to know where you were stepping if you didn't want to knock over a display. The food delivery would be by in an hour and a half, and the workday would start again. In the meantime, what was I going to do to pass the time?

My hands itched for a piano, even though I knew there was no chance they'd let me into the church at this hour. As I sat in the barber's chair, I played different chords in my mind, going through a blues progression in different keys, though it wasn't enough. I got out my silver coin and turned it over in my fingers, feeling the well-worn ridges. I'd had it so long, I didn't need to look twice at it to know each part of it. The shield and crown on one side, and the head on the other, the words rubbed almost to nothing, though you could still make out the date if you held it to the light the right way. *1857.*

I'd found it in our bedroom the morning after the attack, lying there glinting dully underneath my mother's bloodstained sock. I'd pocketed it before anyone else could see it, and I hadn't told anyone else about it until my father saw me holding it two weeks afterward. Even then, I lied and said I'd come across it on the street. He'd checked it then—he had a love for old coins—and told me it was a Spanish picayune. "Might be pirate bounty," he'd said, wanting no doubt to distract me from the memory of that night. "You've heard of pieces of eight? This is worth half of one of those. Not exactly a treasure trove, but lucky to have found it. It's probably worth a dollar."

"Lucky" wasn't the word I would have used, though he didn't know the truth of it. There's only one way that coin could have ended up in our bedroom. The Axeman had dropped it. Enzo had thought it was morbid of me to hold onto it. I'd shown it to him and told him the truth of it, three months after we'd become friends. I wanted to know if he'd found something like it at his house. He hadn't, and I'd never come across another one like it. Had the Axeman really dropped it? There was no way to know, but I was convinced he had.

It might have been morbid, but it also felt right to me. I had something of that monster's, and I'd dreamed of paying him back one day. Giving that coin to him after I'd beaten him—though what "beaten him" looked like was never quite clear. He'd know it was me. That scrawny ten-year-old child he'd terrorized, grown up now to bring him to justice.

And the coin made me feel good. More complete, somehow, probably because I'd held onto it for all these years. I'd thought I'd lost it once, and it had driven me absolutely wild. I'd ransacked my room, desperate to find it, and I'd cried for a half hour in relief once I discovered it lodged into one of the cracks in the floorboards beneath my bed.

Would I really be able to return it to that demon? I closed my hand into a fist around it, then kissed the fist. "Santa Maria, Madre di Dio, prega per noi peccatori, adesso e nell'ora della nostra morte. Amen."

My priest would be appalled to know I said part of the rosary over this coin, but God hadn't struck me dead yet, and I'd always felt like that part fit. *Holy Mary, Mother of God, pray for us sinners, now and at the hour of our death. Amen.* And may his death be much sooner than mine.

I stood, wanting to change my train of thought. It was my fault Papa had slept terribly. I could make it up for him if I had a nice breakfast waiting for him and Mama. Biscuits. Bacon. Eggs. Maybe doing something for someone else would get my mind off the nightmares and the visions and the problems that had been constant for the last few days.

Other than the main room and our bedroom, we only had two

other rooms of the house: a tiny toilet, and the kitchen. So it was in the kitchen where we spent most of our time that wasn't on display to customers during the day. Usually it was a comforting place, full of good smells and happiness. This morning it felt like a morgue. Silent and empty. The electric lights made everything sterile. Dead. Every move I made echoed against the walls. When I cracked the eggs to add them to the biscuits, it reminded me of skulls breaking. The milk sloshing into the batter gurgled too much like the sound of a woman choking on blood.

Making biscuits wasn't proving to be as relaxing as I'd wanted it to be. I'd have to resort to something stronger.

A year ago, Enzo had surprised me with a Victrola. I'd thought about refusing it, but my parents had convinced me to keep it, probably because Mama wanted to listen to music just as much as I did, and we kept it in the kitchen. If I had a recording of Sidney Bechet, I was sure it would sweep away all those nightmare memories. But getting recordings of Black artists was almost impossible, so I had to settle for something by the Original Dixieland Jazz Band. I might have been frustrated the ODJB claimed they'd invented jazz, and their style was a bit stuck-up for me, but they put out a lot of records, and you could get them easily.

When you don't have as much money as you might wish, you find you have to make compromises you wouldn't otherwise make.

So I took out *Clarinet Marmalade Blues* and put the disc onto the platform, making sure to switch the volume on the needle as low as it would go. It made the music sound even more tinny, but with the door closed, the sound wouldn't carry into the bedroom. Our house might have been small, but it had thick walls.

Larry Shields' clarinet began to wail right off, and if the song started off slower than I would have liked, it picked up after the intro. I focused on the beat, listening to the key changes and the way the instruments blended together. It was enough. I turned back to the baking, and the eggs were just eggs again, and the milk clean and white. True, the song only lasted two and a half minutes, but it managed to change my outlook. One day, maybe they would come out with players that could hold more than one song on a disc. What a world that would be!

Papa and Mama got up when I already had the bacon sizzling in one pan and the eggs were just going into the other. It was my fourth record of the morning as well: *Rock-a-Bye Your Baby*, which was a good sign it was time for me to try and buy a few more records, if I ever had the money for it. Al Jolson? I only had the record because Mama had given it to me for my birthday.

"Sixteen hours," Mama said when she walked into the room, still rubbing her eyes.

"Sixteen hours until what?" I asked, flipping the bacon.

"Sixteen hours we have in the day to listen to jazz or make noises in the kitchen. You can do just about whatever you want in those sixteen hours. But is it too much to ask for no jazz for the other eight?"

"You're just grouchy because you haven't eaten yet," Papa said, entering the room. "We couldn't hear a thing. Get a plate, Mama. The produce is going to be here soon, and you'll be happier if you've got some food inside you."

Mama passed on the eggs and bacon, but she had two biscuits with some jam, and she didn't even mention the fact that I'd burned the edges. We talked about the day ahead, and Papa left halfway through to meet the delivery truck. I shoveled in a few more bites of biscuit, and Mama waved me away. "Go help him with the shipment," she said. "I'll clean up here."

When so much of our money depended on the store, our lives revolved around the schedule of others. When the vegetables and fruit would arrive. When people would show up wanting to buy food for the day. You would have thought it would have been regular, but that wasn't how it happened in real life. One day you'd have a large rush of customers first thing in the morning, and the next you wouldn't see the rush come until ten, if it came at all. Sometimes I wondered if everyone hid just around the corner, deciding together when they'd all appear.

Today it started to rain around eight o'clock, and that kept away most of the crowds. Papa had me start working on taking an inventory of the canned goods. Some of the customers had a tendency to have light fingers, and it helped us to keep on top of just what we had in stock.

I was in the middle of counting through the canned beans

when two policemen walked into the store, their blue uniforms and shiny buttons unmistakable, even from the corner of my eye. Papa was out back with Mama going over some of the order records, so I hurried down from the ladder. "Sorry about that," I said, forcing a smile. "What can I—"

"Where are your parents?" the one on the right barged in. He had a big chin and eyes that were too far apart.

"They're back looking at—"

"We need to talk to them," he said. "Now."

I did my best to keep the smile frozen on my face as I turned and left the room. It didn't do any good to antagonize the police. They could make our lives more difficult than they already were. The sooner these two were out of the store, the better. And what were they doing here so early, anyway?

My parents were in the backyard. When I told Papa the police were here, Mama immediately clouded over. "Which ones?" she asked.

I shrugged. "New ones. I haven't seen them before."

"Let me handle it," Papa said. Of all of us, Mama held a grudge against the police the most. She'd never forgiven them for their failure seven years ago, and she'd never forgotten it, either. In her eyes, they were all the same.

Mama came as far as the kitchen, but she stayed by the door, hovering. When Papa limped back into the storeroom, I trailed behind him, heading straight for my ladder again. If I was lucky, they'd all forget about me, and I could listen in. I made a show of moving cans around and consulting my notepad, but all my attention was on the conversation. The room wasn't big enough for them not to be overheard.

"What seems to be the problem?" Papa asked.

"There's no problem," the interrupter told him, his voice much more respectful now that he was speaking with someone over eighteen—and a man. "We've been asked to check in with the local Italian grocery stores. Just a formality. Have you had any suspicious behavior around here lately?"

Papa frowned. I heard it in his voice. "Suspicious? Not that I'm aware of. Does this have something to do with the attack that happened last week?"

"It's an ongoing investigation," the other policeman said. "We're not at liberty to divulge information. What about threats you might have heard toward people in your...community? Maybe someone with a certain organization who might be angry with someone else?"

"There haven't been any—"

Mama barged into the room, hands on her waist and her face already a thunder cloud. She didn't share the "don't antagonize the police" train of thought. "Every. Single. Time," she said. "Anything happens to an Italian that is even one inch out of the ordinary, and suddenly it's the Black Hand this and the Black Hand that. We aren't all part of the Matragna Family. We're just trying to live our

DON'T GO TO SLEEP

lives in peace and quiet. So why don't you stop it with your vague statements and tell us why you're here? It definitely isn't to buy broccoli."

The policemen each took a step back, then glanced at each other. I reminded myself not to stare, turning my focus back to the canned beans, though I couldn't do anything more than hold one in my hand. All the rest of my focus was on the conversation.

"There was another attack last night," the second one said. "Two in less than a week? We think they might be connected, and it's not too big of a stretch to think an Italian crime connection might be at the root of it."

Mama grunted, her lips a thin white line, her arms folded across her chest. She might have been six inches shorter than them, but you wouldn't have known it from their body language. "And when one of your 'normal' New Orleans citizens dies, do you think it must be connected to some of their families?" Mama asked. "It's not as if Italians are the only ones who die in this city, and we're not the only ones who commit crimes."

"I would think you'd be happy we were following leads," the first said, his voice carrying an edge. "After what happened to your family back—"

"Yes," Mama said. "Bring that up again. You always do. *We* were the ones who were attacked. *You* were the ones who weren't able to find anyone—anyone!—who could give you even a hint of who did it."

"Ma'am," the second policeman tried again, "We're sorry for what police back then did. But this is new. A family was attacked last night. A two-year-old child was killed, and we—"

The can of beans I'd been holding clattered to the floor, startling my parents and the police. "Mi scusi," I said, then climbed down the ladder to fetch the can, which had rolled over to stop by the first policeman.

He picked it up and handed it to me. "I'm sorry," he said. "We didn't want to alarm anyone. Are you alright?"

That feeling returned: the memory of the axe coming down and striking that child, and then—

I shook my head slightly. "I'm fine," I said.

"She was ten," Papa added in a soft voice. "When we were attacked back then. It's okay, Gia. Go take a break. You can finish the inventory later."

Half of me wanted to stay and ask the police more questions. To pump them for information and hope I might get some real clues from them. But I knew I was in no condition to speak much to anyone. That memory kept playing in a loop in my mind, and that one memory meant something very significant.

The nightmares might not just be nightmares. They might be visions of reality.

CHAPTER FIVE

An axman murderer, who laid his plans with fiendish cunning and executed them with revolting brutality, chose Charles Cortimiglia, his wife, and their 2-year-old daughter, Mary.

———————————

I COULDN'T STAY IN THE HOUSE another minute. Not with the police there, and not with trying to keep myself from going insane. So, instead, I headed to St. Augustine's. It wasn't my morning to play the piano, but something in my expression made Father Donohue let me in without protest. I made a beeline for the piano, sat down at the keys, and began to play.

When you play an instrument long enough, the boundaries between you and it start to disappear to the point where the thing you're playing is almost a part of you. Where making it do what you want takes no more thought than walking or talking. I still wasn't good enough to get that feeling all of the time, but, every now and then, I got there. The piano would disappear beneath my fingers, and I could just work all my emotions into the music.

I did most of my best thinking when I practiced. Something about going over music, playing different chords and progressions, cleared my mind and let me work through problems in a way just sitting and brooding about them could never do. Of course, I didn't always have access to a piano, so I had to make the most of it when I did. Father Donohue and I had a standing agreement that I could go in and use the piano every Thursday afternoon for two hours. In return for the practice time, I agreed to come and play the organ when the main organist got sick. I didn't mind the organ, but it was far too fussy for me to ever really love it. An organ didn't allow for mistakes. The pipe was either on, or it was off. A piano, on the other hand, could be softer or louder, depending on how you felt. The music could swirl together just how you wanted it to.

Right then, I might as well have been on the organ, for all the nuance I was able to get out of the piano. My fingers felt like bullets, and I couldn't play below a shout, no matter how much I tried to hold back. I'd start off quietly going through some scales, but, by the second time through, I was back to pounding out notes one after another, the noise echoing through the assembly room where the piano lived. Short ceilings, big room. It didn't take much pounding to fill it.

I kept trying to veer off into an actual song, but, after a few bars of *Tiger Rag* or *Rock-a-Bye Your Baby*, I'd be right back in a scale. My brain was stuck on the Axeman and the attacks and what I could do about them. Should I go back to the crime scene? What did I expect would be different from the last time we went? It felt like I was surrounded by a dull roar, with my blood pounding in my ears.

Someone tapped me on the shoulder, and I shrieked and whirled, striking out at whoever was there.

Enzo caught my fist easily and gently. "I thought I might find you here," he said, letting my hand go.

"You heard?" I asked. I pushed the bench back and stood, stretching my legs and checking the time. I'd lost an hour and a half sitting there.

"We have to go over, of course." He said it as if it were the most obvious thing in the world.

"Why would it make any difference?"

His eyebrows shot up. "So you haven't heard?"

I'd thought my spirits were already as low as they could get, but, somehow, they sank even further. "What are you talking about?"

"The attack. It was on the Cortimiglias."

I sat down in shock. There were plenty of Italians in the city, so you wouldn't think the odds were too great that we'd all know each other. But, with marriages and friendships and parties, you'd have been surprised how many we actually knew. The Cortimiglias lived over in the Seventh Ward, only a mile away. Charles and Rosie with their little daughter…"Mary," I said. Knowing which child had been attacked—knowing I *knew* her—made things even worse.

"You had a nightmare about it," Enzo said. It wasn't a question.

"Come on," I said. "I can tell you while we walk. We might not be able to get into their house right now, but the Giodanos live right across the street. Signora babysat my mother back in the day. They'll know more about what's going on."

"It's pouring outside," Enzo said.

"And some water will make me forget this? We'll take umbrellas. Come on!"

I paused when I got to the front doors, however. "Pouring" had been an understatement. The rain was coming down so hard I could have swum across the street instead of walking. I eyed the spare umbrellas the church had by the front door. They were old and not in the best of shape. I grabbed one and squared my shoulders.

"The sooner we go, the sooner we're there," I said.

Enzo nodded, unfolded his umbrella, and we started walking. When I unfolded mine, one of the supports was bent, so the umbrella didn't spread evenly.

The streets were practically empty, though we passed a couple of people wearing face masks, which only reminded me of that strange man from the street car before. As if an axe-murderer on the loose wasn't enough. We really needed to worry about influenza as well? What had New Orleans done to make God so angry?

The rain might not have been that bad if the wind hadn't picked up. It came in strong gusts from every direction, depending on how the streets funneled it. Raindrops whipped in sideways, drenching another part of me with each blast. I was soaked from the waist down in two blocks, but I kept walking. I was *doing* something, and who cared if I got wet?

Out of nowhere, Enzo closed his umbrella and kept walking.

I glanced over at him. "Was it leaking?"

"È una bella giornata, no?"

"You're just trying to distract me."

"Come on, Gia. Where's the girl who loves having fun? Did she get lost somewhere when I didn't see her for a year? It's a bit of rain, sì. But it's eighty degrees out. We're not going to catch a chill. This isn't the Antarctic."

If anything, the rain came down harder. It streamed off his shoulders and pelted his face, and he had to squint just to see where he was going. He knelt in the middle of a puddle and pretended he was bathing, splashing water left and right.

And just like a branch breaking under too much pressure, something about that scene made the tension snap inside of me. One moment I was focused on nothing more than the job at hand and enduring the rain, and, the next, I'd closed my umbrella as well, going over to sit on the curb next to him.

"That water is filthy," I said.

He stared at me for a moment, then smiled at what he saw. "Good thing there's plenty coming down from the sky, then. Come on, we can keep walking now."

I should have been miserable. A day that was already promising to be dismal had turned even worse, but somehow during that walk, the rain washed away my other troubles until it was just me walking along, enjoying the sensation of water on my face and the way my shoes squelched with each step. I used to love the rain when I was younger—before the Axeman had stolen what was left of my childhood. Seven-year-old me would have been so excited to see such a strong storm, and maybe I tapped into that part of me for a little. I forgot about what was waiting ahead and, instead, looked for the deepest puddles to splash through.

We passed several other people on our way to the Seventh Ward. The rain didn't keep absolutely everyone off the street, but the ones we did pass gave us plenty of space. Some of them ignored us, some of them scowled, and a few smiled and said something nice in passing.

Five minutes before we made it to the Cortimiglias', the rain turned off as quickly as if someone had twisted a knob. The sun broke out, and Enzo and I continued on our way feeling, for the moment, at peace.

By the time we made it there, the two of us might as well have jumped in the Mississippi, for how wet we still were. But we were laughing and taking turns bumping into each other, and that half hour was the happiest I'd felt in over two months. Between the Great War and the flu and the nightmares and my parents' store struggles, there'd been more than enough reasons to be worried, but it was the sort of worry that built itself up in little stages, one brick at a time. You didn't think of it as any one big load, but, when you took a step back to see all the worries you were carrying, you wondered how in the world you were even moving forward at all.

That walk in the rain removed the worries for a little, but then the Cortimiglias' came into sight, and all the worries rushed back at once. I stumbled to a halt, staring.

Say one thing for the Axeman: he was consistent. The storefront looked much like the Maggios' we'd visited a week ago. For that matter, it could have been a close relative of my home or Enzo's. Same single story. Same style awning out front. Same fenced-in backyard.

Only this one was surrounded by policemen.

There were four of them in the street, studying the house from different angles while another one stood in the main entrance, perhaps speaking to more inside. Ten or fifteen onlookers had gathered around the building to gawk. They came from all walks of life. Housewives and laborers, white and Black. Maybe it was because it was the second murder in a week, or maybe Enzo and I were just faster getting to the scene this time, but it was a stark difference compared to the group of kids we had to deal with last time.

A tall woman with long brown hair and a scar running down the right side of her face stood out from the crowd, more because, instead of studying the house, she was inspecting the people around her. Her gaze met mine for a moment, and I turned to face Enzo. "Come on," I said. "There's the Giodanos'."

An older man and his son stood in the front yard of the house across the street from the action. I didn't know them as well as I did Signora Giodano, but I waved anyway. When you treated people like old friends, they were much likelier to return the favor.

They noticed us approaching, of course. It was hard to miss two sopping wet Italians, and not just because our shoes squished so much. Signor Giodano was in his sixties with rectangular-framed glasses, a thick gray mustache, and dressed in a brown suit that had seen better days. His son was about our age, though he stood over six feet tall and had to weigh twice as much as me. His eyes were red from crying, and he seemed oblivious to our presence.

"Ciao," I said. With so many strangers and police around, it would be safer to keep the conversation in Italian. "I'm Gianna Crutti and this is Enzo Rissetto. I don't know if you remember—"

Mr. Giodano man nodded, cutting me off. "We remember." He jerked his head at the scene across the street. "Especially on days like today."

I flushed some. "What happened? The police came by our store, and when we heard—"

"The Cortimiglias," Mr. Giodano said. "It was terrible. That demon attacked them. Killed their daughter."

At that, the younger one—was his name Frank?—sniffled loudly and wiped at his eyes. "Mary."

"How do they know it was him?" I asked.

"Who else could it be?" Mr. Giodano answered. "Last night, I heard screams. Not shouting. Not yelling. These were like no noises

I'd heard a human make before. I rushed out my door and hurried over to their house. The back door was open—a panel on it had been chiseled out. Rosie was standing there, her face so covered in blood I didn't recognize her at first. It was like her skin had been peeled away and... Then I saw Charlie on the ground behind her, and I realized it was Rosie in front of me, and she was holding..."

His son took over the story. "Mary," he repeated. "Little Mary. We got the doctors, but I don't see how any of them could survive. Those were axe wounds. Deep. Like someone was hacking at a tree stump instead of a human."

While they were talking, I noticed the rest of the crowd around the Cortimiglias' kept throwing looks our way. At first I thought it might have been at us, but, after a bit, it was clear they were much more interested in the Giodanos.

Signora Giodano—heavyset, with thick white hair and a well-mended dress—came out of the house and stood there surveying the scene. "Is that little Gigi looking like a wet towel? Which would make you Enzo, si? Were you caught out in the storm without an umbrella? And this with Spanish Flu everywhere? What would your mother think? Come in! We need to get you dried and warmed up, and these two need to be inside as well before the police get any more ideas."

She wasn't a woman to argue with. Before I could say anything, she had shepherded all four of us inside their home: another Italian grocery. We were sitting down at her table eating soup and bread, dry towels draped over our shoulders while she bustled around the kitchen. Enzo and I exchanged glances. This could definitely have been going worse.

Plus, the minestrone was excellent.

"Ten years we've been here," Mrs. Giodano was saying. I'd asked them what all the matter was, and that had been all it took for the three of them to launch into it. "Ten years selling fruit and vegetables to these people, and what does it earn us? Nothing. No trust. No respect. We might as well be dirt."

Mr. Giodano waved her off, limping around the room in a way that said he'd had that injury for a long time. "You can't judge people based on how they react at a time like this. The Cortimiglias were attacked. People want to feel safe, so they look for an easy explanation."

"Hah!" Mrs. Giodano said. "More like convenient. And here you are suddenly worshiping those two along with everyone else. When they were the ones who built a store right across the street from ours. We're supposed to treat them like saints?"

"We took their store back from them," Frankie said.

"We owned it," Mrs. Giodano said to me. "We rented it to them. It was never theirs to begin with. And Frankie loved that little girl. Mary. *He's* supposed to have chopped her to pieces? And, if not him, then who? Iorlando can't move faster than a snail, and he's got all the strength of a peanut."

When her husband tried to protest, she kept going. "Don't try to deny it. Who's been running the store these last years? Me, that's who. You do a lot of standing and talking, but I'm doing the selling and getting. If you're able to lift an axe up over your head and cut a family again and again, then you've done a perfect job hiding it."

They went back and forth, bickering in a way that felt comfortable and well-worn. They weren't really angry with each other: they just used their arguing to work out problems and think together.

And they were worried. As Enzo and I let the three of them talk, several points became clear. The attack had happened very early this morning. The Cortimiglias had bad blood with the Giodanos, and Mr. Giodano was the first person to find the bodies, which increased suspicion around them. People were already claiming they'd used the Axeman attacks as a way to cover vengeance on the new family.

It didn't add up, however. There was no way the old man sitting at the kitchen table would be able to brutally attack anyone. I didn't see Mrs. Giodano handling the weapon, either. And Frankie? The boy was practically a puppy.

We visited for a while longer, but their store business picked up eventually, and they had to leave to go tend to customers. Between the rain and the minestrone, I was feeling like a new person. "We'll head out in a few more minutes," I told Enzo.

"Head where?"

"You're going to distract any policemen who are left, and I'm going into the Cortimiglias'."

"This soon? What are you going to look for?"

"Maybe nothing, maybe something, but I didn't walk all this way to not even bother trying."

"That's a terrible idea, Gia."

"You're just saying that because you didn't think of it."

"What was there to think of? It took you all of what—five seconds? We don't want the police paying attention to us."

"So be a good distraction, then. We're Italians. It's not like they bother learning our names or faces. Besides, you heard the Giodanos. The cops already are half convinced *they* did it. If we get caught, at least we'll be taking the attention away from them for a little while."

He held my gaze for a few seconds, then sighed. "And people say *I'm* the impulsive one."

"That's why I like you, Vincenzo Rissetto. You know when it's useless to try and talk me out of something."

"Got any ideas for a distraction?"

"You're an Italian boy who can pick up a picnic table with one hand," I said. "I don't think distracting the police is going to take too much effort."

CHAPTER SIX

*Police authorities frankly confess they are puzzled to determine
whether the murders were the deeds of a single degenerate, or are
the outcome of a vendetta among Italian people.*

———————

"Y OU REMEMBER THE QUESTIONS?" I asked Enzo as we walked
over to the Cortimiglias'.

"This is still a terrible idea. The tactics here are way off."

"There's only one policeman left. You have to stand there and
talk to him for fifteen minutes. I think you can manage it." The
storm was completely gone by now, though the street was still more
than half puddles. My shoes were mostly dry, at least.

"What if he doesn't want to talk?"

"Then make something up. Bring up what it was like seven
years ago. Forse dovrai improvvisare, ma ho fiducia in te."

"Improvise? I'm not one of your jazz friends, so maybe your
faith is a bit misplaced."

We had turned left out of the Giodanos', planning to walk

around the corner and come from different directions. Now we were about to split up, so it was my last time to calm my friend down before the plan began. "Enzo, what will happen if you ask too many questions?"

"He'll get suspicious."

"Exactly. And what does a suspicious policeman do?"

"Keep an eye on me."

"Right. So, if that happens, and you run out of things to talk about, or the policeman won't talk anymore, just…ti celi un po'."

"Lurk around?"

"Yes. Lurk. That's the word. You lurk around, and he'll be suspicious, so he'll be watching you instead of the store. That's all you are, Enzo. A distraction. I'll be taking care of the rest, sì?"

He wasn't nervous. He just didn't like that we hadn't come up with anything better. But we didn't have all day. I patted him on the back, shoving him forward so that he'd start walking again. "Fifteen minutes. Anyone can do anything for fifteen minutes. I'll come out when I'm done, and then you can leave."

"Fifteen minutes." He headed off toward the store, his face a scowl and his shoulders hunched. If that didn't make the policeman suspicious, I had no idea what would.

I gave my friend a thirty-second head start, and then I followed. All I had to do was wait until the policeman wasn't looking my way, and I'd be able to sneak into the backyard just as I'd done in Freret. For all Enzo had groused ahead of time, when he actually came to the policeman, he started talking right away and didn't seem to have any problems.

The policeman distracted, I moved forward in a steady stride to the backyard fence. Not too fast to draw attention, but I wanted to get behind the man as soon as I could. "Distracted" only went so far, after all. That worked without a problem, but when I went to open the gate to the backyard, someone had locked it. The fence was at least six feet tall, with rough wooden planks lined up right next to each other, the tops cut into triangles.

I shook the door again, thinking it might have just been stuck. The fence rattled, and Enzo's voice got louder for a moment to cover my mistake. They were only twenty feet off, though the policeman was facing away from me. I froze for a moment, pointing to the gate and looking to Enzo to make sure he understood what was going on.

This was our only chance. It wasn't as if I'd be able to have Enzo be the distraction again in the next hour or two. We'd have to wait for the shifts to change, and, even then, I'd be in the same predicament: a locked gate and no way over.

But I hadn't grown up lifting bags of flour and rice and beans for no reason. I raised my eyebrows at Enzo and jerked my head back in what I hoped he understood as a message. Without waiting for him to acknowledge it, I turned back to the fence, got a firm grip on the top, and pulled myself up in as close to a smooth motion as I could manage.

It shook and teetered with my weight, not built to stand up to a hundred and ten pounds of Gianna. The triangles scraped at my stomach as I went over, and there was a sickening moment when they caught on my blouse. My momentum stalled, and I thought I'd be stuck there for anyone to see. I pushed forward, and my blouse tore, but I managed to land without too much noise.

I crouched in the Cortimiglias' backyard, listening to my breathing and waiting to hear if the policeman came over. Enzo's voice asked another question—not loud enough for me to understand—and the policeman answered in a rumble that didn't sound concerned. I had done it.

My blouse wasn't as torn as I'd worried it might be. Two rips across my stomach, and my skin was bleeding slightly from the scrape, but it wasn't anything I couldn't cover up by folding my arms in front of me, should the need arise. I could mend it and probably not get in too much trouble with Mama.

Better yet, the back door was open. I should be able to get into the house without any further problems.

I took a deep breath, stood, and padded over to the back porch.

Once again, the door had been chiseled open. It was like most of the doors down here: a solid wooden frame, but with four rectangles where the wood was thinner—to make the door look nicer, I supposed. It also meant anyone with a sharp tool could cut through those thin spots without too much trouble. Maybe we ought to start replacing our doors.

Where the carnage in the Maggio home had been confined to the bedroom, a trail of blood greeted me as soon as I entered the kitchen. Red footprints pacing back and forth in the room, leading from the main store. They weren't worker's boots. No tread on them to speak of, and they made me think of my father's Sunday shoes. I placed my foot next to one of them: mine were only an inch smaller. You could almost see the Axeman leaving the crime, walking through the kitchen, pausing to stare at…what? I tried to picture what might have caught his eye. The sink? Or had a dog barked outside, and he'd frozen with fear, worried he might be caught?

I didn't get even a hint of fear from him, however. Those footprints weren't as large as I thought they'd be, but they showed no hesitation. No shuffling. A small pool of blood next to the door indicated where he might have set his axe down after he was done with the attack. It was gone now: taken by the police?

If the kitchen had some trails of blood, the main storeroom was a cityscape of it. More of the Axeman's shoes striding straight through the place, crisscrossed by a smaller set of bare feet accompanied by a stream of trailing blood, as if someone had been pouring it from a jug as they went. Splashes of red, congealed on the floor. Mrs. Cortimiglia, running to the door as best she could carrying the body of her dead daughter in her arms. With the amount of blood she'd been losing, it was a miracle she'd been able to make it that far.

I pictured their daughter, remembering what it had been like for me seven years ago. I'd been ten, and I still woke up in the night drenched in sweat, the image of that bloody axe sinking into my father's shoulder fresh as when I'd first seen it. Was it a mercy Mary had been killed in this attack? Nonsense. Would I have rather been slain seven years ago?

There were signs of the police, as well. Fainter footsteps that had tried to stay out of the main pieces of evidence and had largely been successful.

I stood in the main room for a full minute, trying to clear my head and tap into whatever it had been that I'd connected with back at the Maggios'. What had I done before? It had felt so easy then, as if my mind had been waiting to reach out to the crime. I remembered the eagerness that had washed over me when I'd seen the blood there. How it had made me nauseous but…excited.

This time, I felt empty. Lost. Like I was standing back in the middle of where the Axeman had attacked my parents, watching the past and unable to do anything about it. I'd thought this trip would make some piece of information click into place, even if I hadn't known what, but if I'd been expecting the universe to whack me over the head with inspiration, then the universe had other plans.

What was I doing? Who was I to think I could do anything against this brute? I was no one special. Just a silly girl with night-mares. Someone whose mind couldn't get over the trauma of an attack seven years ago. And now, to try and feel important, I was going where I didn't belong, sticking my nose into other people's tragedies.

I was a fake, and this was proof. No visions were coming to me in the store. I was everything people accused Signora Caravaggio of being. And, if I had half a brain, I would leave now and—

No.

I shook my head. That wasn't me thinking those thoughts. That was the voice that liked to talk to me at night when I was lying in bed, trying to sleep, dreading the nightmares that might follow. The voice that loved so much to remind me of the mistakes I made and the stupid things I said. The one that wanted me to fail every minute of every day. Papa had told me about that voice when I was thirteen and felt like the world was against me.

"There are plenty of people who are going to tell you you're nothing," he'd said. "There will even be a part of yourself that will believe it. A voice that says you're a failure. And all it takes for that voice to be right is for you to pay attention to it. Don't do that, Gianna. Don't let other people tell you who you are and what you can do."

I clenched my fists and strode toward the bedroom, filled with newfound determination. I would go right to where the attack happened, and I would see if anything else came to me. I had dreamed about a little girl being attacked, and it had to have some sort of a connection to everything that—

Something…called to me. Like metal drawn to a magnet. I paused and studied the floor on my right for a moment. A glint of light caught my eye. Something shiny that had fallen between the floorboards. I bent over to fish it out, though I knew what it was the moment I saw the gleam.

An old silver coin, with a crown and shield on one side, and the head of Charles III on the other. I couldn't make out the date, but it was a Spanish picayune that would match the other one in my pocket like a twin.

My hand clenched into a fist around it. The room blurred, and I stumbled to my left, careening for a moment as I struggled to find my balance. I closed my eyes and took a breath, and when I opened them, the room had changed. It was cloaked in darkness, and it took a moment for me to gain my bearings. I was still in the main room of the store, in the same place I'd paused before, as if I'd backed up ten feet and 12 hours.

And I was furious. As soon as that emotion hit me, all other thoughts were swept from my head.

I edged forward, the shaft of the axe handle smooth in my hands, its head a comforting weight at the end. A promise of things to come. The room was silent, and only a few cracks of light filtered in through the shutters, remnants of the streetlights from outside.

One of the floorboards creaked as I put weight on it, and I froze for a count of twenty, waiting to hear if it had woken any of them up. A tiny groan wafted toward me from the room ahead of me: the noise of the little one settling back down.

I wanted to rush in. To start swinging and hacking, to feel the release that came with the feel of the axehead cutting through flesh into bone. *That jolt as it made contact. The way the bone pulled against it when I went for another stroke. I needed it, and having it this close was almost unbearable.*

But, at the same time, the wait made it all the sweeter. The anticipation of what was building inside me, waiting to break out. It was the difference between finding a surprise present, beautifully wrapped, and shredding through the wrappings to see what they hid.

All parts of the process were a joy. One that couldn't be rushed.

Six more steps brought me to the bedroom door, left slightly ajar. I shut my eyes and waited, listening for confirmation of even breathing. The male's deep sigh. Proof they were all ready for me.

I eased the door open. It squeaked halfway through, and the little one fussed again. A light sleeper. "Mary?" the female said, her voice thick with sleep. "Stai bene? Dorma, cucciola."

The spoken Italian was enough to push me over the edge. Made me want to jump in early and dive into what was waiting for me. But it had to be from the shadows. If they were awake, it would ruin some of the experience. So I tucked myself to the side of the doorframe, mindful of how their eyes would be adjusted to the dark and might see me as a backlit shadow, looming.

My palms began to sweat. To have it all so close and not be able to start yet was almost too much. I focused on counting in my head. Calm and steady until I reached fifty, and then I moved forward again.

There was enough light to see three forms on the bed: the little one was sleeping with my prey. I'd take the male first. He'd be more likely to

*cause problems for me later on, and I didn't want to have to worry about
any resistance.*

*I inched forward until I was practically touching the bed with my
thighs. My heart hammered in my chest, the pressure building as I raised
the axe up and back, just like I was chopping wood growing up, but so
much sweeter. I allowed myself a few moments of pause in that position,
reveling in what was about to come, focusing on my target: the male's
shoulder. I didn't want to kill him. Not right away, at least. It wasn't as
pleasurable if they didn't scream and flail.*

*And then I brought the axe streaking down, cutting through the
air and thunking into flesh and bone in one swift motion. The sudden
movement startled the female awake. She gasped—they always did—and
called out, "Charles? Mary?" Panic already seeping through her voice, even
though she'd barely had enough time to sense what might be happening.*

*The male groaned in pain instead of screaming, which was a bit of a
disappointment. I wrenched the axe free and attacked the female.*

*From there, the rage took over as it always did. My axe rising and
falling almost of its own accord. Warm blood on my hands, splashing
onto my face and splattering onto the floor. I lost all sense of control,
lashing out at everything and anything in the darkness. The little one
might have cried out at some point, and one of the axe blows crushed
something small and light, but I had to keep going. Had to keep—*

The room blurred and spun again. When I blinked my eyes
clear, it was daylight again. I was lying on the floor in a shadowed
room, and someone was shaking me by my shoulder.

"I said, what's all this?"

The policeman from outside was crouched next to me in the Cortimiglias' bedroom, and his scowl could have curdled milk. Enzo stood behind him, peering down at me with a concerned expression.

My mind was still reeling from what I'd experienced, trying to make sense of it all. That hadn't just been a vision. It had been like I'd actually been there. Seeing what the Axeman was doing. Feeling what he felt.

I wanted to throw up. To go take a long bath, or at least scrub my hands. I could still remember the way the blood had felt when it hit my face. The feel of the axe as it—

"Well?" the policeman said. "Are you listening?"

"I—I didn't—"

He wrenched me up, and I scrambled to my feet. He grabbed Enzo with his other hand. "I don't know what the two of you are up to, but you'll both be coming with me. All very suspicious is what this is, and I know a few people who'll want to ask you some questions."

I should have come up with some sort of an excuse. Some way to convince him to let us go, but, at that moment, it was all I could do to put one foot in front of the other and keep from falling down. I didn't understand what had just happened, but, whatever it was, this was much more than just a simple quest to catch a killer now.

And I still had that second picayune clutched tight in my fist.

CHAPTER SEVEN

In every case except one the victims have lived back of corner groceries, their homes have been entered in early morning hours, entrance has been effected by removing a panel from rear doors and an ax, in nearly every case left on the premises, has been the weapon of the murderer.

THE DRIVE TO THE POLICE station did not go well. The officer who caught me insisted on staying in the back with me and Enzo. We weren't allowed to speak, though I don't know what I would have told Enzo if I could have said anything. Admitting to what I'd just gone through? What sort of a person has a vision of a killing and remembers how wonderful it felt?

When we got to the station, we were separated and led to different rooms. I sat there, flushed and confused, with no idea how much time had gone by. There were no clocks. No one checked on me, though I did make a fuss at one point until I was allowed to use the toilet. Other than that, I waited. Watched police officers in and out of uniform walk past the single window in the room. Listen to muffled conversations that wafted through the door. No one seemed to be taking special interest in me, but I had no idea what happened to a person once the police got involved.

The whole thing had been foolish. We'd risked so much, and now what might come of it? The police would almost definitely contact our families. What was I going to tell my parents? They knew all about my nightmares seven years ago, but I'd seen what that knowledge did to them back then. After six months of them worrying and not understanding, I had just told them the nightmares had gone away.

Occhio non vede, cuore non duole. The eye doesn't see, the heart doesn't hurt. Though Americans said it as "what you don't know can't hurt you."

Well it would hurt them even more now, to know I'd lied to them for all this time and now brought the attention of the police down on us again. Italians in New Orleans had trouble enough without the police making more of it. And, when you have nothing but time on your hands, there are plenty of other worries that can come to you. What if the other Italians blamed me for making the police more suspicious? What if my name got in the papers? At that point, there was no knowing what might come of it.

Signora Caravaggio had warned me my future looked dark, and what had I done? I'd gone searching for the darkness. She'd told me it was up to me to get through it, and I'd thought that was what I was doing by acting with Enzo. Had I only made it worse, instead?

My mouth was parched, and my stomach was a tight knot of hunger. It had to have been at least four hours I'd been stuck in that room. Had the police already sent someone to speak to my parents, or were they just wondering what had happened to me?

I took the time to study the new coin, though it had no hidden mysteries. This one was from 1846, but the writing was clearer than my old one. DEI GRATIA CAROLUS III, the one side said, followed by HISPAN ET IND RMFM on the other. I'd said enough Latin prayers to know it was talking about honoring Charles III and Spain and...India? I wasn't sure about the last bit with the initials, but knowing that wouldn't magically unlock the rest of the puzzle for me.

The Axeman had to have dropped it. It was the only thing that made sense, since I'd found the same coin at his attack on my parents so long ago. It didn't seem like he'd placed it there on purpose. Was he just carrying a bag of old coins with him? Maybe he was some sort of collector. Should I tell the police?

For a moment, I thought my imagination was making up the smell of freshly baked bread. Rye, just like Mama would bake each Monday morning. But the scent got stronger, and then a woman stepped past the window and stopped at the door, saying something to someone out of sight before opening the door and brining the scent in with her. I slipped the coin back into my pocket.

The woman was of average height, with long dark hair in a bun, blue eyes, and a set to her jaw that said she wasn't someone who put up with much from anyone. The scar she had running down the left side of her face only added to that feeling, and, the moment I saw it, I remembered seeing her at the Cortimiglias'. She was still wearing the dark blue skirt, though she'd removed the leather jacket, revealing a simple white blouse that came to her wrists. She had a picnic basket draped over her right arm, and she set it on the table in front of me before closing the door and sitting across from me.

Without speaking, she opened the basket and removed a tablecloth. She set the basket on the floor and unfurled the cloth across the table. That done, she set her elbows on the table, rested her chin on her hands, and stared at me.

I stared back, confused.

"It's from when you were a child, isn't it?" she asked me in a low alto that made me wonder how good her singing voice was. I always preferred altos, but why was that occurring to me now of all times?

All I knew was I had no desire to talk to this woman, since she wasn't even with the police. Maybe she was some goody-goody attached to them. I didn't know, and I didn't care.

"I don't English," I said, keeping my face blank.

The woman didn't even blink. "Your obsession with crime scenes. Or is it with the Axeman?"

I felt the blood rush to my face, and I sat back, hoping some shadows might hide the reaction. "Solo italiano."

"Nonsense," she said, then reached into the basket and took out a cutting board, followed by a bread knife, a plate, and a large loaf of rye bread. The scent got even stronger, and my stomach growled in response, loud enough to be heard in the hall, most likely.

I licked my lips. Maybe I just needed to spout out more Italian. Most people got frustrated when you said things they couldn't understand. "Lei può provare a corrompermi con il cibo, ma non funzionerà. Non le dirò niente, pazza."

She smiled, though I couldn't tell if it was from my stomach growling, or from what I'd said. Was there a chance she spoke Italian?

"Your name is Gianna Crutti. Born March 23, 1901. You live with your mother, Harriet, and father, August. Your family was attacked by an unknown man on August 13, 1910. He came into the house and hacked into your father before waking your mother and demanding money. Five and a half feet tall, clean-shaven, dark hair, broad shoulders, mid-thirties. September 20 of the same year, the man attacked Joseph and Conchetto Rissetto. Their son, Enzo, is next door, wondering what you're doing and what's going to happen to him."

So she knew our history. Anyone could have found that out by looking through the papers from back then. "I no tell nothing," I said. "Non penso nemmeno che lei sia con la polizia."

She blinked once and answered in accented but very fine Italian, "I can switch to Italian if you insist, but I think this would be easier for both of us if we stuck to English."

I blushed again. "You shouldn't make people feel stupid."

"Agreed," she said, then sliced off the end of the bread and offered it to me. When I declined, she shrugged and began to eat it herself. "You'd be surprised what I know about you," she said in between bites. "But none of that really matters. What does matter is that I know you didn't have anything to do with these murders, and I've already spoken to the police about letting you go."

"How can I trust you?"

"I don't care if you trust me. Once I'm done talking to you, you're going to leave the police station with your friend, and I'm never going to see you at another crime scene again."

"Who are you?"

"Not relevant. You and your family have already paid enough to this Axeman. I'm here to make sure you don't end up paying more. You're trying to catch him, aren't you? Catch him or kill him?"

I folded my arms and sat back in my seat, angry that I felt like I had no control over this conversation.

"I can relate to the feeling," she continued. She cut another couple slices of bread, then took out a plate and some fixings for sandwiches. A jar of mayonnaise. One of spiced brown mustard. Knives to match. "You think, if you can finally confront him, that all of your problems will disappear. Maybe you've even made yourself a promise about it. I'm here to tell you you're wrong."

"How am I wrong?"

She took out some sliced roast beef, along with a second plate. "Are you sure you don't want one?" she asked, offering me the bread and the knife. "You're not punishing me by not eating, after all. I thought you'd be hungry, but, if you aren't, you—"

"You think I'm going to just eat lunch with you while my friend is starving next door? Or is someone in there giving him a sandwich, too?"

She stood without another word, packed a few of the fixings back into the basket, and disappeared. A few minutes later she returned, setting the condiments out again. "He's eating now. Is that better?"

I waggled my hand back and forth in front of my face. "Better would have been me seeing his face when you showed up with the basket. But it'll do." I grabbed the bread and started sawing off my own slices. If the food was free, I might as well eat it instead of sitting around starving. But she wasn't going to get any information from me. Then again, maybe if I played my cards right, I could get something from her. "How am I wrong?" I asked again.

"There are two things that might happen if you try to face the Axeman. The first is that what you have planned will backfire. You'll draw his attention, or you'll stumble across him while you're nosing around. When that happens, you'll meet a man who has already proven he isn't just willing to kill, he prefers it. You and your friend will almost certainly die. You might think life is bad now, but it's much better than the alternative. That's the sort of thing you don't understand until that alternative is staring you in the face."

The two of us focused on our sandwiches for the next while.

Whoever this woman was, she'd brought an impressive array of meats, cheeses, and vegetables. I couldn't have made a sandwich this nice if I'd been in my own store. A few policemen walked past the window while we were silently at work. Judging by the looks they gave us, they were as confused by this woman as I was.

"What's the second thing that might happen?" I asked at last.

"You'll get what you think you want."

"How is that a problem?"

"It depends on what it is you think you want. If you want him dead, you'll have to live with the memory of killing him. If you want him caught and brought to justice, you'll find that justice doesn't magically fix things." She stared down at the corner of the table for a moment, lost in thought. But, before I could comment on it, she refocused, grabbed her sandwich, and took a large bite.

"You aren't with the police?" I asked her.

She shook her head, her mouth still full.

"But you're investigating the Axeman. I saw you at both the Cortimiglias'."

"I'm not telling you anything more than you already know," she said. "What I want you to do is tell me what *you* might know about this case. Then you can finish your sandwich, and we never have to see each other again."

"Why should I tell someone I don't even know anything, let alone things about myself?" I asked.

"Fair enough," she said, then wiped her hand on her skirt

and offered to shake mine. "My name's Etta Palmer. I'm with the Pinkerton Detective Agency, and I investigate…unusual crimes."

I shook her hand, mainly because I didn't know how else to get her to put it down without being rude. "What do you mean?"

"Killers, mainly. Or those who are exceptionally cruel. I find them and catch them before they do anything else."

"You must not be very good at it, if it takes you seven years to even show up for one of them."

The wry grin she gave me puckered the scar on her cheek. "There's only one me, and America is a big place. I have to choose where I can do the most good."

"And what?" I asked. "Now that he's back killing, he's more interesting to you?"

"I'm not here to be badgered by a seventeen-year-old," Etta said. "You're too young to really—" She checked herself, and the smile that followed that seemed much more genuine. "Let me see if I can guess some of what has you so motivated," she continued. "Humor me."

I shrugged and polished off a few bites of my sandwich. That was some of the best salami I'd ever had. Peppery, but not enough to make your eyes water.

"When that attack happened seven years ago, it changed you," Etta said. It was a statement, not a question, so I didn't say anything back. "Your life was turned upside down in a moment, and you wanted the old one back."

"E' inutile piangere sul latte versato," I said.

"No use crying over spilled milk?" She thought about the statement for a moment, then shook her head. "No. You might try to say that to make me think you believe it, but that's not what you're showing me now. Most people who have something happen to them like what happened to you don't go hunting it down years later. I've talked to people who have been in those situations. They'd do anything to avoid it."

"You've talked to people, but you've never been attacked like that," I said. "So what would you know? You can be a detective. You can go around running after murderers, but you've got no, how do they say it? Skin in the game?"

Now it was her turn to take a bite of her sandwich. She chewed it with her eyes closed, swallowed, then opened them again. "You think I don't know what it's like to be helpless? To have your entire life held in the hand of someone else. To know that, if he wanted, he could end it all with a flick of his wrist or the stroke of his axe?"

"Is that where you got the scar from?" I asked. "From a man?"

"I got the scar from thinking just because I'd faced down one monster and lived that I was ready to go after all the others. For thinking no one else could possibly be as evil—as dangerous—as he had been, so everything else would be safe. But you're not safe, Gianna. Just because you lived through one attack doesn't mean you're invincible."

I set my plate down and pushed it away from me, my appetite

suddenly gone. "You think I want to be safe? Invincible? I don't think you understand me after all."

She put her palms on the table and leaned toward me. "I *know* you want to be safe, but that's not all you want. You want to turn in at night without checking the locks three times. You want to be with your family without remembering their screams. You want to sleep without nightmares, and you think, if you can just catch him, then it'll all go away. But it doesn't go away, Gianna. None of it. We're only as safe as we let ourselves be, and doing what you're doing is only asking for more pain, not avoiding it in the future."

That had all been too close to home for comfort. How had she known about the nightmares? "You talked to Enzo first, didn't you?" I asked, the conclusion clicking in my head. "You forced him to tell you about me, and then you come in here with your basket and your bread and—"

"I haven't said a single word to your friend. I handed him some food, and I left."

"Then how do you know all about that? You talked to my parents?"

"I know because I've been you. Sat where you're sitting. Wanted what you want. Go back, Gianna. Give it up. From what I've seen poking around a bit, you have a good life. Sure, your family could use more money, but who couldn't? You have to appreciate what you have before it's too late."

"You've been me?" I asked, incredulous. "What sort of a line is that? You think I'm supposed to believe it? You don't know me, no matter how much snooping around you've done. And, even if you've been in some sort of a situation like mine, you didn't follow the advice you just gave me, did you?"

She paused, then shook her head. "No. I didn't."

"Then why do you think I'd run away from this now?"

"It's not running away."

"Call it whatever you want, but we both know what it is, if you really think you understand me."

She hung her head, and her shoulders drooped. "You're right. Of course. You're going to do what you're going to do, but at least stop going to these crime scenes, alright? I can step in this time, but the police won't listen to me more than once. The Pinkerton name gets some respect with them, but I have to be careful not to use it all up until I need it."

"I'm done with the scenes," I said, and meant it. I never wanted to experience something like that again.

Etta studied me for a few seconds, then nodded. "I believe you. Now is there anything you can tell me about the Axeman that might help me find him?"

Now it was my turn to slouch. Because what did I really know about that demon that the police didn't? "No," I said at last. "I didn't see him seven years ago, and I haven't seen him now. I don't know what he looks like, and I don't know where he's hiding. I don't know why he's doing this." But I did, didn't I? Except how could I explain that to this woman? I appreciated that she was straightforward. If I were to tell anyone about this, it might be her, but she would laugh me out of the room. Psychic visions? I'd be lucky if she didn't put me in an institution.

Etta weighed what I said, maybe wondering if she believed me. But at last she concluded. "Finish your sandwich, then go get your friend. The police know to let you go. But, if you think of anything else, you come to me. You and I want the same thing. Will you do that?"

I grunted, unwilling to commit to anything. "Thanks for the sandwich," I said.

She smiled. "There's more where that came from if you come talk to me again."

I smiled back. "Oh, it was good, but it wasn't *that* good. But I'll think about what you said at least, sì?"

"Fine," she said, standing. "Just remember one thing, Gianna. People like the Axeman… It's not a game to them. He'll kill you if he can. Don't put yourself or your family in any more danger. One attack is enough." And, with that, she turned and left the room.

CHAPTER EIGHT

MYSTERIOUS PERSON'S NOTE DATED 'HELL,' SIGNED 'AXMAN': Immunity Promised All Families Who Have Jazz Band Playing in Their Homes When "Fell Demon from Hottest Hell" Flies Over City.

═══════════

MY MOTHER REFUSED TO ACKNOWLEDGE the appeal of newspapers.

"All those pages, every day? Maybe there wouldn't be so much news if people didn't have to sit around coming up with articles to write all the time. Who cares who won what game and what someone said in New York? We've got problems enough of our own right here."

Which was definitely true, but didn't make the newspaper any less important. We sold the *Times-Picayune*—the name's significance was not lost on me—which came out in the morning, and *The State*, which was an afternoon paper, and it was one of the biggest perks of the store. Being able to see what was going on in the city and the world first thing. I would always keep an ear out for the delivery: the rumble of the truck that brought them by, followed by the heavy, soft *thump* when the newspaper bundle landed on the curb. If I was home when it came, I was always the first outside to get it and bring them in.

Even a few months ago, I was mainly looking through them to find where the next concerts would be and if there might be any touring musicians coming through. These days, I was much more worried that another attack might have happened, or impatient to find out if the police had any more leads. My nightmares hadn't gone away, but they hadn't been specific since the attack on the Cortimiglias'. More…expectant than bloody, if that made sense. If they were a window on the Axeman, then he was planning something, and I was desperate to find out what.

My conversation with Etta had only made that keener.

So I was more eager than ever to scan the morning and evening news each day, and I had been since the beginning of October. I'd told my parents that it was for word of when the Original Dixieland Jazz Band might be in New Orleans next, assuring them I'd heard a rumor it would be any day, but I was really only focused on finding some clue that might lead me closer to the Axeman.

If that clue existed, it had slipped past me so far. It hadn't put me a step ahead of him before he'd killed baby Mary, and I worried I'd keep lagging behind him for the next ever.

My mother was right about one thing with news, however: it

seemed like there was always too much of it. Word from the front, with Enzo hanging on every syllable: fighting in Meuse-Argonne, which left maybe more than 20,000 Americans dead; and a key battle at St. Quentin Canal, which Enzo had assured me was vital, since the Americans, British, and Australians broke through something called the Hindenburg Line. I'd raised my eyebrows and nodded at him and hoped he would drop the subject.

The influenza in New Orleans was also getting more threatening. A steamer had brought 56 infected sailors into port on the 2nd, and they'd put them in the Belvedere Sanitarium over in Algiers, since the naval base's hospital was already overflowing with cases. That wasn't too far from Signora Caravaggio, and I worried about her over there on her own, surrounded by sickness.

Except the influenza hadn't stayed there. I wanted to flinch every time I heard a cough or a sneeze, and I'd seen three different fights break out in the city when someone who looked sick had gotten too close to someone else. It didn't help that the city hadn't made it mandatory to report cases until the 7th, so there was no way of really knowing how many people had it here. One article I read estimated 7,000. That would be more than 2 percent of the city in just a week or two.

Could it get much worse? It was hard to believe when so much of life just kept moving forward. They'd had another war rally on the 5th in Lafayette Park. 50,000 people had crammed into the place. Surely, if the influenza were that bad, something would have gone wrong with an event like that.

And what did it really *do* to you? I'd heard plenty of stories. Enzo had said your lips turned blue and you suffocated to death because your lungs couldn't breathe, but two of our customers had been talking about how it made you bleed from your eyeballs. With people believing that, it was no wonder you'd see so many different precautions being taken. Some people swore by wearing face masks. Other people said face masks made it even worse, because you couldn't breathe as well. And then there were people walking around with strings of onions around their necks, since they thought the influenza was repelled by the scent.

I remembered Signora Caravaggio's vision of me, and my stomach sank further. How bad could the epidemic really get? And was that what her vision had meant, or had it been aimed at the Axeman?

Or was it both?

Between all those different worries careening around in my head, it was no wonder I had trouble sleeping. The morning of the 9th, I was up by 4:00, lying in bed and listening to my parents snore on the other side of the curtain. Sometimes you know sleep will never come back to you. You go from asleep to awake like lighting a match. And, as I lay there, I knew the longer I stayed there alone with my thoughts, the more I'd worry about them.

I was sick of thinking about things. I wanted to *do*. To take real steps and make real progress, and since I knew I wouldn't be making any real progress about the Axeman or influenza or even the Great War, I got out of bed and padded into the storeroom to take inventory of canned goods.

My father had made up a chart to help him keep track of what needed counting when. It wasn't a complex process: you stood there and looked at each can or bag or item and made sure it still looked ready to sell. Then you counted off how many of them were in the store, noted it, and moved onto the next. My father used that information to know what was selling and how quickly. He'd also used it to catch a thief who kept coming to the store two years ago, walking off with canned food and selling it down the street.

But, while Papa was good at making charts and having intentions, he often didn't find time to follow through on them. That morning, I was going to do it for him. I found the notepad and the pencil, dragged the ladder over to the canned goods section, and climbed to the top to start with the canned bread that some of the sailors from Ireland or England or even Boston came looking for. "You can't sell it if you don't have it," my father would say, and he had six cans of the stuff right now, each one covered in dust. I wiped off the tops, checked for dents or bulging in the cans, and scribbled down the number.

For the next while, I lost myself in the work. It was so much easier to focus on something that had a beginning and an end. I could watch myself getting closer to finished, even though it might have been taking more time than I'd expected. There were no customers, so there were no interruptions. I had made it to the beans by the time Papa came into the room, wiping sleep from his eyes.

I checked the clock: 5:05. Still twenty-five minutes before he was usually up. "I'm sorry," I said. "Was I too noisy?"

"Noisy?" he said, then switched to Italian. He always spoke Italian when he was too tired to manage English. "You were quiet as a mouse. When did you get up?"

"An hour ago. I couldn't sleep. Do you want some breakfast?"

He stared up at me, watching for a moment, before breaking out in a smile. "What did you do, Gianna?"

"Scusi?"

"Up at four in the morning, doing inventory? Either you killed my daughter and took her place, or you're my Gianna and something is wrong."

"Why would something have to be wrong?"

"Come on, daughter. I've lived with you for seventeen years. Mal comune mezzo gaudio. How would the Americans say it? A trouble shared is a trouble halved? Tell me what's wrong."

And I wanted to. Staring down at him, looking at the man who'd always been there for me to protect me and to pick me up and solve my problems and kiss my scrapes and give me a hug when I needed it, the thought of running to him and telling him all about the nightmares and my worries and Signora Caravaggio was almost overwhelming. But would he do with them? I would just be throwing worries on a man who'd had more than his fair share of them throughout his life.

"I've been gone from the store more than I should have the past week," I ended up saying. "I wanted to show I was sorry."

He thought about my words for a moment before smiling, nodding once, and crouching down by the ladder, taking out cans of tuna fish one at a time to count them up. I wasn't sure he'd believed me, but he'd gone along with my explanation. The two of us sat there working together for an hour and a half, and we were through a good chunk of the inventory when a truck rumbled by outside, followed immediately by that tell-tale thump of a stack of newspapers hitting the ground.

I tried to ignore it, and I thought I'd done a good job of it until Papa said, "Go. Find out if your jazz band is playing yet or not. We're about done with inventory for now, anyway."

While I might have wanted to pretend it wasn't that important to me, I couldn't stop myself from setting down the cans of lima beans, giving Papa a quick hug, and running outside to get the papers. I brought them into the storeroom, sliced off the string that tied them together, and took the top copy into the kitchen to read while I ate some oatmeal.

I skipped over stories about the Hindenburg Line and fighting in Europe. Enzo would take up enough of my time telling me about that already. But even my desperation for news of the Axeman couldn't hide the story about a quarantine: 56,000 cases of influenza in New Orleans? I leaned forward, trying to read the article as quickly as possible while still understanding what was going on.

All schools were shutting down, as well as churches, theaters, movie houses, and "other places of amusement." No more sporting events or funerals or even weddings, though somehow saloons, ice cream parlors, and restaurants were still okay? But there were strict laws against spitting? It didn't entirely make sense, and I thought I'd read it too quickly at first, but going over it a second time confirmed my first impression. Places of amusement had to mean jazz halls. A pit gaped open inside me as I thought what that would mean. One of the only things keeping me sane had been music. If churches were closed, too, did that mean I wouldn't be able to go practice piano?

I hadn't even considered any of that might be a possibility. Music and church and theaters and schools and sports—all of that was just part of life in the city. I'd been worried about death and the impact it might have on people, but, somehow, I hadn't thought it would cut into life as well.

Papa came in. "So? What's new in the world today?"

"Influenza," I said. "What did we do to deserve this?"

"Sometimes God wants to try us. It doesn't always have to be a punishment."

"This, though. This is different. It's like one of the plagues from the Bible. People go from being fine to being dead in the space of a few days. Sometimes as fast as a few hours!"

"All the more reason to make sure we're prepared to meet God," Papa said.

"Think about it," I snapped, trying to make him focus on something other than religion. "You have a tickle in the back of your throat. A few hours later, two mahogany-colored spots appear on your cheekbones. From there, your face turns blue, your limbs turn black, your lungs fill up with liquid, and you die. And that's if you're lucky. If you aren't, you might get some of the other symptoms: bleeding from your nose, ears, and mouth."

"I don't want to think about it," Papa said. "I want to still have some appetite when I'm eating breakfast."

I turned the page of the paper, lost in thought, dizzy, and confused. Then the next article hit me:

Hell, October 9, 1918

Editor of the Times-Picayune, New Orleans:

Esteemed mortal: They have never caught me and they never will. They have never seen me, for I am invisible, even as the ether which surrounds your earth. I am not a human being, but a spirit and a fell demon from hottest hell. I am what you Orleanians and your foolish police call the axman.

When I see fit, I shall come again and claim other victims. I alone know whom they shall be. I shall leave no clue, except perhaps my bloody ax, besmeared with the blood and brains of he whom I have sent below to keep me company.

If you wish you may tell the police to be careful not to rile me. Of course, I am a reasonable spirit. I take no offense at the way in which they have conducted their investigations in the past. In fact, they have been so utterly stupid so as to amuse not only me, but His Satanic Majesty, Francis Joseph, etc. But tell them to beware. Let them not try to discover what I am, for it were better that they never were born than for them to incur the wrath of the axman. I don't think that there is any need of such a warning, for I feel sure that your police will always dodge me, as they have in the past. They are wise and know who to keep away from all harm.

Undoubtedly you Orleanians think of me as a most horrible murderer, which I am, but I could be much worse if I wanted to. If I wished to I could pay a visit to your city every night. At will I could slay thousands of your best citizens, for I am in close relationship with the Angel of Death.

Now, to be exact, at 12:25 o'clock (earthly time) on next Tuesday night, I am going to pass over New Orleans. In my infinite mercy, I am going to make a little proposition to the people. Here it is:

I am very fond of jazz music and I swear by all the devils in the nether regions, that every person shall be spared in whose house a jazz band is in full swing at the time I have just mentioned. If everyone has a jazz band going, well, then so much the better for the people. One thing is certain and that is some of those persons who do not jazz it on Tuesday night (if there be any) will get the ax.

Well, as I am cold and crave the warmth of my native Tartarus, and as it is about time that I have left your homely earth, I will cease my discourse. Hoping that thou wilt publish this, that it may go well with thee, I have been, am and will be the worst spirit that ever existed either in fact or the realm of fancy.

The Axman.

The rest of the world fell away as I reread it three times, my oatmeal forgotten, and each time through I got more confused and angry. Was this real? The *Times-Picayune* said they'd gotten the letter two days ago and debated posting it, but decided, in the end, it was better if they did. I wasn't sure which was worse: if it was authentic or fake. If it was authentic, and the Axeman was using jazz against the city, it felt like a personal attack. I wanted nothing in common with that devil. If it was fake, and someone was using these attacks as a way to make a joke or promote some idiotic song or who-knew-what, then I wanted to find that person and claw his eyes out.

Next Tuesday? That would be the fifteenth. My mind bounced back and forth between thinking this was a hoax and nothing to worry about, and panicked that it might be real. After all, I already knew he was somehow fixated on picayunes. A letter to the paper that bore its name might be exactly what he'd want to do. If another attack happened—*when* another attack happened—that would almost certainly mean another nightmare. Another vision and connection to that demon.

And, if this letter was a fraud, would that make the Axeman angry? I could almost picture him sitting in a room, reading over this story and seething with rage. Wanting revenge on whoever had written it.

Papa sat down with a plate of eggs and bacon as I was starting to go over the letter a fourth time. "Che c'è?" He asked, worried. "You look like you're about to faint."

There were some things I could wave off and dismiss, or try to talk Papa out of believing, but I knew I was in no state to do any of that over this. I thrust the newspaper away from me, turning from it in disgust. "That demono stronzo is writing letters to the paper now, and those imbecilli decided to print it."

It was a sign of how worried he was that he didn't even comment on my language. He grabbed the paper and put his glasses back on, moving it back and forth in front of his face for a moment to find the right focus. His lips pressed together, and he crumpled the paper before throwing it on the floor and spitting on it. "Don't bother with that trash. It isn't him. It's just some bastardo americano trying to make money off the whole thing."

"It doesn't matter though, does it?" I asked, standing up and pacing around the kitchen. "People will read it. People will talk about it. *He* will read it. And it will make him do something."

Papa came over and grabbed my shoulders, stopping me in mid-turn. "Gia. This isn't your fight. We paid our price to him years ago. I feel bad for those who may be paying it now, but there's nothing we can do."

For a moment, I'd forgotten what Enzo and I were doing was secret. I panicked, wondering if I might have done or said something that would have tipped Papa off. As my thoughts raced over what had happened in the last few minutes, I was fairly sure I hadn't. Still, I had to gain control of my emotions, something that sometimes was a struggle. I took a few deep breaths and closed my eyes, willing myself to calm down even as I wanted nothing more than to find someone responsible for this and throttle them.

Papa patted my on the shoulder and let me go. "Take the morning off. Take the day, if you want. Go find Enzo and search out a few new musicians in the city. Something that will take your mind off this for now, sì? Things will look better when you've had some time to process it."

My first instinct was to flare up again. To protest that I wasn't a child and didn't need to be treated like one. But that was just my irritation showing itself. And, after all, wasn't I overreacting in Papa's eyes? He didn't know anything about my nightmares and our investigations.

I leaned over and kissed his cheek. "Grazie, Papa. Tell Mama

I'll see her tonight. She was looking for a wider set of knitting needles last night. Maybe I'll look through the stores and see if I can find some."

He smiled at me and nodded. "Doing something for someone else is the best way to forget about yourself."

Which was why I'd offered that as my plan. If there's one thing Papa liked, it was when I took his favorite sayings to heart.

The news that might have affected me was the letter from the Axeman, but the city had been far more changed by the sudden quarantine. That only sunk in as I had time to walk through the streets, noticing the shuttered stores and the way the few people who were out this early tended to shy away from each other. I counted ten people in face masks before I'd walked more than five blocks. I'd have to tell Papa to look into carrying some in the store. Maybe Mama and I could make some in our spare time.

News had spread quickly, and, as I thought about it, it made sense. 56,000 cases? If that estimate was right, almost a fifth of New Orleans had caught this influenza in less than two weeks. It had to be overstated. At that rate, the entire city would be sick before the end of the month.

As I had time for the information to settle even further in my mind, so many other questions rose to the surface. Were the symptoms I'd told my father really accurate? It just didn't make sense that someone could go from walking around, fine as can be, to bleeding from the ears and dying a day later. I'd heard the young could die from it even more than the old. Even though I was normally so worried about germs, I'd been so focused on the Axeman, I hadn't even considered Enzo or I might be impacted by illness more than by a murderous killer.

How long did it take to catch it from someone else? Should we be closing the store? The thought of my parents sitting there all day with strangers coming in from all around, coughing or sneezing or putting their dirty hands onto everything in the store, made me squirm. But, if we closed the store, how long would we have to keep it shuttered, and how would we pay our bills in the meantime? We had nothing saved up. We needed today's money to pay tomorrow's bills.

Forget planning on selling masks. I needed to buy my parents some now, so they could start wearing them right away. I started checking in at the few stores that were open, but all of them had already sold theirs or hadn't thought of carrying them in the first place. It was only eight o'clock in the morning, but I felt like I was running in circles without a plan or even a general idea of what to do.

This was all happening too quickly. I needed time to think. To brainstorm ways we might find out more about the Axeman and get a handle on how to keep my family safe from the influenza. And, to do that, I needed to talk it out. Needed someone who knew what we were doing and why.

It all snapped together, and I wondered why I hadn't thought of it earlier.

I needed Enzo.

CHAPTER NINE

Persons coming into proximity of the patient should wear
a gauze of cheese-cloth mask. These may be ready made in
the simplest form. Simply cut the gauze the size of a man's
handkerchief, and have a sufficient number on hand. One
of these is folded on the bias, passed across the face just
under the eyes, and the ends tied behind the head. This is a
simple method which will protect the nurse, as the double
fold of gauze across the face will arrest the droplets.

M Y FEET HAD BEEN TAKING me to Enzo's without my mind even knowing. When I made the decision to go see him, I was more than halfway there, with Lafayette already in the distance on the left. Enzo's family's store was more toward the Garden District, just off St. Charles Avenue, though on the poorer side of it. But "poorer" was relative. The houses here were much bigger and better made, and, if you traveled farther down St. Charles, they turned into full-blown mansions with pillars and fences and carefully tended properties. You'd have to go out to the plantations to find things more extravagant, and many of those were worn out these days.

St. Charles was where the truly rich people of the city stayed. The Rissetto family store was on the outer edges of that, but even the outer edges were enough to make a significant difference. Were they rich? No, but they were much better off.

It still confused me, how two families who had started out in such similar situations could end up on different ends. But then I had to remind myself that we hadn't been the same from the beginning. The Axeman had made us more similar, but Enzo's parents had been born in this city and had advantages my parents never had. Mama and Papa didn't move to America until they were both in their teens, and it's harder to get a toehold when you're just starting out.

When I arrived at Enzo's, I froze in the doorway. His store was in the middle of a lull, and it was just him behind the counter, his eyes haggard, the way he got after working with the public too much. Some people weren't as comfortable talking to people as I was. But what really drew my eye was the wooden box attached to the wall behind him, a black metal tube and microphone jutting out from it.

"You bought a *telephone?*"

Enzo had smiled when he saw me come in, then he glanced behind himself. "About a month ago. Papa heard some of the stores further down are letting people phone in orders so they're waiting to be picked up. He decided we could start offering delivery for extra."

"Have you used it?"

"I don't have anyone to call," Enzo said. "And Papa doesn't like anyone else touching it. When I picked up the receiver a week after we got it, he looked ready to kill me."

"Seems smart to me. Talking to someone you can't see is a good way to get yourself in trouble. How do you know what they're really thinking if you can't see their eyes?"

"You don't mind the Victrola."

I walked over to stand in front of him, lightly touching the spindle they kept by their register. "With music, you speak with your soul. Nothing can stop that coming across. Telephones? No thank you. I'd rather run across the city instead."

"Maybe one day you'll need to talk to someone faster than a sprint will let you."

"Then I'll figure out how to use one then. If your father doesn't kill me first."

Enzo's store was larger than ours. The goods newer. The floor not as cluttered. His mother liked pouring out potpourri into little bowls around the store, and it all smelled like cinnamon. The scent threw me back six years, making me think of the summer Enzo and I took one of those bags and tried to brew tea from it to sell to customers. We failed spectacularly.

But I was stalling. Before I could bring up why I'd come, however, the lull ended. Three different women came in at the same time, all of them with a long list of items they wanted Enzo to help with personally. Enzo stood there, eyes darting from woman to woman as they each tried to speak louder than the other.

I clapped my hands three times. "Ladies," I said, making something up on the fly. "Thank you so much for coming in. We actually are running a special on sardines today. A new shipment in direct from Lisbon. Very exclusive, because we aren't sure if they're worth the extra money. Would any of you be willing to try some— free of course, if you'll tell me honestly what you think of them and how much you think we should charge?"

That caught their attention. Use the words "free" and "exclusive," and anyone might begin to wonder just how big of a hurry they were really in. Enzo, meanwhile, singled one of the women out and began getting her order while I distracted the others. From there, the two of us were kept hopping from customer to customer, with the line at the register sometimes getting five people deep.

I didn't ask where his parents were and what had happened. I just stepped in and started filling orders. The building might have been bigger and better-stocked than the room I'd spent my morning taking inventory in, but I'd been to Enzo's often enough that I knew where most things were, and the few times I was confused, I only had to ask him for directions.

"Have you read the *Picayune* yet this morning?" I managed to ask him between customers. It was one thing to help. It was another to forget why I was here.

He shook his head, and I ferreted out a copy and opened it to the letter, then took care of a woman who'd come in wanting to buy 50 cans of creamed corn. Sometimes I was glad I didn't have to know what people planned on doing with the items they bought from our stores. She refused to believe all Enzo had in stock was 34, and, even by the time I persuaded her to leave, I'm fairly sure she thought I was still holding some back.

When she was gone, Enzo told me, "It has to be fake."

"Does it matter if it's fake or not?" I asked him. "What are we going to do about it?"

"It might be a good chance to smoke him out."

Another three customers came into the store, and I sighed and straightened, but murmured to Enzo before heading over to take my share. "I can't just sit back and wait for that demon to always be making the moves. We have to do *something*."

I wanted all these people to disappear. Why should I have to waste time listening to a woman argue with me that I'd weighed her fruit wrong, when the Axeman was out there planning a new attack? And what did it matter if I was wearing a mask or wasn't wearing one? I had three customers complain to me in the space of a half hour, despite the fact that, even yesterday, seeing masks in the city was much more an exception than the rule. But here people were, treating me like I had a whole bag of face masks just ready to put on all along, and I was choosing not to.

"Where are your parents?" I finally asked Enzo. We'd been going for two hours straight. "What were they thinking, leaving you to run this all by yourself?" Their bedroom door, which opened right on the main storeroom, the same as mine back home, had remained closed the entire time.

His eyes followed mine over to that bedroom door for a moment, then flicked back to me. "They…" He pressed his lips together the way he did when he was making an important decision. "No," he said at last. "No lies. They're here in bed. They're both sick, but they didn't want anyone to know. We don't *think* it's the influenza, but, if word gets out, it might cause a panic."

"Panic" was right. The moment he said they were ill, I'd had a strong urge to flee from the store. But this was Enzo's family. Sure, I might not have seen them in over a year, but they were still friends with my parents. I'd grown up around them. You didn't abandon family when time got tough. You grew closer.

"You should have told me right away," I said. "Here I've been angry with them all afternoon."

"I know I should have. I was just worried you'd go away."

"Sometimes you can be a real imbecile. You know that, right?"

"I'm reminded of it often," he said.

I let that comment slide. "Do they need anything?"

"You're doing more than enough by helping out right now. I'm sure they'll be back on their feet in no time."

That reminded my how serious this could really be. It all seemed so imaginary, but people really were dying, no matter how little I might have seen of it in the real world so far.

"What do you think?" Enzo asked, changing the subject. "Should we try seeing if any other stores have some of those masks for sale? I've had a dozen people ask why we aren't carrying any."

"I was talking to a nice old nonna who said she'd seen a tailor over on Terpsichore Street who's been cranking them out."

"When did you have a chance to hear that?"

"While we were talking about dress styles that might be coming back into fashion," I said.

"Dress styles?"

"Vincenzo Rissetto, we've been over this before. You can't go through life only giving people what they ask for. If you don't get something from them other than money, why are they ever going to want to come back to your store instead of another?"

He held up his hands in surrender as he walked over to the cash register. "I'll risk watching the store solo if you'll go buy us twenty of those masks. I don't care how much they cost. We'll just pass the price onto whatever we charge."

I went without protest. He knew what his customers would want better than I did. What would it be like to have so much money you could just casually take some out to buy something you hadn't even planned on needing? As I walked the few streets over to the tailor's, I wondered if my own parents were struggling today. Still, if they knew what Enzo had been facing on his own, they would have sent me over to help out, and they'd understand when I explained what happened once I came home.

Once I was back, we each took a mask and put one on. Some of the customers had been complaining that we weren't masked. "Setting a bad example," they'd said. Now other customers complained we were wearing them. "Fearmongering," they told us, even as they kept buying items off their grocery lists. If you got enough people together, there would always be two opinions about anything, even breathing.

The masks weren't perfect—they tended to slip down my face when I spoke, and I had to keep retying mine. I also wondered why in the world I should be wearing a mask when I wasn't sick. Shouldn't they be putting them on people infected with the virus? But then again, maybe it would keep some of the coughing off me, and, if it did any good at all, it was worth the money. Though thank goodness we were wearing them in the fall in New Orleans. Masks in the summer would have been brutal.

Enzo's parents never came out. "Do you want to stay to see if they're okay?" I asked him as we counted out the money in the till and checked our figures for the day.

He shook his head. "They were sleeping the last time I went in. I don't want to wake them. I'll leave them a note, and then we can go." He disappeared into their room a final time. I waited, idly poking at the tip of the spindle they had next to their register: the pointy silver one shaped like Apollo's arrow. It was built into the counter: strong and immovable. Right now, it felt like many of my problems were just like the papers on this spindle. They'd been speared and left waiting for the future. Not gone, just paused for the moment.

Now they were back with a vengeance, and they only seemed to be multiplying.

What would I do if my parents got sick? If they died? I took out my coin and rubbed it to ward off the bad luck.

We'd debated the next steps we could take. Enzo had been for more brute force, which was hardly surprising. If at first you don't succeed, just keep trying until you do, even when you want to scream because trying the same thing hasn't done any good yet at all. That was how the American saying went, wasn't it?

"We need to know where to start," I told him as he locked the doors and I gave the front porch a final sweep. "Maybe he has a tattoo. Maybe he's got a scar or a birthmark or…anything. If we had some sort of hint to go from, then it would make sense making more investigations, but, right now, we'd just be walking through the city hoping to stumble across that madman by accident. And we wouldn't even know if we did, because we don't know what he looks like."

"So you really think you can use the supernatural to do get that clue? What—is a ghost going to whisper it in your ear?"

I bit my lip for a few seconds, forcing myself to remember we were both tired and stressed and that yelling about old arguments wasn't going to get us any closer to solving this. I kept sweeping, the broom strokes filling the silence for the moment. "I think it's worth trying," is all I ended up saying.

"But you've tried to have nightmares before," he answered. "It didn't work."

I hadn't told Enzo about what I'd seen at Signora Caravaggio's, or how she'd had me do the reading myself. But I *had* shown him the second coin I'd found. "That was before I had the new picayune. Maybe with something else of…*his*, I'll be able to succeed where I haven't before. It's another connection."

"It's a coin," Enzo said. "There's no connection there."

I threw the broom down and glared at Enzo. "You talk about how much you care about me, but you insist on treating my belief about this as some sort of made-up game."

"You make fun of my interest in the army," he came back. "How is that different?"

"We've had this fight before, Enzo. Why do we have to have it again?"

He glared at me for two seconds, then broke abruptly, taking a deep breath and loosening his shoulders. "You're right. I'm sorry. I swore I wouldn't make a deal about it this time, now that we've been seeing each other again, but…I guess I'm not that good at keeping promises to myself."

I blinked. The Enzo I knew didn't back down that easily. I swallowed all the arguments I'd already started working on, remembering instead how grateful I was to have a friend here to see this through with me. "Thank you," is all I managed to get out.

"Something's going on with you," Enzo said. "Your nightmares, the way you know things before they happen. I might be skeptical, but…it's worth checking out. How do we do that?"

That took me even more off guard. "I—we—Signora Caravaggio had me do a reading last week. Showed me some of how she uses objects to see things. With the second coin, I was thinking maybe I could use that as a way to connect to him."

Enzo crouched down with the dustbin and swept up the pile I'd been working on. "Okay. We'll try it in a cemetery."

"A cemetery?"

"That's where people always are able to make connections in the stories, isn't it?"

Yes, I thought to myself, *but those stories are made-up.* I didn't say that, though. Not when my lifelong skeptic of a best friend was actually making some effort to support me. I grabbed the broom off the floor. "Good point. The cemetery it is."

With both of us in agreement, it didn't take long to iron out the details. Lafayette Cemetery No. 2 was a mile and a half in the opposite direction of home, but that was as big of an advantage as it was a disadvantage. I could catch the streetcar back from there, and we'd be even more certain not to run into anyone we knew. Going to a fortune-teller was one thing. Explaining to my parents what I was doing in a cemetery was something entirely different. My father was too good at knowing when I lied.

And I liked cemeteries, anyway. At least the ones they had here in New Orleans. I wasn't sure how I'd feel about the ones

you read about in books, where the bodies were buried under-
ground, with nothing but crosses or small stones to mark where
they lay. In New Orleans, we buried people in stone vaults. A
graveyard looked more like a city than a park, with tiny white and
gray houses lining its paths. When the area had first been settled,
they'd tried to bury their dead the normal way, but dig a few feet
down anywhere, and you hit water. The coffins all floated, even
when they were weighed with rocks. So, eventually, the people
took the Spanish route.

The city had changed again while we'd been in Enzo's store.
The streets were emptier, and the people who were out either wore
masks or glared at the ones who didn't. A sense of panic crack-
led in the air. There were no street musicians. No casual strollers.
The sun was shining, but it felt harsher, like the flickering candle
you find right next to a bookshelf, the flames tickling the spines,
moments away from setting the whole thing on fire.

When we got to the cemetery, it was as empty as we'd expected.
There was a wide central path leading through the middle of the
grounds, with vaults in various states of repair on either side. Many
of them had stories about the families they held. How they'd died.
What they'd been like. The richer families had huge sepulchers,
complete with dozens of spaces for coffins, while the poorer had to
make do with reusing the same few spaces over and over, clearing
out the oldest deceased to make room for the new, with the family's
bones all mixing together in a container beneath.

Who would want to be buried under the ground, anyway? It would be like being in prison by yourself for the rest of eternity.

It took some time to find just the right place: tucked somewhere even more private, with a spot to sit down. Everywhere we went, it felt like invisible eyes followed us. Carved angels on the vaults. Statuettes on ledges. Or maybe someone was just behind one of the tombs. Watching. Waiting.

Enzo and I didn't talk about it, but neither of us felt safe until we'd walked up and down a row three times, searching it completely. Many of the vaults had short iron fences around them, but some plots could only afford a raised bit of ground big enough to hold a few coffins inside. As long as we just perched on the edge of those plots, it wasn't really sitting on a grave, was it?

I sat down, though Enzo refused.

"It might be a while," I said. "I don't know what I'm doing."

"I'll keep an eye out for anyone coming. You don't need me looking over your shoulder the whole time."

With other people, that might have just been a way for them to get out of doing something they wanted to avoid. With Enzo, I knew he genuinely wanted to help, and he was practical enough to know what he could actually do. I forced a smile and nodded. "I'll call you when I'm done," I said, trying to sound optimistic, but still feeling like this was a terrible idea. If I didn't really want it to work, then why in the world would it? And a cemetery? I felt like the kind of charlatan Enzo made fun of.

But part of me was terrified this would work in spite of my wishes. That was even worse.

I fished around in my pocket for both coins, bringing them out and holding them next to each other. Was the Axeman a collector of some sort, then? Or maybe this was a ritual he went through. Some sort of payment he gave back to the families he ruined.

What had Signora Caravaggio done with me and that stone before? She'd had me clear my mind. Focus on what was there. But, then again, the memory of that experience wasn't exactly a positive one. When I'd done it before, I hadn't known how disturbing it could get. Now it felt like the difference between brushing up against a hot stove on accident, and grabbing hold of a glowing ember on purpose.

I wanted nothing to do with the Axeman. Why would I try to get a stronger connection to him? And, if it worked, would that mean he'd have a stronger link to me?

That fear might have been enough to stop me even now. It probably would have, except for the memory of that little body being chopped into by the axe. I knew that feeling would be with me for the rest of my life. If I didn't do this, and another memory like it came along, how much worse would it be, knowing I might have prevented it if I'd only tried harder?

I clenched my eyes closed, gripped one coin in each hand, and tried to clear my mind. Let it focus on the coins and yet wander where it wanted. Deep breaths. In. Out. In. Out. The silver warm and smooth. If I concentrated enough, I could feel the ridges on the inside of my palms.

Where had he gotten them? A picture popped into my head: a swamp at sunset, Spanish moss hanging from the trees, the air so humid it was tangible. Mosquitoes swarming my face, and up ahead, a dull red glow coming from the open door of a ruined church, its steeple lying broken and half submerged in the swamp.

Another image: inside the church, now, its floor rotted away. The same red glow shone up from the cellar, though water had flooded it completely. I glimpsed a man with empty eyes and sunken cheeks, staring up at me through the water.

It startled me, and I jumped. Just like that, I was back in the cemetery, my hands in fists around those coins, my temples throbbing with a dull ache. Where had that vision come from? Maybe trying to do this in the middle of a cemetery was letting my imagination get carried away. Or maybe that had been a sending from one of the bodies around me. I could just picture myself surrounded by ghosts and specters, their forms hovering over my shoulder, wanting to reach out through me to touch the world again.

Signora Caravaggio had warned against trying to see the future again. Did this count?

But my mind was made up. I closed my eyes, focusing not on the coins, but on the man who had touched them. Who had thought so much of them that he'd carried them around and left them as a sort of payment or exchange. I tried to push out the pain of my headache. This was working. I could do this if I only tried a little harder...

I was in a room with expensive drapes: burgundy with gold stripes and black frills, the window looking out over a river that could only be the Mississippi. It was a view I'd seen before, or one close to it. I could see the ferry crossing over to Algiers, with the telltale silhouette of that area cast against the sky. Where would that put the room? Somewhere near the Vieux Carré, or right in it. High enough that you'd be able to see the river over the berm. If I could look out one of the other windows, I was sure I'd be able to pinpoint the location within a few blocks.

If only I could see something else. I tried to focus on moving my view, but the headache that had started with the other vision came back with a vengeance now, battering its way into the vision, coming in waves of pain sharp enough to make me wince. I realized I wasn't just there in spirit. I was in a body, larger than my own. Thin, and wiry. My hand reached up to massage my temples, and I saw my arm covered in thick dark hair.

Could this be the Axeman? As soon as the thought occurred to me, the headache tripled in strength, to the point that I felt on the verge of passing out. The Axeman called out, putting his head down between his knees and cursing in pain. The pain overwhelmed me, and my vision went dark.

The agony continued, needles shoved in the corner of my eyes. I kept hoping I would pass out, or that I'd find myself back in the cemetery with Enzo. Anything other than this constant suffering. But my vision didn't return. An overwhelming weight settled onto my chest, as if I were being crushed to death in a vise. I couldn't breathe—couldn't even move my lungs to inhale. I wanted to thrash around to try and clear some space for myself, but, the more I struggled, the more it felt like I was suffocating. Minutes passed, each second feeling like an eternity, without even the relief of passing out. I began to wonder if I'd be trapped like this forever, bound in some hell that I'd stumbled into out of my own foolishness.

I should have listened to Signora Caravaggio. Trying to do this on my own and been a mistake. Who was I to think I could—

The paralysis went away, the weight disappearing. At first I was so relieved to be sucking in breaths that I didn't notice anything else. Those details filtered in one at a time. The fact that I still couldn't see. That my movement was restricted. When I tried to step forward, I met a wall not six inches in front of me. Edging to my left and right proved just as impossible. If someone had created a coffin just my size and stood it upright, I couldn't have been any more constrained.

Sounds came from outside: the heavy fall of an axe splitting wood. The steady beat, blow after blow. I could almost *see* the axe's movements. Coming back over the head, pausing, and then slashing down to tear at the wood with a sound like rending flesh. Somehow I knew with the certainty that only comes in dreams that what was going on out there was just practice. That I would be let out of this box, and, when I was, it would be to face the Axeman one final time.

I screamed.

"—okay? Gia?" Someone was in front of me. Above me. The box was gone. The sound of the axe disappeared. My eyes fluttered open. Enzo was crouched next to me, a thread of anxiety laced through is voice. Somehow I'd slumped off my perch on the edge of the vault, and I was sprawled across the cemetery pathway.

I struggled to sit up and batted him away. "I'm fine," I tried to assure him, but my headache was stronger than ever. Even moving made me want to cry out. My voice echoed in my ears, as if I were underwater. Even the thought of that was enough to put me back in that vise, unable to breathe. I shuddered and tried to forget that. "It's just my head. Hold on."

He gave me some space, and, after a minute or two, the pain had subsided to the point that it didn't feel like someone was boring into my right eyeball with a rusty hook. I was free. There was no box. No suffocating pressure. Whatever had happened then, I'd gotten out of it, though I swore I'd never try something like that again.

At last I nodded, taking deep breaths. Willing the pain to go away. "I saw something," I managed to say.

"The Axeman?"

"I think so." I winced again. The pain was enough that I wondered if I might throw up. No sooner had the thought came to me than I lurched to the side, just getting clear enough of my dress that I didn't splatter vomit all over it. I heaved once, then again, bringing up everything that was in me. I coughed, my mouth bitter and my throat burning.

"We need to get you to a doctor," Enzo said. "Or get a doctor to come here."

"No," I said. The nausea had passed, and the pain had already lessened some. "I just need to rest, and I...I don't think I can do that again. He sensed me, I think. For a moment at the end, I was sure he knew I was there, peering out through his eyes like some kind of parasite."

Enzo's eyes widened. "Do you think he might—"

"He was hurting the same way I was. I don't think he'll have any desire to try doing it back to me. And all he would have sensed from me was this cemetery." Which made me doubly grateful that we'd chosen the one so far from our homes.

"So was it worth it at all?" Enzo asked.

I looked up at him, and, even through the pain and how terrible I must have looked, I could still feel the despair welling up inside me. What had this really bought us? I forced myself to think through the pain and panic, my mind still struggling to overcome that last vision. I'd gone into this searching for clues. What had I seen? "I know he's thin and wiry. Hairy arms. I only saw his left hand. I didn't see any tattoos..." I trailed off. *Think, Gianna. Think!*

Inspiration hit. I was focusing on the wrong things. Knowing what the Axeman looked like would have been great, but maybe I had an even better clue. I straightened, nodding to Enzo. "I know he was in a room with a view of the river, probably in the French Quarter. But I know something much more important than that."

"What?" Enzo asked.

"I know the color of his drapes."

CHAPTER TEN

ALL SHOWS, CHURCHES ARE ORDERED CLOSED TO FIGHT EPIDEMIC: CASES IN THE STATE TOTAL 100,000. State and City Health Board Heads May Take More Drastic Steps and Close Other Places—Complain That Failure of Physicians to Report Cases Handicaps Them in Their Work—Demand for Physicians Greatly Exceeds the Supply.

N EW ORLEANS WAS A BIG city, but everything gets smaller with experience. I remembered the first time I'd crossed the Mississippi to get to Algiers, I'd thought the river was neverending. Now I crossed it all the time, and it seemed like no big deal. True, every now and then it struck me: the sheer amount of water going through it every second of every hour of every day. But mostly it was just wallpaper to me now.

That's how the French Quarter was. I still marveled to hear tourists talk about how its streets blended together, and how they would confuse Royal and Bourbon, and how sprawling it seemed to be. For me? Give me a glimpse of one house, and I could tell you where I was. Period. True, the angle of view from the Axeman's window wasn't exactly like that, but it was still close enough for me to tell the location of the room within a few blocks.

It was late in the afternoon, but I couldn't stand waiting any longer. "This is the best lead—the *first* lead—we've had," I told Enzo. "The sun's still up. All we have to do is walk up and down a couple of blocks, looking for maroon drapes with gold stripes and black trim on the second floor of a house. In thirty minutes, we can know where he's living. Less than that if we pick up the pace."

We'd started back for the city center as soon as I'd had my head on straight. The headache had lessened to a dull roar, and I chose to shove my attention to the excitement of our first real lead in our search. If I was lucky, I'd never have to think of that black room, the axe chopping down outside. Over. And over.

"I'm not saying it will be difficult," Enzo told me, snapping me back to the present. "I'm saying we need to know what we're going to do when we get there. If you really just saw him, then he's there right now. Will we just knock on his door and tell him we know who he is? What do you think will happen then? He isn't just going to come with us to the police station."

That slowed me down. "You could overpower him. All those pushups you do have to be good for something."

"I don't know anything about him. That's a terrible idea."

I stepped into the street to get around a delivery truck that was parked in the middle of the sidewalk. A car I hadn't seen honked at me, and I darted to safety.

"What do you want to do, Enzo?" I asked. "Are we supposed to tell the police? Tell that Etta woman? They're useless. They always have been, and they would have no reason to believe us. As soon as they start asking questions, we'll be laughed out of the room. If we want this demon stopped, we need to do it ourselves, and, if we wait too long, he might not be there anymore."

"Sure. But there are other ways of going about it. If we find his room, we can wait to see if he comes out. Once we know what he looks like, he can't get away from us as easily."

As much as I wanted to do something this instant, I had to admit Enzo was right. This was our one chance. If we blew our surprise and let the Axeman know we were onto him, then he might disappear again into the ether. I didn't want another seven-year reprieve. I wanted him done.

By the time we reached the Vieux Carré, Enzo had me down to a leisurely stroll. Just two people out for a walk in the evening air. In the middle of an epidemic. We had our masks on, so it wasn't as if we'd be easy to recognize, and we took turns glancing up at the windows of the buildings we passed.

After the first trip through the streets checking for drapes, I thought we must have just been sloppy. After the second trip without finding anything maroon or gold, I began to worry if I really had seen anything at all in that vision.

The third trip through, a gust of wind caught the curtains of a room on the second floor of a building at the corner of Chartres and Toulouse, billowing them outward for a moment. Long enough to reveal, that while they were a plain beige on the outside, the inside was maroon with gold stripes and black trim.

We had him!

It was all I could do not to stop in the middle of the street and point it out to Enzo. I steered him left down Toulouse until we were out of sight of anyone who might have been up there. "It's here! He's here. Probably right above us this second. And you want to just sit around and wait?"

"There's nothing wrong with being patient. We can pick a spot where we can see the door, and we can take turns watching it to see who comes out. Then we'll—"

I grabbed his elbow and pulled him back to the house with the drapes. "That will take too long. People are dying, Enzo."

"I'm not letting you go in there unless you give some something like a plan that will work."

"He doesn't know who we are," I said. "All we need is a good reason for knocking on his door. We…could be fundraising for the poor. Because of the epidemic. We knock, he opens the door, we see him. That's how doors work."

His feet lost their reluctance. "Gia, that's actually a really good idea."

"Improvisation can be a wonderful thing."

It took going in a couple of wrong doorways before we found the one with the staircase leading to the right room. And then I was standing in front of a black door with a neat gold knocker, and my insides were roiling. This was it. After so many years, I'd finally be face to face with this monster. Once we knew who he was, we were halfway to stopping him.

I knocked on the door.

We waited for ten seconds. No one came. I knocked a second time, then a third.

"He must have left," Enzo said.

I pounded on the door in frustration. That demon couldn't do this to me.

"I don't think that's how fundraisers knock," Enzo said.

I wanted to kick something. Lash out at someone. Anyone. I bit back the remark I wanted to say to Enzo, then forced myself to take a couple of deep breaths. "We're so close," I hissed.

"We can come back later."

Later. Everything was *later* in my life. I wanted now. I reached out and tried the doorknob.

It wasn't locked. The door started to swing open freely, and Enzo snaked a hand out to stop me from opening it further. "We can't just go in," he whispered.

"He's not home," I said. "We'll dart in, peek around, then leave. It's his fault for not locking it."

And, as reasonable as my friend prided himself on being, he'd been waiting for this as long as I had. He glanced behind us, then nodded. "But quickly."

The two of us entered on tiptoe.

I don't know what I'd expected out of the Axeman's house. Bloody weapons or stained clothing or some signs that a fiend lived there. Instead, the apartment was neat and orderly. Spotless, almost...sterile. There were no picture frames. No loose change on the dresser. Nothing on the kitchen counter. It didn't look lived in at all. Bare white walls, dark wood floors, a living room, a kitchen, a bedroom, and a bathroom. It took all of twenty seconds to walk through. The only thing noteworthy about any of it was the drapes.

The closet was empty and so were the dresser drawers. There wasn't a sign anyone had lived here at all.

A voice spoke from behind us. "You here for Mr. Brown?"

I whirled to see a fat middle-aged man standing in the main doorway, looking at us with a slightly confused expression. "Mr. Brown?" I repeated.

"You just missed him. He took his suitcase about a half hour ago. Seemed in a rush, though you have to sort of assume that, with people like him."

"What do you mean?" Enzo asked.

"Salesmen," the man said. "I get a lot of those come through here. Settle in for a week or a month or longer, but they never stay that long. Mr. Brown always paid in advance, and I told him he wasn't getting any of it back. I have rules on that."

"You're sure he's gone?" I asked.

"When a man takes his entire suitcase with him and it weighs as much as that suitcase does, he's not doing it for fun, you know. What did you need him for?"

"He's our uncle," I said. "We hoped to see him while he was in town. But I'm not even sure this is his room. His name is Russo, not Brown."

The man shrugged. "Sometimes people give me false names. I don't ask too many questions. That's why people feel comfortable staying here. As long as their money's good, and they understand they're not getting their deposit back if they duck out on short notice. I have rules on that."

"A tall man?" I asked. "Thin, with dark hair?"

He frowned. "That's not Mr. Brown. He was more average height. Maybe five foot seven? Dark hair, sure, with a big scar on his right forearm. Looked like a war wound or something."

"Yes," I said. "That's our uncle, alright. Everyone looks tall when you're shorter than they are. But who could forget that scar? Did he say where he was going?"

"I don't ask questions like that," the man said. "That's why people—"

"You've been very helpful," I said. "I'm sorry we missed him."

Enzo and I hurried out without another word. My stomach

felt like it might sink through the floor. "Gone!" I exclaimed the moment we were outside. "He must have known I'd seen him. He got scared off."

"It doesn't matter," Enzo said. "We know what he looks like now. A huge scar like that? People will have seen it. If we start asking around, we'll find him."

I tried to believe him, but I still couldn't help feeling disappointed, wondering if I'd done something wrong. Maybe I could have been more cautious reaching out to him. I could have asked Signora Caravaggio if she had experience with it, or…tried to practice first. But, even as I felt the regret, I knew it wasn't justified. I was doing my best, and we'd gotten unlucky. Enzo was right. We had something more to go on now.

And, from what I'd felt when I'd been inside the Axeman's head, he didn't feel like someone who'd stop killing just because he was drawing attention. He'd fled so he could keep going. I knew that in my bones.

We'd find him, and I prayed it was soon.

Over the next few days, Enzo and I went around to some of the different Italian groceries, asking questions. We started with the ones we knew, then branched out to different parts of the city, from Carrollton to Bywater and as far north as Fairgrounds. It didn't help that it was harder to just wander the streets now. Between the influenza and the talk about the Axeman's letter, many people had taken to staying inside as much as possible. Those who were out moved quickly, heading to their destination with no detours. Storekeepers didn't like you standing around in front of their building, and they even discouraged browsing inside their stores. I saw several older men wearing holstered guns, as if we were living in the middle of a cowboy drama. Never mind that this was New Orleans, not the Alamo.

At the back of my head, a clock was ticking, counting off the seconds until the 14th. Each time we asked around and came up empty, it got louder. Every morning it was there as soon as I opened my eyes. Sometimes it even woke me at night, and I lay in bed, staring at the ceiling, trying to come up with a way to make that clock stop.

The city felt it, too. Enzo and I ended up making a list of all the Italian grocers in the area, and it was depressingly long. Far too many for the two of us to hope to be able to cover, especially when we had so many other things that needed doing. The grocery business didn't just shut down because of the epidemic. In many ways, it got harder. People were more demanding. They bought more food and supplies, and then the ones who had missed out complained when those supplies were gone, as if it were our fault for not ordering more. I was tempted to tell them there were only so many cans of sardines out there, and having ten in your pantry wasn't going to make the influenza any easier to bear.

Somehow, I managed to keep my mouth shut.

In our spare time, we turned our attention to visiting those grocery stores, dividing the list in half and dropping by as many as we could. The Axeman had to be doing the same thing, sì? If you wanted to catch a shark, it made sense to swim with its prey. You could watch those storekeepers get more and more nervous as the days went by. Fewer of them let their children out of the house, and some of them had grandparents or neighbors sitting outside with loaded shotguns.

It felt like I had gone back in time seven years ago. Everything was happening again.

All our efforts did nothing to stop the days from progressing. The 14th was four days away, and I told myself there was still time. It was three days away, and I scoured the newspapers for some shred of a clue about who the Axeman might attack. It was two days away, and Enzo and I stayed out past midnight visiting more stores. It was the next day, and I went through my work in a daze, at a loss for anything else I might try. I felt like I was standing beside a railroad track, watching a train get closer and closer to hitting children walking along those tracks, and there was nothing I could do.

No one had seen anyone with a scar on his right hand. People looked at us like we were dim-witted when we asked.

My nightmares had grown worse, though if they were from the Axeman or just from my worries, I couldn't tell. I'd wake up drenched in sweat, my clothes sticking to me despite the chill in the air, my mind racing from the memory of a child screaming as someone beat her to death. Or I was in the middle of a maze, trying to escape as a beast crept up behind me.

It didn't take Signora Caravaggio to tell me what those sort of nightmares meant.

On top of all this was the influenza. Everything shutting down more and more. Enzo's parents got better, and I wondered if they'd even had it to begin with. I woke one morning to a tickle in the back of my throat, and I was panicked for the next three hours, convinced my cheeks were going to get that mahogany hue any minute. It didn't happen, thankfully, but that just showed what was always on my mind. On everyone's mind. You'd see black armbands practically everywhere you looked, and ambulances constantly on the streets. Hospitals couldn't keep up with the sick, and people suffered in their homes.

I hadn't gotten it yet, and my family hadn't, either. How long could that last? And, if we did get it, what version would we get? Some people just had what seemed like a bad cold, but, in other families it wiped out the lot of them. Were there two different versions? Did one family do something the other family didn't? So many questions, and so few answers.

Then Mama got a telegram from Signora Caravaggio's neighbor. My friend was sick with the influenza and failing fast. I was on my way to Algiers the moment I heard. The woman was there all by herself, and it wasn't as if Mama or Papa had the time to make the trip. The whole time on the ferry, I worried what I might find when I got there. Sometimes the influenza carried off its victims in a matter of hours. Would I already be too late?

I arrived at her house, breathless and panicked. The animals were all growling and hissing, snapping at me as I walked past. Six cats rushed me the moment I opened the door, and I had to dance between their curling forms to get through to Signora's bedroom, my stomach a rock inside me. For her not to have fed any of the animals, it had to have been bad. Checking my face mask was tight around my mouth and nose, I opened the door, prepared for the worst.

She had the lights off and the windows closed. It smelled of mold and stale air and something else I couldn't place. At first the room was deathly still, but then she coughed: wet and hacking. I tried the light but it didn't turn on, so I grabbed a candle from the foyer, lit it, and went in.

In the flickering orange light, Signora's face looked like she'd rouged her cheeks dark brown, almost skeletal. Blood trailed down her check from each side of her mouth, and her whole face had a blue tinge. She stared at the ceiling with vacant eyes, and, if it weren't for her wheezing, I would have sworn she'd already passed.

It was all I could do to keep standing, seeing her in that state. For a moment, I had a strong urge to flee. Anywhere to be safe from whatever this *thing* was that had my friend in its grip. But I straightened my back and went to work, forcing brightness into my voice. "Signora," I said in Italian. "It's far too stuffy in here for you. You'll feel better once we've got some air in here and you can see the sun."

She turned to face me, struggling to speak.

"Hush," I said. "Save your strength for getting better. You can tell me all about it when you're through with this." Inside I wanted to wail with despair. I'd never seen someone look so close to death. How was I going to do anything to help?

But I did what I could, opening the windows, washing her face, changing her pillow and her comforter. I went to the kitchen and cooked up some chicken broth, and I fed the animals and cleaned up the messes they'd made. All the while doing what I could to convince myself Signora would improve.

It took two hours of solid work, but, by the end of it, the house smelled livable again. The heavy spirit that had been waiting for me the moment I opened the doors seemed to have been banished for now, and Signora looked much more like herself. I chattered away as I fed her the broth, keeping my mouth moving so my thoughts wouldn't dwell on anything.

"You can't be here alone," I told her. "And I can't make it here each day to take care of you. Which of your neighbors likes you the most?"

She struggled to respond, and I signaled she should save her strength. "I'm sure I can find someone who will work," I told her. Someone had telegrammed Mama, after all. I should have checked with her before I left, but I'd been too worried.

It was nothing a bit of door knocking couldn't suss out, however. I could be persuasive when I needed a light touch, and the second house I tried directed me to a woman four houses down who was a regular patron of Signora's. She was worried about the influenza, but, when I told her what a state my friend was in, she agreed to check in on her three times a day.

Would that be enough? I tried to convince myself it would be. I explained to my friend who would be coming and when, and she even managed a smile at me before I let her drift back to sleep. But, when I closed the door to her bedroom, I wondered if I would ever see her alive again.

The Axeman might be threatening strangers, but the influenza was after someone who was essentially family to me. I needed to know she'd be alright, and I remembered where she kept her crystal ball—the one that had brought me all those dark visions back when all this started.

Would it be safe to try it again?

For this, it had to be worth it.

I hurried into Signora's office. The sooner I was through with this, the sooner I'd know. It took some rifling through drawers to find the stone again, sifting through dried chicken feet and ivory dice and a wide selection of matchboxes from all over the globe. Once I had it, I settled myself into a chair—careful to leave Signora's open. I wasn't taking her place. I was still just a visitor.

Calming my nerves, I removed the rock from its cloth wrapping and stared at its glinting colors again. My stomach was a twisted mess of nerves. Fear or nausea or something else? I did my best to clear my mind and focus on what I wanted to know: would Signora recover? Could I resume my search for the Axeman? What was the right choice?

Other thoughts flashed through my head. What would my

priest say if he saw me here again? Even if I saw an answer, how could I know it was true? Couldn't the devil use this to twist me to his purposes? And, as that thought came to me, a vision popped into place.

A flooded cemetery at midnight, the tops of the gravestones poking out of the water. The swirl of an alligator's back and tail as it sunk back beneath the water. And up ahead, a church with a leaning steeple, a fiery red glow streaming from the door and windows.

I floated toward it, the building growing larger almost on its own. As I grew nearer, I caught snippets of voices chanting in an arcane tongue. Inside the church. A group of people were kneeling in front of a man bathed in shadow. They each had a small bag in front of them, and they filled the bag with different items as they chanted. I caught a glimpse of some of the objects: rocks, crystals, amulets.

Silver coins.

I gasped when I saw those, and the group looked up at me all at once. They stood, glancing back to the man they'd been addressing. He pointed at me, and his finger was more of a claw or talon than anything human. They turned back to me and began clambering over each other to get to me as soon as—

Someone slapped the stone from my hand. The room spun and my eyes struggled to focus. "I told you looking again was a risk, Gia."

Signora Caravaggio stood over me, leaning against a chair for support, but her eyes blazing with anger. I struggled to come up with something to say. Anything. "I didn't—"

She waved at me in dismissal, and then all the strength evaporated from her at once, her knees buckling. I hurried to catch her before she fell to the floor.

"Knew you were up to something," she managed to murmur. "Could feel it."

"Let's get you back to bed," I said.

Once she was situated, she was fading back to her stupor again, all evidence of that energy almost vanished. "You need to go take care of this, Gia," she told me in a breathy, tired voice. "I'll manage on my own."

"But I can't—"

"You're in too deep now, and things will be much worse for you"—she took a deep, shuddering breath—"than they'll be for me, even if it all goes perfect. He's got his hooks into you now."

"Who does?"

It didn't seem like she'd even heard me. "Beware of looking too hard at what you don't understand," she managed to say. "Sometimes they lie." She drifted off to sleep again, though some of the color still seemed to have come back to her.

It was a long walk home, full of thoughts and second-guesses and hopes that I'd be able to see my way through this somehow.

And then the day of the 14th arrived. We'd had messages from the woman I'd left in charge of Signora. My friend was well on her way to recovery, getting better almost as quickly as she'd fallen ill. The only thing about this sickness that made sense was the fact that it didn't make any sense.

The sun rose, just as it did every other day. The weather was too cheerful for a day I'd dreaded so much. No clouds in the sky. Birds singing on rooftops. I skimmed through the newspaper, hoping, perhaps, the police had caught the Axeman or had some leads I might follow up on. They mentioned the demon's letter, of course, but people were still torn about what to believe about it.

Mama and Papa tried to keep me occupied the whole day. We churned through our customers, one after another. I'd grown used to wearing my face mask now, though I still had to take breaks from time to time, retreating to our bedroom so I could take it off and breathe normally. They must have been getting tired of it, as well. Papa seemed especially winded, and he kept clearing his throat. Was he sweating more than usual? Mama watched us with a permanently concerned expression.

"Maybe you should stay in tonight," she told me as the day came to a close and we began packing up the street displays.

I shook my head, trying to dismiss my own fears. My parents would be fine. I kept seeing the influenza everywhere I looked, and it hadn't been anywhere real yet. Besides, I had other evils to fight. "I'm not letting that beast steal another minute of my life. And that's if the letter was even from him. I think it's nothing more than some ciarlatano idiota wanting to make some money off people too foolish to know better."

Mama nodded, then hesitated. "Tell Enzo not to keep you out too late, then. There'll be more work in the morning, and your father's wearing himself ragged. I wish we could just sleep in peace for once, but we'll be up with the rest of the city, playing some of your jazz songs on the Victrola. Your father thinks it's silly, but—"

I rushed over to throw my arms around her. In all my focus on finding the Axeman, I'd lost track of what my parents might be thinking about all of this. Was she really thinking I was just seeing Enzo each night for fun? But better that than knowing what I was actually trying to do. "It'll all work out," I told her, then forced a smile. "Maybe you'll even become a fan. I could take you to some concerts that would make even a stone start to move."

She smiled back, though it didn't reach her eyes. "Maybe," was all she said. She paused a moment more, then kept going. "Gia, your father and I know you're up to something. We debated telling you to stay in tonight, but you're seventeen, and you're well past the age we can tell you what to do. But be careful, okay? I know you want to help, but don't do anything that might—that might put you in danger."

I nodded, though I didn't trust myself to speak. While I wasn't planning on throwing myself deliberately into a situation I couldn't get out of, I also didn't have it in me to shy away from it. Not when I knew what sort of an effect the Axeman could have on the people he didn't kill, let alone the ones he murdered in cold blood.

CHAPTER ELEVEN

Axman is Invited to Small, Select Party:

The Axman is invited to a stag party at 552 Low-
erline Street tonight at 12:15. He'll be as welcome as the
flowers in May, according to an invitation extended him
through the Times-Picayune by Oscar William Morton,
William Schulze, Russell Y. Fairbanks and A. M. LaFleur,
Jr. They sincerely hope he won't have his social secretary
send regrets.

———————

ENZO AND I WERE TO meet at the Butcher's Hall in the French Market. For once, I beat my friend there by fifteen minutes. I might have felt from my work in the grocery store that the entire city was panicked because of the influenza, but you wouldn't know it from the line in front of the Café Du Monde, even at six o'clock. The lights were already on the awnings, and the air was full of the scent of fried dough and coffee. Men and women and families, out waiting in line. Most of them masked, though plenty of them with their masks down below their noses or even tucked underneath their chin. Wearing a mask like that was like wearing a skirt hiked up to your waist. Technically you had it on, but it wasn't really doing anything it was supposed to.

At least the spitting laws were being strictly enforced.

When Enzo came, I was ready to give him a hard time about being late. But his hair was out of place, and he had bags under his eyes. Sometimes you know at a glance when good-natured joking is a bad idea. "Did everything go okay today?" I asked him.

He nodded and smiled. "Just a long day. I'm sure you can relate."

I wondered what I looked like. With the amount of sleep I'd been getting, maybe just as bad as my friend.

"Are you hungry?" he asked. "We could get a beignet or some coffee."

The thought of eating made my stomach turn. He might as well have suggested we gnaw on wood, for all the thought did for me. He must have seen my face blanche, because he continued right away. "Me neither. Let's go."

We'd mapped out a route for us to follow, starting in the Vieux Carré and weaving out in a spiral to hit most of the stores we'd already been keeping an eye on. By starting this early, we should be able to get to all of them twice, and the French Quarter itself we should be able to get to a third time. Yes, the Axeman had attacked elsewhere. We couldn't cover Algiers, for example, and the farthest parts of the city were out of reach, but this was something.

Sitting around tonight doing nothing would have been impossible. And, by being out, maybe we'd have a head start on anything that happened. With so many people on the lookout for him, finding someone he could attack would have to be almost impossible. Wouldn't it? Enzo and I had warned who would listen to us to be on the watch for a man with a scarred right hand, but who knew if anyone would really pay attention.

As we walked along the streets of the French Quarter, I was amazed how many people were treating the evening more like a lark than something to worry over. The city might have closed all the dance halls, but the saloons were open, and plenty of restaurants had live music inside on a normal night. With the streets buzzing about the Axeman, it seemed like all the bands and musicians in the city must have been hired for the night.

I saw many people I knew well, musicians and fans alike. None of them seemed to be worried the same way I was. Then again, the Axeman hadn't been after Black families, and there weren't nearly as many Italians who were into the jazz scene the same way I was.

The later it got, the more raucous people became, with dancing spilling out onto the streets. It was as if all the worries of our time had been bottled up for the evening, and that energy escaped with people dancing and forgetting about everything for the moment. In many ways it reminded me of Mardi Gras. And maybe that made sense, since the real festivities had been canceled this year, and who knew if they'd be held again next year. People in this city lived to celebrate, and the epidemic and the Great War and the Axeman seemed like a challenge in some ways. The city was rising to meet it, even if doing that would make things worse.

The sky grew pink and then deep red. The air got cooler, but the people only grew louder. By then we were out past Hoffman Triangle and Fontainebleau and over into Gert Town and Mid-City. My feet were aching, and it felt like someone had taken a dagger and started drilling it into my right temple.

Out this far from the Vieux Carré, there weren't as many restaurants and saloons to draw the people, but that hadn't stopped them from breaking out instruments or Victrolas. I lost count of the houses that had their windows open, jazz music blaring from their apartments as they proved to the world they were listening.

Some of them—the Italians, mainly—had their faces lined with worry. Others seemed to be doing it just for something different to do. Alcohol was joining the celebrations, as it always did, and people had begun dancing and singing with varying degrees of skill. Enzo and I passed a man dressed only in pants, standing in the middle of the street, singing "Over There" at the top of his lungs. He slurred most of the words and mumbled the ones he didn't know, and it wasn't even remotely related to jazz, but that didn't stop his neighbors from shouting him on and laughing at him.

"Do you think they even believe anything might happen tonight?" Enzo asked me.

I rolled my eyes, unable to keep my thoughts out of my expression.

"They're bambini. Little children who are bored or scared or who knows what. And, if the Axeman does attack tonight, they'll go to bed telling each other how dangerous it all was. How it could have been them, even though we all know it wasn't and it couldn't."

I massaged my temple, willing the pain to go away. Maybe I should have agreed to that coffee.

As we walked, I kept checking myself, wondering if the frustration I was feeling came from me or from the Axeman. Was he out there somewhere, just as mad at these people as I was? What did it feel like to him? Did he think this was the city mocking his warning, or did it make him happy to see how much his letter had changed New Orleans for a night? Or was he enraged that someone had used his attacks as an excuse to peddle jazz records?

Maybe it was my frustration, or maybe I'd just been walking too much, but it felt like it was getting hotter the later it got. Where was the cool night air? Why did my clothes feel so stuffy? It was like the world was tightening around me. Everything was narrowing down, and I wanted to scream or yell at something to stop it.

By the time we made it back to the French Quarter, the entire area had transformed even more. The masks and the precautions from earlier in the day had vanished, and people thronged the streets, calling out to each other, dancing, and singing along with so many bands I lost count. Normally, I would have loved this. It was everything I dreamed New Orleans could be. But, tonight, it sent a new stab of pain searing through my head.

I glared at everyone we passed, my emotions burning hot inside me. A woman careened into me, and I shoved her away. For a moment, her boyfriend looked like he wanted to do something about it, his brow furrowing, and his hand balling into a fist. But then he stared at me a second more and just laughed, bursting out with a wave of bourbon-scented breath.

Enzo took me by the elbow and pulled me away. I shook him off, but I let myself be shepherded. "It's not real to any of them," I said, mopping my forehead.

"Why would it be?" Enzo asked. "They aren't the ones at risk."

He nodded at one of the groceries on our route. A man with a shotgun stood on the porch, his door open behind him. All the lights were on in his house, and a Victrola was playing its tinny music as loud as it could, while his wife stood inside, cradling a crying baby in her arms. The man's eyes were wide and constantly moving, and his knuckles were white.

What was I doing out here, leaving my parents to fend for themselves?

"Are your parents worried about it at all?" I asked Enzo, trying to somehow feel like anything other than a failure.

He took a moment before he responded, and I wondered if he was thinking the same thing. "My parents...They know I'm doing what needs to be done."

Something about the way he spoke felt off to me, but I was too tired, too worried, and in too much pain to track it down right then. "I can't…" I shook my head, walking over to lean against a lamppost. I wanted it all to stop. Just to be someplace quiet, with all of the craziness of the past year gone.

I realized I'd taken my silver coin out of my pocket at some point, and it was now in my fist. Enzo was repeating something that might have been my name, over and over, and I just wanted him to shut up and, if I had to, I'd beat him into silence along with everyone else on this street and in this city where no one cared and they all deserved what they were getting because I promised and you always have to pay your debts and—

The street disappeared in an instant, replaced by me, standing in the middle of a dark grocery store, an axe in my right hand, casually swaying back and forth like the pendulum of a clock. The pain that had been troubling me all afternoon and night had vanished, and I no longer felt worried or conflicted.

I was free to do what I always wanted to do. Needed *to do.*

In five quick steps, I rushed to the door in front of me and kicked it open. A man shouted inside, startled. I was into the room, laying about me with the axe in a rage. The first few blows swung wide, hitting what might have been a dresser or the bedframe. In the darkness, it was almost impossible to tell. Light streamed in from the open door behind me, but with all the chaos that was happening, it was hard to keep track.

The man rushed toward me, and I elbowed him off before swinging the axe at him again like a baseball bat. He lunged backward, avoiding the blow but losing his balance in the process and tumbling to the floor where he ended up right in the line of light from the door.

I got a moment's glimpse of his eyebrows raised in terror before I took a step back, cocked the axe, and swung it over my head to bury it deep in his left temple. Blood welled up around the wound before I'd even wrenched the axehead free. When I did, it splattered along the floor and into the darkness, a sloppy line of red.

The axe came up for another blow, but it hung there for a moment, behind my head, ready to attack.

No!

I came to myself just long enough to remember who I was. Gianna Crutti. And I had recognized the face of the man I'd just attacked: Mr. Romano. He was one of Papa's best friends, not some person to hack into. I was here to stop the Axeman, not commit his crimes with him. I poured every ounce of determination I had into making that axe drop from my hands. Who knew what was happening or how it all worked, but I was in this demon's body for a moment, and if I even had a chance of stopping him, I had to take it.

The axe stayed frozen. My eyes stayed fixed on the lifeless man before me, blood pouring from the inch-wide gap in his skull. My fingers tightened and muscles tensed, but the blow never came.

"Who are you?" I said, though it wasn't me who had thought it.

Fear lanced through me. It was one thing to be watching through the Axeman's eyes, but, to know he was aware of me in return...I could feel that emotion echoed by the Axeman as well.

My hands released the axe, and I turned to run from the room. I thundered through the kitchen and rushed through an open door into the night air. I got a glimpse of houses and heard jazz music playing a few houses down. As I jumped the fence, someone screamed.

I paused at the top of the fence and glanced back to see Pauline, Mr. Romano's fifteen-year-old niece. I had played with her and her sister for weeks each summer until I was thirteen and the Romanos moved farther away. Where had it been to? Someplace farther north, wasn't it? Now she stared at me in horror, her outline silhouetted by the light coming from the kitchen as she stood in the doorway I'd just escaped.

"Assassino!" she called out. "Help!"

I flipped the rest of the way over the fence and sprinted from the house. I caught a glimpse of a street sign: Tonti and Gravier. A thrill of success washed over me, enough to kick me out of the vision or possession or whatever it was I'd just been experiencing.

Enzo was back, staring over me as I lay on the street, surrounded by revelers. I blinked twice and batted away his hands. "Help me," I said. "I've got to get up."

My legs were weak, but I managed it. "What happened?" Enzo asked. "You—"

"Andiamo!" I called out. "I just saw it. He's less than a mile away!"

Fighting off nausea and dizziness, I pulled Enzo after me back the way we'd come.

CHAPTER TWELVE

Romano's skull had been fractured with the flat side of the ax which was found in the kitchen. He died two hours later at the Charity Hospital. The slayer, who entered the house by jumping the fence from an adjoining alley and opening the kitchen blinds by putting his hand through an opening caused by one of the slats being out, had taken the weapon from the rear shed.

M Y MIND FELT LIKE IT was as dizzy as my body was. With all the people in the streets and the loud noises coming from everywhere, it was a struggle just trying to remember which way was north. It felt like the entire city of New Orleans had been put on a boat, lurching back and forth beneath my feet as I stumbled my way toward where I knew the Axeman had just been.

I might have been pulling Enzo at first, but it didn't take more than a block before he was pulling back. "What happened, Gia? You're not—"

"Tonti and Gravier," I said, though it took me a couple of tries to get the words out. "It's over by the—"

"The Romanos' store?" he asked.

I nodded, still trying to force my feet to keep moving, even if my balance was gone. "He attacked Mr. Romano, but Pauline came out. She screamed. He's running away, but he's running toward us. Maybe we can catch him." I couldn't spare time to think about Mr. Romano's kind smile and the way he'd always brought me candy whenever he came by to visit Papa. There'd be time for that later.

Enzo only hesitated a moment, glancing from me to the way we needed to go. "Come on," he said, and he began to drag me instead. I could have kissed him.

As we ran and my blood got moving, whatever it was that had been affecting me started to dissipate. The dizziness went away, and the strength came back to me until I wasn't leaning on Enzo like a crutch anymore. And with that feeling of strength came something much more important.

Anticipation.

Tonti and Gravier was back behind the hospital, just fifteen blocks or so north of the Orpheum where Enzo and I had gone to the concert two weeks ago. If the Axeman had headed north from there, then he would have had too big of a head start on us for me to hope to catch him. But he'd gone south, instead. With people chasing after him, he'd want to go someplace with more people.

Someplace like the Vieux Carré. What were the odds he'd pick the same street Enzo and I were on? Not great, but they were the best odds we'd had since we started this hunt.

"You collapsed," Enzo said as we ran. "You were having a seizure, thrashing around. It wasn't like that before. I didn't know what to do."

Maybe that explained how I kept getting injured in the middle of the night. If I was having seizure episodes whenever I started seeing what the Axeman was seeing, then it would be easy for me to hurt myself.

"I'm fine," I said, focused on running. An entire group of revelers had packed themselves in a cluster on Common Street, and Enzo and I had to elbow our way through, losing at least half a minute in the process and earning a number of swears and dark looks.

By now, I realized we couldn't just keep sprinting. Even if the Axeman were still running, it would be too easy for us to pass him, or for him to notice us running in the first place. It wasn't enough to find him. We had to *catch* him. What was the plan—run into him and then tackle him until the police showed up? I knew how strong he was. Enzo might be able to handle him, but I'd rather something more concrete to be sure we got him if we found him.

I slowed to a jog, then stopped altogether, panting from the sprint. The night air was cool in my lungs, and all traces of dizziness and the stuffy feeling I'd had all evening were gone.

"What are we—" Enzo started, but I held up my hand.

Why did it feel like I was still running? And not just trying to get somewhere. Trying to escape? The feeling was getting stronger. A panic that I might get caught, but a thrill as well. Like I was really alive in a way I never could be. The rush of adrenaline of the feel of that axe connecting. The warmth of the—

I blinked. Those were the Axeman's thoughts, and they were getting stronger. Because he was coming closer to me? I'd never even considered what it might be like to be in the same area with him. What sort of connections did this link of ours give me?

A plan jumped into my head from nowhere. Risking our entire investigation on a chance encounter in the street was a fool's errand. But, if we could set up a trap of some sort—meet that demon on our own terms—then we might have a much better chance of nabbing him. And, if I could tell where he was and what he was thinking, I might be able to get him to go where I wanted…

I turned to Enzo. "We can't just rush at him together. We have to trap him. If I get his attention, do you think you could circle behind him and tackle him?"

Enzo's face clouded over. "Get his attention how?"

"Never mind that. Could we catch him like that?"

"If I can get to him and he doesn't know I'm coming? He won't be doing much after I club him over the head hard enough."

"Good," I said. "Then you follow me by about twenty feet. Far enough away that he won't see you, but close enough that you can get to me in time, sì?"

"More improvisation?"

"We don't have time for anything more than that. I can *feel* him, Enzo. I know where he is, and I think I can lead him into this trap."

"What if he finds you first?"

I forced a smile. "That's why you need to be close, but not too close." The sense of urgency—of fear—inside me was weakening. The Axeman was getting farther away, or he was calming down. Maybe I only had this connection when he was upset or feeling strong emotions. "Let's go!"

It was one thing to have a plan pop into your head in the middle of a crisis. But I hadn't had time to think it through to see if it would work. Once I ran off into the darkness, a thousand different doubts rushed in to keep me company. What if I couldn't actually track the Axeman? What if I did, but Enzo lost me instead? You know you're in trouble when you're worried that your plan will work and that it won't work at the same time.

But I was done with waiting and done with worrying. It was like when I'd had a toothache for weeks. At first, I'd been more worried about the dentist than I was about the ache, but, once it got bad enough, I couldn't wait to get into that chair.

I hurried down the street, paying more attention to that voice inside my head: what I thought of as the part of me that was connected to the Axeman. Was it getting louder? Stronger? It took some trial and error—making a few wrong turns and then backtracking—but I got better at it. It felt like I had a double bass somewhere deep inside me, the lowest note being plucked every now and then, sending shivers down my spine. The closer I got to the Axeman, the more constant that note became. What would he look like? What would I do when I found him? How could I, a seventeen-year-old Italian girl, make a devil like that do anything?

The note felt stronger, to the point that it almost never stopped. It began to be difficult to tell what I was thinking and what he was feeling. *I was proud of myself. Content for the moment, although already a few doubts were creeping in. I'd run away too soon from the attack. I'd let that girl see me, and I hadn't gone back to finish her. I'd have to do better on my next try. I'd promised I would, and if I didn't keep that promise—*

I blinked a few times, forcing myself—Gianna—to focus. The Axeman had to be somewhere on this street. Maybe only ten or twenty feet away from me. There were a number of street parties going still, even this far from the center of town. Word hadn't carried about the attack yet, and everyone was still laughing and singing. There had to be a hundred people around me. How would I be able to find him? The more time he had, the calmer he would become. I wasn't sure if my connection with him would stay strong, so I had to do something now.

He'd have blood on him, wouldn't he? I tried to remember what exactly I'd seen in the vision, but it was all jumbled together in my head. The streetlights cast strange shadows on everyone, and it was impossible to tell what things really looked like. He wouldn't be talking to other people, I didn't think. He'd be alone, walking down the street, ignoring everyone else, maybe seeming too pleased with himself, or lost in thought. Was he that shorter man leaning against the brick building on my left? Maybe just waiting for the rush from the attack to die down? Or he could be the muscular man heading toward me. I even tensed up as he came closer, but he passed without a glance my way, and it wasn't as if the pull inside me got any stronger as he did.

This wasn't working. What if I were just making all of this up? Convincing myself I was seeing and feeling things because I was so desperate to actually be making progress?

I spun around, frantic to find a hint anywhere. A scarred right hand. A man with suspicious eyes. Enzo trailed me, and, seeing his bulky form back there made me stand up straighter. We had a plan. I just had to make it work.

Taking a deep breath, I closed my eyes and tried to ignore everything but the feeling of that note inside me. The thoughts that seemed to come off the Axeman like the reek from a sty. They weren't from my right. Not in front of me. Not...behind me? No. More to my left. I imagined that note being played by an actual musician, and with my eyes still closed tried to pinpoint exactly where those noises were coming from.

When I opened my eyes, I was staring at a man across the

street, standing with his arms folded. He was wearing a workman's cap that cast his face into shadows, but I could feel his eyes on me. A surge of emotion shot down my spine, and I knew I was staring at him the same way I knew my own name. More than that, he recognized me as well. Not necessarily that he knew who I was, but he knew we were connected.

His arms dropped to the side, and he took two steps toward me.

I fought the urge to check for Enzo. It was one thing to picture yourself as bait, but this was the demon I'd had nightmares about for years. Those had been about a nameless thing. A myth. This was a man at least three inches taller than me, with an athletic build. A real live monster, actually in front of me.

For all my bluster about swearing I'd catch him, I wanted nothing more than to run and hide. But fleeing would leave him still out there. The only way I could be sure he'd take interest in me—and hopefully miss Enzo coming in to ambush him—was if he knew I knew who he was and what he was doing.

I got off the lamppost and walked toward the man. He was strong, yes, but so was Enzo.

He came forward as well, taking his hat off and smiling at me. After all these years and so many sleepless nights, I'd half expected him to roar like a werewolf. But he had no fangs or claws or bristling hair and wild eyes. He had a strong chin and a confident set to his shoulders, like a cat that's just been fed milk. He cocked his head to the side, studying me. "You're the one who's been nosing around in my head, aren't you?" he asked, his voice an even tenor. "You're Italian? What are you doing following me?"

Just keep him distracted long enough for Enzo to get him, I reminded myself. "That was Papa's friend you just attacked, and you think you can just chat with me in the street? You're a fiend."

He smiled, and it was an open grin. One that had to make him popular with women. "So you're here to stop me. That's brave for a girl your size. You think just because I don't have an axe, I can't do anything to you? Or maybe you think you're safe with all these people around? People are sheep. As mindless and as easily led. I could take you away from here, and no one would even blink twice."

My mouth had lost all moisture. I thought myself good with people. I could talk to anyone anytime about anything, but something about this man made my stomach twist. He wasn't a cat. He was a slimy lizard. A snake sunning itself on a rock after a big meal.

He tilted his head to the other side, eyeing me up and down. "So you've been in my head. Did you like what you saw there? Is that why you wanted to meet me?"

It was all I could do not to put my hands over myself as if he'd found me as I'd just come out of the bath. "You—you attacked my family," I stuttered out, not quite sure what I was saying, only knowing that I had to keep him looking at me. I could barely remember why. Where was Enzo? Had he lost me somehow?

The Axeman raised his eyebrows, and his smile grew wider still, as if he'd just made a huge realization. "You're me," he said.

My thoughts scattered. "What?"

"I can see it now. You and me, we're the same. Different sides of the coin, maybe, but we share the same thoughts."

I backed up a couple of steps. "I'm nothing like you."

"It's nothing to be ashamed of. You liked what you saw, didn't you? Liked the way it made you feel when you're bringing the axe down. The panic in their eyes. There's nothing wrong with it. We're just doing—"

Enzo leaped out behind him, lashing out straight for the Axeman's unprotected head. Somehow he dodged, like a fly that's gone before your hand's even a third of the way into the swat. He spun to meet Enzo, ramming his fist straight into my friend's stomach. Enzo's breath exploded out of him, but he still tried to envelop the Axeman in a bear hug. Instead, the Axeman slipped through the blow again, punching Enzo three times in his kidneys. Enzo grimaced with pain and fell to his knees.

The crowd out on the street ignored us. Just another brawl on a wild New Orleans night. And the Axeman was still smiling at me. "You brought a friend," he told me, then took another step forward.

The way he'd handled Enzo wasn't human. This really *was* a demon, and I'd been a fool to think I might do anything to stop him. All thoughts of capturing the Axeman fled in a panic. I had to do something to get away. Anything.

I screamed out into the night as loud as I could, echoing the same noise I'd heard Pauline make in my vision. It was high and wailing, more piercing than I'd expected and enough that even I was startled.

Everyone around me froze, the celebratory air gone stiff and tense. I pointed at the Axeman in front of me. "Murderer!" I called out. "He's got an axe!"

Absolute panic broke out, as my screams were echoed by ten others, and then fifty. Everyone began to push and shove to get away, all the fears of the Axeman's warning boiling to the surface. I used the opportunity to turn and run as fast as I could—away from Enzo, away from everything. I didn't care where, as long as it was away from *him*.

The pocket of chaos I'd caused by yelling only lasted for a block. People farther away hadn't heard it and didn't seem to care there were some people running away from something. The streetlights cast strange shadows here, more spaced out than they were in the Vieux Carré. With all the revelers out singing and dancing, I had to weave back and forth to make my way down the street. It wasn't as crowded as it was in the city during the day, but it was darker, too, and I was sprinting. I ran into three people in the first two blocks. One of them grabbed me by the hands and whirled me into a dance move, laughing and smelling of beer. I struck at his face, and he cursed me and shoved me away.

I stumbled and nearly fell, but I caught my balance in time and sped back up, risking a glance behind me in hopes, perhaps, I'd lost the Axeman.

He was only ten feet back, his face covered in shadow, his arms pumping. I caught a wave of intent from him: he wasn't frightened of being caught. He was excited and relieved he'd get a second shot at a kill tonight.

Behind him, the shadows of the street seemed to multiply, making it look like I wasn't just being pursued by one man, but by four or five.

My fear intensified, and I found speed I never knew I'd had.

The world around me seem to slow down, and I lost track of everything but what was directly in front of me. Zig to the right to avoid a man kissing a woman on the sidewalk, cut to the left to get out of the way of a passing wagon. I shot through two men arguing in the middle of the street, and they called out angrily as I passed, followed almost immediately by the sounds of a scuffle as the Axeman barreled through them as well.

I wasn't sure if it was just because I was moving faster or because I was ducking through spaces that were harder for him to fit through, but the next time I checked, he was 20 feet away, but just as intent on me as ever.

My lungs burned, and I'd only been running for five blocks. Who would get tired first, me or him? Where might I go to be safe? I'd initially thought I'd cut over to Tulane Avenue, which would be better lit and give me more room to run, but, with the way the Axeman could race, I stuck to Gravier instead. I needed the chaos and confusion.

The lights from the hospital passed by on my left, taking Tulane

University with it. No wonder so many people were out here. The college students were living it up. In the distance, Duncan Plaza was coming up: a small park that ended on Loyola. My mind scrambled. If I could make it there, the Orpheum Theater Enzo and I had gone to was only four blocks further. I might be able to hide in there.

I ducked my head down and ran faster, my mind racing. It was like my body was wholly set on escaping but this voice at the back of my head was questioning everything. What if I just screamed out and told everyone he was the Axeman? Wouldn't the whole street come to help me?

Or would they run away in fear, just like the crowd had scattered when I'd screamed before? Or would they think it was a joke? It was too big a gamble. If I couldn't even trust the police to catch this man, how could I assume regular people would do it?

My legs had begun to feel rubbery. I'd walked in a big loop around the entire downtown tonight, and now I'd been running for two miles. How much farther could I force myself?

The buildings fell away on my right. I'd reached Duncan Plaza! It was empty, perhaps one of the few places the police had broken up parties? Or maybe people wanted to be closer to their homes tonight. Somewhere with a thick door and a dead bolt close by, just in case. My footsteps thundered on the sidewalk, followed by the echoes of those behind me, though they bounced off buildings in some way to make it sound like I was being chased by a small crowd and not just a lone man.

I could do this. I was going to make it. Just another—

Fingers caught at my hair, at first just a stray touch, almost like a bird had sped past my back. But then a hand grabbed hold of a whole clump and pulled back.

I lost my balance, my legs kicking out in front of me as I fell to the ground. The shadow of a man filled my vision as the Axeman loomed over me in the darkness. I tried to scream, but he clamped a hand over my mouth.

So I bit him, getting a good grip on a finger and grinding my teeth through the meat, twisting my face back and forth and tasting blood. He cursed and slapped me. I brought my knee up between his legs and made solid contact, though he must have gotten in a shot at me as well, as my stomach exploded in pain. The man yelped and dropped to the side, down on his knees for a moment.

This was it! Blinking back tears, I shook my head clear of the pain and got ready to attack the fiend in earnest.

But then I looked up and saw my imagination hadn't been adding pursuers to the mix. A second man was barreling toward us. In the panic of the night, I questioned if the person who I'd been scuffling with was the Axeman, or if it was this new figure. The area was covered in shadows.

If this were someone who could help me, maybe it would be safer to change gears. But what if this new man were the actual demon, or if he had an accomplice? Behind the second man, Enzo's form rushed in, his silhouette unmistakable.

That made my mind up. I'd already felt guilty for running away and leaving Enzo behind. There was no way I was going to do that twice in one night. Who knew who the other two attackers were? We could fight them and figure it out later.

The next while was a blur of kicks and jabs. I knew Enzo had been wearing corduroy trousers, and from the feel of it, the other two were in denim, so I wasn't worried the demon had escaped and I was just fighting my friend. I was still meeting plenty of denim in that struggle, though more corduroy than I would have liked.

"Stop or we shoot!"

A voice called from somewhere outside the brawl. Not mine. Not Enzo's. Not the Axeman's.

Etta's. She unshuttered a lantern in her hand, casting light into the darkened area. A glance showed me several police officers in uniform surrounding us.

All four of us froze, leaving me panting, but exuberant. Enzo and I had done it! Except then I got a good look at the other two men involved in that street fight. Neither one of them had the strong chin and easy smile of that fiend.

Enzo and I had been fighting complete strangers. Somehow the Axeman had gotten away.

CHAPTER THIRTEEN

Squads of policemen, detectives and armed citizens scoured
the neighborhood, but found no trace of the man, who wore
a blue jumper, cap and dark trousers. He carried a dark
coat under which something seemed to be concealed.

———————

E TTA RUSHED UP TO ME. "Did you see him? Do you know
what he looks like?"

I blinked up at her, still overwhelmed with the disappointment
and fear of the last half hour. "What?"

"The Axeman!" she snapped. "What does he look like?"

"Five foot eight. Light hair. Big chin. Handsome. He's got a
scar on his right hand. Looks like it was a knife wound, maybe."

Her shoulders slumped, and some of the police around her
murmured to each other. Etta glared at them. "It's dark. It's not
unheard of to have different descriptions of the same person." She
proceeded to direct groups of the police to spread out looking for
anyone suspicious, but you could tell her heart wasn't really in it,

and the police seemed doubtful as well. Some of them grumbled about following a "fake woman detective," and they did it loud enough that I could hear it. Etta must have caught it as well, but she ignored the comment.

Enzo and I were ushered to a bench, forced to sit there quietly while the police did their work. One by one, the groups Etta had sent out came back. None of them had anything new to report. Around twenty minutes later, a new man showed up trailed by a couple of uniformed policemen. He pulled Etta to the side, and the two of them began talking. Judging by Etta's expression and the way she was moving her hands, it wasn't going well for her.

The man broke off the conversation by clapping his hands and yelling, "Alright, everyone. This goose chase is over. Let's go back to the Romano store and do some actual detective work. McClellan, you take the boy back to his home. Get anything of use out of him that you can. I've told Palmer she can handle the girl."

And just like that, it was over. Enzo tried to protest, but there wasn't much to be done with all the police there. Etta came to stand by me, then jerked her head to the side. "Come on. We have to get you home."

I followed her without protest, my face hot with shame, and my legs still wobbly from all the walking and running. It was almost midnight, and I'd been going full speed since early this morning. No wonder my head was pounding and I was fighting off a sniffle. I wanted nothing more than to find a bed, curl up, and sleep for the next three days. There were a thousand different regrets flashing through my head. Second-guesses for what I could have done differently. True, Enzo and I hadn't been killed, but just because the night could have gone worse didn't mean it couldn't have gone better.

Etta's lantern was still out, so we weren't in darkness. "Who knows if they'll ever trust me again," she said, staring off in the direction the head policeman had headed.

"What happened?" I asked.

She turned back to me. "No. My questions get answered first. What were you doing here so close to where the attack happened? And don't tell me you don't know there was another attack. You know far too much for me to believe that."

"You wouldn't believe me if I told you," I said.

"Try me. You might be surprised about what I can believe."

I walked in silence, debating. My head was spinning, and it was hard to think straight. I didn't want to fight anymore. I'd tell her the truth, and she'd think I was insane, but at least, then, I'd be able to say I'd tried.

"I've been having dreams," I said at last. "Nightmares about the attacks. I see where they're happening and what he's doing, ever since he first attacked my family seven years ago. You wanted me to be done with this? You warned me about him, I know. But I can't just give it up. If I do nothing, then I know the next attack is another one I'll remember for the rest of my life. How can I do nothing? I have to at least try."

"Dreams," Etta said, her voice flat.

I rolled my eyes. "See? This is why I don't tell people. Because of that tone in your voice."

"I know what it's like to have the police not believe you," she said. "Like I told you before: you reminded me of myself. I once thought I was the only person who could do anything. I almost died because I insisted on doing everything on my own. You and your friend could have had the same thing happen to you tonight."

"I had Enzo with me," I protested. "He would have—"

She pulled me forward again. "He could have died right next to you. Or, if he didn't, he could have had to live the rest of his life wondering what he might have done differently to save your life. Or what if he'd been the one to die instead? This isn't a game, Gianna. This man knows how to kill, and he does it for pleasure. He wouldn't stop just because you confronted him."

"Who is he? You act like you know."

"I've met people like him. If I knew who this particular one was and where I could find him, neither of us would be here right now. The police here haven't exactly been a fountain of help. It was all I could do to convince them to listen to me tonight. I pulled every ounce of credit I had with the Pinkerton name. They wanted to focus their forces in the richer parts of town. I got them to spread a wider blanket. We had men three blocks away from the Romano's. If he'd only attacked a little earlier or a little later, we would have had him."

"But I know what he looks like," I said. "I've seen him. Talked to him."

She nodded. "And the Romano niece said the man was short, stocky, and dark-skinned. Never mind that people see what they want to see, and that it's hard to keep a level head in the dark when your uncle's just been attacked. The police don't want to believe me, and I led them to you, so they won't want to believe you, either."

We walked in silence again. I stopped worrying about seeming so independent, choosing to lean on Etta for support, instead. My legs felt like they might give out soon. It was a good thing we weren't too far away, now.

At last Etta spoke again. "With your dreams, maybe we can find him together. Yes, it could have gone better tonight, but it could have gone much worse. He still doesn't know who you are, though now he knows you're trying to…"

She trailed off, feeling me stiffen as she spoke. "You spoke to him, right?" Etta asked, her voice resigned.

I nodded.

She scrubbed at her face with her hands, then grimaced and looked up at the rooftops. "Why do we always have to talk?" She looked back down. "What did you say?"

I wanted to throw up as I realized just what a fool I'd been. "I told him he'd attacked my family before, and…"

"No," she said. "What did you say *exactly*?"

I tried to remember. "What do you mean?"

"Did you say who your family was, or when you were attacked?"

"I think it was just general. That he'd attacked us. I can't remember. I wasn't thinking well."

Etta closed her eyes and breathed a sigh. "If you'd given him an exact time range, it would make it that much easier on him."

"But he only attacked three families back then," I said, panic bubbling up inside me. "It won't take him that long—"

"You'll have some time. That's better than the alternative."

"Why is he even doing this?" I asked, feeling overwhelmed and voicing the question that had been on my mind ever since the first attack. Etta seemed like the first person I'd talked to who might actually be able to give me something like an answer.

"People like the Axeman…it depends on each case. Sometimes it's to feel powerful. Sometimes it's sexual. Sometimes I think something just doesn't line up right in their head. They think they're talking with the Devil, or they're convinced God has spoken to them. In this case… Have you heard of the Church of Sacrifice?"

"What?"

"In 1909 in Rayne, Louisiana, Edna Opelousas and her three children were found, murdered by an axe. A grisly killing that drew plenty of attention but went unsolved. There were others. The Byers in West Crowley. The Andruses in Lafayette. The Casaways in San Antonio. At one point, twelve murders happened in the space of about sixty days, all axe-related.

"Police arrested Raymond Barnabet. He went to trial in

October 1911, and his mistress and two children—Zepherin and Clementine—both testified against him. While he sat in jail, another family was killed. The Randalls. Six total. All with an axe.

"So the police kept investigating. It turned out Clementine had a dress in her closet, covered in blood and splattered brains. They arrested her, but the killings still didn't stop. In January, just two months later, three families were killed in separate attacks. The press went wild with stories of Voodoo murder cults. A preacher in the area, Reverend King Harris, was brought in for questioning.

"Clementine Barnabet confessed to seventeen murders. She said she'd gotten a Voodoo charm that made her invisible, and that was part of a cult bent on murder and destruction. Later, she confessed to killing thirty-five."

I glanced over at her. "Rayne?" I asked. "Crowley? Those places are hours and hours away from here. San Antonio is twelve hours or more. You can't think those murders are related to the Axeman, can you?"

"Between 1884 and 1885, seven women and one man were murdered in the area, with another eight people injured in the attacks. The killer was never found. Want to guess what weapon was used?"

"An axe?"

"Each time, victims were attacked in their beds. Each time, attacked with an axe. All that's missing is the Italian angle."

"But that's over the course of thirty years!" I said. "What—do you think these crimes are all committed by the same person? He'd be in his sixties now." I thought of Iorlando Giodano, hobbling around his kitchen. There was no way a man like that would be able to do all this. And the man I'd just fought had been much younger than sixty.

Etta continued, "I'm not saying they're all done by the same person. But I *am* saying there's more to this than simple coincidence. Because, while the police might not have been able to connect them, I have resources that aren't available to them. The local police don't care about anything farther away than their jurisdiction. They don't have the time to worry about crimes that might cover a larger area. With the Pinkertons, I have the freedom to investigate more broadly."

"You can't believe they're all connected," I said, more to convince myself of it than to argue with her. "It doesn't make any sense."

"This coming from the girl who just told me she's been having dreams where she sees what the Axeman is doing as he's doing it?"

She had a point. "Then how?" I asked.

"I've spent the last three years looking into these crimes. When they first happened, I was...otherwise occupied. But I've made it a point to investigate things like this. People who murder not just for passion, but for pleasure. I first picked up the trail with Clementine Barnabet, and I've been interviewing and researching all the other crimes ever since."

The fevered pitch that had gripped New Orleans earlier in the night was gone. There were still a couple of parties hanging on for dear life, with a few patches of revelers in the street and snippets of music carried on the wind, but, by and large, the place had emptied out.

Etta kept glancing at me, apparently trying to gauge how I was handling everything.

"I'm not a porcelain doll," I said. "That's the fourth time you've checked on me."

"You're breathing heavily. Are you feeling okay?"

"It's been a long day," I said. "I was up early, I couldn't sleep, I ran across half the city twice, and I fought with a murderer. I'm tired."

"You're sweating."

"Stop looking at me like I might break. You said you had something that connected all these axe murders besides just the same kind of weapon. What is it?"

"It's just guesswork," she said, "and it's a stretch at that, but too many stories keep having snippets of the same information for me to pass it off as nothing but rumors. There's a church somewhere to the west of here, probably an hour or two outside the city. The ruins of a church, actually, right in the middle of a large stretch of swamp. I don't know who built it or why, but there's something there that attracts people of a certain mindset."

I stumbled in surprise, remembering the image that had flashed through my head at Signora Caravaggio's: the church lit with glowing embers. "Who does it attract?"

DON'T GO TO SLEEP

She shook her head. "Some people say the Devil holds court there, and, if you find the place, you can sell him your soul in return for whatever you desire. There are too many stories about crossroads and soul selling for me to completely dismiss them. Maybe there's some truth to all of it, or maybe the story's just that: something people have come up with to explain where evil comes from. Clementine Barnabet certainly seemed to believe she'd gotten something to help her in her crimes. People call them different names. Mojos, conure bags, tobys, or jomos. They're typically made of flannel and filled with items depending on their purpose. Roots, animal parts, coins, or crystals. She believed hers made her invisible."

I thought of the paired coins, sitting even now in the pocket I'd sewn into my skirt. We'd reached the edges of the Vieux Carré again. Only a few more blocks till we made it home. "And you think…What?" I asked. "That all of these people visited this church and agreed to kill?"

"I think there's a power in belief, and, when enough people believe in an idea, it can make that idea as real as anything else in this world."

"People didn't just magically believe an evil church into existence."

"Are you religious?" she asked.

"I go every week."

"But do you believe?"

I rubbed my eyes, trying to keep this conversation straight. It was too late and I was too tired to have this deep of a discussion. And besides—I barely knew Etta. Why would I tell her all these things about myself? Except, somehow, it felt like we had a deeper connection. Like she understood *me* in a way I'd only felt from my parents or Enzo.

"I don't believe the way my priest would want me to believe," I said at last. "I mean, I believe in God. That there's someone or something out there more powerful than any of us. I also believe in the Devil. Some people call it superstition, but I've seen Signora Caravaggio be right too often for me to not believe. I don't claim to understand how it all works, but yes. I believe. But I don't believe God likes Bach more than jazz."

That last bit just slipped out without me even thinking about it. Old habits die hard.

Etta smiled, but it was a tired grin that didn't show any teeth. "I grew up believing. There wasn't any doubt God existed, this despite having what I think anyone would call a rough childhood. At first, I blamed myself for that. I must have been doing something wrong to make God want to punish me. Then, I blamed God. Why should an all-powerful being take such pleasure in putting so much pain in front of a young girl?"

"And now?"

She stopped. My house was just down the road, thank goodness. I felt like I might collapse any moment. "Belief has power. Like you,

I don't pretend to know how it works. I just know that it does. Is there an evil church in the swamp somewhere? I don't know, but, at the very least, something about that story is inspiring people to commit all manner of atrocities, and your Axeman is just the latest. I was too late to stop the others, but maybe, if I can find him and stop him, I can learn enough about what's happening to put a stop to anything it might cause in the future as well. But it's late, and you're tired. I'll be by tomorrow after we've both slept some more, and you and I can make some plans for what comes next."

Etta turned and left without another word. I watched her walk away, suddenly overcome with an even more severe bout of dizziness. I'd pressed myself too far, and I'd be paying for it tomorrow. Still, tonight might not have gone like I'd planned it would, but, somehow, I felt like I was closer to catching that demon than ever before. With Etta's help, maybe this would work out after all. That was something.

The lights in my house were still on, which surprised me. It must have been my parents staying up, worrying about when I'd be home. A pang of guilt stabbed me in the stomach. I hadn't thought about what they must have been thinking this whole time. Typical Gianna: worried about herself and never thinking of others.

I circled around back and let myself in. The stove was on, with a kettle simmering. A number of washcloths were wadded up in a pile in the sink. Was Mama doing…laundry? The feeling of guilt twisted, changing to one of concern in an instant. Something was not right.

When I came into the main room, our bedroom door was open. Mama was perched on the bed next to Papa, stroking his head with a damp cloth. She looked up at me, her face lined with concern. "Put your mask back on, Gia," she said. "Your father's come down with influenza."

The shock washed over me and took out whatever it was that had kept me going for so long. I crumpled to the floor in a heap, and I blacked out.

CHAPTER FOURTEEN

*Arrangements for the opening of a large emergency hospital
and the adoption of more drastic sanitary regulations were
the most important developments in New Orleans Thursday
in the fight against the epidemic of influenza.*

━━━━━━━━

I WASN'T SURE WHAT HAPPENED NEXT. Time melted from one
scene to the other. I had to have been feverish—it's the only
thing that could have explained the series of visions I had. One
moment I was in my bed in the corner of the room, listening to
Mama tend to Papa. She was crying, or he was, or it might have
been me, and then I was walking through a swamp, each footstep
squelching deep into the mud, and water up to my waist. Ahead
of me stood a rotting church, shifted on its foundations so that
it looked almost like a sunken pirate ship more than a house of
worship. The cross had fallen off its steeple and lay buried upside-
down in the muck beside the building.

Something red glowed inside.

Then I was back in my bed, staring at the ceiling and wondering what time breakfast would be ready, and if Papa might let me go play in the fountains. I was so hot and sweaty right then, and I couldn't get comfortable. If I could just find some water, I was sure I'd feel better. I would dive right into it. Hold my breath and then let it go a little at a time as I watched the bubbles float to the surface.

Except Papa was sick, wasn't he? And he'd been attacked. The memory of the Axeman's visit to our family all those years ago flooded back, but, this time, I was the Axeman, bashing through the door and chopping into my family like kindling. My mother's screams filling the air, and somewhere a ten-year-old child sobbing uncontrollably. I turned my axe from my father to the house itself, hacking through the walls and doors, leaving gaping holes that could never be repaired, while a group of policemen stood outside, peering in through the holes and laughing at the pain they saw inside.

Enzo visited me, I thought. Or was it just the memory of him? He sat by my bed and brushed the hair out of my face, and he kept saying he was sorry over and over and over, and I wanted to ask him what he was sorry for, but my throat was too dry and sore, and my mouth didn't want to form the words. And why had I ever told Enzo he had to leave? As my vision faded away again, I wanted nothing more than to tell him it would be alright, and he should stay. But then it was black, and I was back in the swamp.

Signora Caravaggio stood next to me. "I told you," she said, her voice lower than usual. "Heartache and misery would follow in his wake." She might have meant Enzo, which is who she'd always meant when she said that phrase, but this time she nodded toward the festering church, now only fifteen feet in front of us. A man stood in the doorway, outlined in red and holding a dripping axe. He pointed to a pine box, standing upright on my left. I walked into it, unable to make any other choice.

Someone nailed a lid in front of me, each hammer blow shaking my body to the core. At first, light leaked in around the edges, but, with each nail, that diminished until I was back in pitch-black. I deserved this. It had always been waiting for me.

Outside the box, an axe began its steady staccato. Except now it wasn't chopping into wood. Someone screamed in panic. *Mama.*

I struggled. When it had just been me, I had been resigned to my fate, but knowing Mama was out there with *him* was too much. I wriggled my hands up in front of my face and pounded on the coffin lid, pushing at it as hard as I could. I might as well have been pushing against a building.

Except light streamed in through a small opening. I must have knocked a knot in the wood loose. I pressed my face up against it, standing on my tiptoes to be tall enough, though even then it was just out of reach. I could catch glimpses, but only of the top of the room. Enough to see the axe glisten in the firelight as it swung up, but unable to see where the blows landed.

Mama kept screaming. Why had I let myself be trapped like this? Why wasn't I helping her? What sort of an idiot—

My eyes sprang open, my mind clearer than it had felt in hours. The box was gone, and I was back in my bedroom. Mama was crying in a way that made me squirm, my sheets covered in sweat and clinging to me, even though I was shaking from cold. Something about that cry made me want to hide under my covers and never come out. Except, when I looked for Mama, it was Papa sitting by my bedside that I saw instead. He was smiling at me, and he looked healthier than I'd ever remembered. As if the years since the Axeman's attack had dropped off him at last, and he was pain free again.

"I'm sorry, Gia," he said, stroking my face and making me wonder if he wasn't Enzo here again and I was just confused. In the background, Mama's sobs continued. Heart-wrenching wails of grief, punctuated by a hacking cough.

"Sorry for what?" I asked him.

"I have to go away for a while, but you'll be seeing me again. Don't worry about that. I want you to know I'm proud of you and what you're going to do. You were always the strongest one of us. Thank you."

He reached his hand out to me, and I took it. He squeezed three times, and I squeezed four, and then he was gone. In his place were two men carrying something large wrapped in a blanket, and Mama had left the room, though her cries still echoed through the house, mixing with Enzo's "sorry" repeating itself over and over.

I lay there thinking of jazz transitions, my hands aching for piano keys as I wished I could lose myself in music. If I could be playing for just a half hour, I was sure I would feel better and start thinking straight again. I even got out of bed, stumbling through the room and out into the main room, where it was dark. Was it still the same night I'd come home? It might have been, or it might have been a week or a month later. Light trickled in from the kitchen, and I tottered my way to see who was there.

Mama looked up. Her face was pale, and her hair disheveled. "Gia! What are you doing out of bed? You need to—"

"Papa's at the church," I said, and I wasn't sure at first if I meant the one in the swamp or the one with my piano, but then the memory of the swamp escaped me, leaving me wondering what I'd even been thinking of. There was only one church, and the priest had said I could play the piano there.

But Mama wouldn't hear of it, and she forced me back to my bed. I was too weak to resist, though I asked her to get Papa first. He wasn't in bed, but I was sure, if he came back, he'd tell her it would be better for me to go practice. I wouldn't ever play on stage if I never took time to practice. Mama only started crying when I asked about Papa, which somehow made me cry, too.

Because he was gone, and for some reason I worried he wasn't coming back, even though he'd promised me we'd see each other again.

I lay down in bed, Mama pulled the covers up over me, and I surrendered to sleep once more.

CHAPTER FIFTEEN

Despite the fact that schools, churches, theaters and practically every other center at which crowds congregate have been closed, the disease continues its alarming spread, both in the city and in the state.

———

WHEN I WAS ABLE TO think again, it seemed like I woke up to a world that had changed. I lay there on my bed, staring at the ceiling and doing my best not to think about everything that had happened while I was sick. If I didn't think about it too much, then there was still a chance it was all just another fever dream. That wasn't too unbelievable, was it?

I'd been in and out of nightmares the entire time I'd been sick. I'd had so many visions of the Axeman that I couldn't remember if any of them were new or if they were all just a repeat of what I'd seen before. His attacks all blended together. The same type of stores. The same screams. The same blood. It was like his Victrola had become stuck, and he was repeating the same passage over and over and over. An ugly song in a minor key that never ended.

If I'd had all those visions, then why should the memory of my father being taken out of the room, covered in a sheet, be any more real than the memory I had of that church in the swamp with the glowing windows?

Staring at the ceiling was safer. As long as I didn't take my eyes off it, I didn't have to see the rest of the room. If I stayed in a zone where I only suspected something, I didn't have to deal with actually *knowing* it.

Except no one can stay in that zone forever. Even as I lay there, I recognized the memories of those men coming into my room were too complete. How Mama had been crying. How my sheets had been so scratchy, and how I'd been sweating from heat and shivering from cold at the same time.

How my father's hand had fallen out from underneath the sheet as they moved him. Limp. Lifeless.

I remembered what the Axeman had done in his attacks, but there was still a sort of filter between me and them. Those memories felt different, like playing music someone had written versus playing something I made up as I went along.

At last I had to know. Had to be sure that the pit in my stomach was justified.

I took my eyes off the ceiling, swung my legs out of bed, and teetered to my feet. My muscles were shaky, but I staggered forward and moved aside the sheet that separated my part of the room from my parents'.

There was only one pillow on my parents' bed.

You wouldn't think a simple detail like that could carry much information, but, the moment I saw it, my legs buckled and I fell to the floor.

Mama found me there, sobbing.

The next while passed in a different sort of blur. I might not have been as fevered as before, but my mind didn't seem to want to actually do anything. I found myself lost in thought, thinking of everything that had been happening. The choices I'd made. The ways my family had been hurt.

Thinking about Papa.

It was like when the Axeman had first struck our family with tragedy, except this was an enemy I couldn't see. Couldn't confront. Couldn't blame. The influenza didn't care about us. It hadn't picked Papa over someone else. It spread its tendrils into every corner of the city, and you had to just hope and pray it left you alive.

Except why had it taken Papa? I found myself resenting everyone else I saw or heard. I stayed holed up in my bedroom for long stretches of time, hating the customers for coming in and pretending nothing had changed. Why should they need flour or sugar or canned sardines? Papa was dead. Why should they feel they could complain about how their cheese had been moldy? What did moldy cheese even matter?

They were alive to whine about cheese.

And Papa was dead.

His death hadn't just taken him away from me. It felt like it had stolen so much more along with it. Thousands of possibilities, now gone. Things that should have been commonplace, ripped away. I would never hear him complain to me again about my songs being too loud. We would never take inventory together. I'd never be able to walk next to him and bat his hand away from mine when he tried to hold it.

It had robbed me of my memories of him as well. I couldn't think of even the most basic things without feeling like my insides were on fire. Like there was a hole in my chest that just wanted to swallow my body.

Enzo came by at some point to talk to me. I told Mama not to let him in, but he dropped off a lasagna from his mother. The thought of eating made me nauseous. Normally I loved his mother's cooking, but now it smelled…off. Like she'd used the wrong spices. Mama forced me to try it, but the whole thing tasted like cardboard. She must not have been that hungry, either. I found her plate with the whole serving still on it. She'd only nibbled at the edges.

The rest of it went into the garbage.

I lay in bed, wishing the world would swallow me up so I could disappear. I kept thinking of things I could have been doing to help Papa instead of running after the Axeman. What good had that done, anyway? My entire life, I'd blamed that demon for so many of my problems. My family had been happy, and then it had been torn open by a stranger. It had all seemed so unfair.

But this proved that wasn't so unusual after all. All those people I'd been reading about in the paper—all the deaths—each one of them was another Papa. Another family's life blown apart. People died every day, and it could all happen in a matter of moments. Maybe it was a murderer, or the influenza, or getting hit by a street car, or drowning in the river. But what difference did it make in the end?

At times I thought back on the visions I'd have of the Axeman's crimes. Lying in my bed, I envied him. He knew what he wanted, and he went out and grabbed it for himself. I'd always thought of myself as direct and fearless, but it had been a mistake for me to do that. I should have stayed home. What if all my roaming around the city had brought this illness back to Papa?

I might have killed him with my carelessness, despite all my worrying about disease. Clearly I hadn't really been concerned, and this was the price I paid for it.

So my hours blended together still, just in a different way than they had while I'd been so ill. Mama brought me food I didn't eat, asked me questions I didn't answer, and reminded me to do things I ignored.

Papa was dead. Why should I do anything else?

Etta came by to check on me that afternoon, and that was one thing that spurred me to action. Mama poked her head into my room and told me I had a visitor.

"I don't want to see Enzo," I said, turning my back to the door and pulling the covers up over my shoulder.

"This is someone different," Mama said. "A woman with a scar down her face. I think she might be police, but she won't admit it."

In a flash, I whirled back and leapt out of the bed, thundering past Mama, glaring around the main room until I saw Etta. "Out of here!" I yelled at her. "Out! I don't want anything to do with you!."

Her eyebrows lowered in confusion, and she held up her hands almost tentatively, as if was worried she might break me. "Gianna, it's been three days. I just hadn't—"

I stormed up to her and had to check myself before I fell on top of her. My body still wasn't completely recovered from the illness, and the quick movement had made me dizzy. "I'm done with that," I said, wishing I were six inches taller so I could loom over her the way she loomed over me. "My father is dead. I want to be left alone. The next time I see you…"

Any suitable threat escaped me, so I just left the words hanging there between us as I turned and stalked back to my room, hoping it wasn't too noticeable that I was so shaky on my feet. I slammed the door behind me, wishing we had enough money for thicker doors that might make a bigger boom.

Etta didn't come back, and I didn't come out of the room again until I had to use the bathroom that evening. She'd left a card behind with her name and a telephone number written on the back: Hemlock 1138. I stuffed it in my pocket and forgot about it.

Mama was in the kitchen, cooking or eating dinner or maybe taking care of something to do with the shop. I crept as quietly as I could, hoping she wouldn't hear me so I could just go back to my room without speaking.

The loose floorboard by the dry goods section gave me away, squeaking even louder than normal. I winced.

"Gia," Mama called out to me. "I know you don't want to eat, but you have to come in here and put something in your mouth. You're going to waste away."

I considered ignoring her, but my conscience wasn't up to it. It seemed, no matter what I did, I felt like I should be doing something else. More. If I stayed in bed, I felt like I was failing my mother. If I came out, I felt like I wasn't honoring my father mourning properly. So I compromised between the two, slinking into the kitchen and sitting down at the table without saying anything.

"I made some soup," Mama said. "Minestra d'orzo, your favorite."

The memory of the foul-tasting lasagna made my stomach turn again, and I wondered if this might be another repeat of that experience.

I must not have been successful at hiding my reaction.

"Enough," Mama said to me out of nowhere, slamming a bowl on the table and looking down at the spilled soup that had sloshed over the side.

I backed up from the table, glaring at her in confusion. "What was that for?"

"I can't do this anymore, Gia. No more."

"Do what?" I asked. "We haven't been doing anything the whole day."

"Is that really what you think? I've been taking care of you. Taking care of the store. Taking care of—of your father. Not just today. Three days I've been doing this."

Even the mention of him was enough for that wave of guilt consume me again. If I'd been here instead of out with Enzo…"Those are just normal things," I said after a moment, then added, "Other than Papa, I mean."

"Yes. Normal things. Things that need doing. Does the deliveryman care that August died? What about the customers? There are other shops in the city, Gia. People might feel sorry for us, but they still need to eat. They still need to live their lives, and they'll find a new way to live them if they have to, no matter how bad they might feel for us. You think we're the only people in this city who have lost someone?"

"No," I said, and that sense of guilt grew larger. As she was speaking, I was noticing other details that had escaped me before. How flushed she looked, for one thing. She was sweating, despite the chill in the air. Was it from overworking, or something else?

Mama rushed over to me, took my chin in her hand, and forced me to look up at her. "I didn't raise you to be a depressa. You think being sorry for yourself is going to make this any easier?"

I batted her hand away, irritation flashing over my face.

She smiled and jabbed her finger at me in the air. "Yes. That's right. That's the Gia I need. The one with fire inside her. The one who won't stop at anything until she gets her way."

Just as quickly, that fire died. "I can't go back to that," I said. "If I hadn't…"

"If you hadn't what?"

I shook my head, unable to force the words out around the invisible stone that had somehow lodged itself in my mouth.

Mama pulled a chair out from the table and sat next to me, sliding over until she could put her arm around me. "If you hadn't what?" she repeated, softer.

"It's my fault," I said, the words bursting out of me like a dam breaking. "I should have been here. I was so obsessed with my own worries I didn't even pay attention to Papa. I should have been here working the store with both of you. Been here when he came down sick that night. You needed help, and I was running around town instead."

"He got sick, Gia. You being here wouldn't have stopped the influenza any more than me standing on the shore would stop the Mississippi. You got sick, too. I'm just glad you weren't taken from me as well."

"But he's *gone*," I said. "He's gone, and I didn't even get to say goodbye. I keep expecting to see him or hear him or talk to him. It's not fair, that so much should change just like that."

"No," she said. "It's isn't fair. But there's nothing we can do about that now, and we have enough problems that we need to focus on dealing with the ones we can fix. Our family has practice dealing with sudden changes. I wish it weren't so, but there we have it."

"Someone else should take their turn with them," I said.

She rubbed my back some more. "You know it doesn't work like that. Your father spent his whole life on this store. This house. When the Axeman tried to take it all away from us, we talked about moving back home. We still had plenty of family in Italy, after all, and it seemed like maybe America wasn't what we'd hoped it would be. The city didn't care about us, the police practically blamed us for our problems, and it all felt like too much."

"Why did you stay?" I asked, thinking what life might have been like if they'd chosen differently. To be in a place where everyone was like me, and I didn't always feel like someone different. Part of me thought that would be wonderful, but a bigger part cringed from the idea. I'd always liked being different. I was proud of it.

"We stayed because we're Cruttis. We don't give up. Everyone is going to have tragedy in their life. It might not be a murderer wielding an axe, but it'll be something. You can depend on that as sure as you know the sun will rise, and never mind any clouds in the sky. Tragedy wears different clothes, but he comes to visit everyone on the street, you know? He lives in Italy the same as he lives in New Orleans. We'd made the decision to live here, and so we stuck around."

"And what do we do now?"

She casually waved a hand in front of her face. "What do we do now? We stay. August wouldn't want us giving up because of this. I had some time to talk to him before he passed. We'll stay, and we'll succeed, but, with just you and me now, we can't afford to have only one of us actually working. We need to be a team more than ever, and I need your help."

She was right. I could see that, even if I couldn't feel it. At last, I nodded.

"Good," Mama said. "So you can start pitching in by telling me what, exactly, you were doing with Enzo that night."

There was being part of the team, and there was begging your mother to kill you. If she found out I'd been going after the Axeman, I could kiss being independent goodbye. She'd chain me to the cash register. "Nothing," I said.

Mama smiled, pushing a lock of hair out of her face. Her forehead was clammy, but, before I could ask her about it, she said, "Gia, the best thing about you is that I remember being you. Remember how much easier it was to lie than to tell the truth. I thought I was smart then, too. Smarter than my parents, that was for sure. If they knew half of what I'd been doing with August back then, I thought they'd have killed us both. But my parents were smart. They had to have known, just like I know you were out looking for that bastardo."

"I didn't—"

"You did, and don't lie to me right after I just told you I know the truth. That Etta woman came by, and she and I had a long talk."

If I'd been feeling even a little more like myself a moment ago, that was gone now. I wondered if Mama would even let me get together with Enzo anymore. "So what's the price?"

"What?"

"I already know what you're going to say. I was stupid. I was rash. I risked my life. So what do I do now? You're going to make me stay inside the store the whole—"

"Gia, if you're so smart, why do you even ask me anything?"

"Well isn't that what you were going to say?"

"It should be. Sometimes I wonder what sort of a mother I am, to let her daughter do the things I've let you do. And maybe I would have kept you in here for the next eternity, but there are several reasons not to, even if I might be reconsidering them right now."

She stood up, moving around the room the way she did when she wanted to fight but didn't want to let herself. Her steps seemed less sure of themselves, however. She almost tottered at one point, but perhaps she'd just lost her balance. "For one thing," she continued as if nothing was wrong, "you're seventeen. If my mother had tried to keep me inside the house at your age, I think we both would have killed each other. Your father would tell me that if he were here, and he'd be right. For another, the doctors said you need fresh air, so you *should* be taking walks around the city, even with that madman out there chopping into people."

Her tone made it clear there was more to her list of reasons. I waited her out.

"When Etta came, she had questions about the Axeman. What

he looked like. What I remembered. I didn't like her at first, but she grew on me. I even answered most of her questions. She thinks she's pretty smart. Too bad she's practically police."

"What's going on, Mama?"

"What did you tell the Axeman when you saw him?"

I was glad I was sitting down, because I would have fallen over right then if I were standing. "I didn't—I—"

She laughed, though there was no humor in it. The she closed her eyes, grabbed hold of an empty bowl sitting by the sink, and squared her shoulders. "If we didn't need every dish," she said, "I would throw this on the ground. I want to."

"Mama, I—"

"I've talked to Etta, girl. I know. You didn't just go after him. You met him. The truth, Gia. All of it!"

"Why?" I asked, still hoping somehow I might hold back something.

"You don't get to ask that. First the truth."

Between my illness and Papa and how quickly this conversation had been changing course, I couldn't keep track of anything anymore. "Yes! We found him, or he found me, and he chased me." Once I started talking, there was no stopping. I told her about the whole night, and the visions, and the fight on the street. She sat down at some point, staring at me with a fierce expression, asking questions now and then when something wasn't clear.

"And that's everything," I said once I was finished. "Everything I can remember, at least. But can you tell me what's going on?"

She sat back in her chair, chewing on her lower lip, her eyes downcast, moving back and forth slowly, almost as if she were reading a book.

"Mama," I started again.

"There was someone outside our house last night. I saw him on the street, lurking around. I yelled at him, and he ran off, but it made me feel...wrong."

She closed her eyes and opened them again, wide, as if she were trying to wake herself up.

I stood, seeing it all for what it was at last. Mama was sick, and she'd been forcing herself to keep going long past when she should have been in bed. And here I'd been, moping about myself. What sort of a daughter was I?

"You need to be in bed," I told her.

"I can't," she said. "Not when it's all unfinished. Not when he's out there. If he's after us again, someone needs to—to stop him."

"Let me handle it for now." I grabbed her by her elbow and pulled her to her feet, gently but without giving her an option. She went along with it, falling into me as she lost her balance again. "When did you come down with it?" I asked quietly.

"Two days ago," she said, not bothering to deny it. "It hasn't been as bad as what you and your father had. I just need to sleep for a full night. I'm sure I'll—"

Her eyes rolled back in her head, and she slumped to the floor.

CHAPTER SIXTEEN

The cry of "axman" was heard again Tuesday night in the neighborhood of Rocheblave and Canal streets, when persons living in the square bounded by Cleveland avenue, Rocheblave, Canal and Dorgenois streets, reported they had seen a man jumping over their back fences. Detectives and policemen surrounded the block and made a thorough search, but found no trace of the intruder.

———————

I YELLED AT MYSELF FOR MOST of the evening. When I wasn't taking Mama to her bed and trying to make sure she was as comfortable as possible, that is. How could I have been so focused on myself that I hadn't noticed my own mother was pushing herself past the breaking point?

A lot of the fuel for those yells came from the very real fear of what would happen if she were to die as well. I'd just lost Papa, and I'd thought that was as crushing of a blow as I could imagine. Now, thinking what life would be like with just me to face it, it was all I could do to not drop into a sobbing heap on the floor.

I had almost died. I remembered Signora Caravaggio's face when I'd tended to her. How close she'd seemed to passing. That could have been me. It could have been my body they'd carted out of the store alongside Papa's.

Who would keep the store open? What would I do if it closed? Where would I go? How could I afford to pay for anything? I'd viewed myself as an adult, fully ready and capable of facing the world on my own, but, faced with the possibility of becoming an orphan in the space of a few days, I suddenly wanted nothing more than my parents back to take care of me and tell me everything would be all right.

Instead of giving myself time to think too much on my future, I threw myself into work. Now that I was forcing myself past my depression, I noticed all the details I hadn't seen before. The unwashed dishes piled up in the sink. The dirty sheets stacked behind the house, the top few still stale from sweat, but underneath those a set of stained, rust-colored sheets. I stared at them for a moment, confused Mama could have been so careless to spill so much paint on the fabric. Then I realized they were from Papa.

I burned them and wondered what she had been thinking, holding onto them.

It was already late, and I was dizzy from a combination of anxiety, exhaustion, and lingering effects of the illness, but every time I found myself with time to think, I didn't like where my thoughts led me. I kept checking on Mama, convinced each time I peeked into the room that her cheeks would have turned the same purpled hue Papa's had when I saw him last. But she stayed asleep, even if she was fitful.

At last, I had to force myself to bed, though I dreaded the thought of lying there with nothing to do but think. I was falling asleep on my feet, so I hoped I'd pass out as soon as my head hit the pillow. For once, my plan went as expected.

Except my dreams were just as troubled as my waking hours. Papa came to me, his skin pale, with a trail of blood from the corner of his mouth and his bedclothes stained a bright scarlet. "This is your fault," he said. "You abandoned me."

I jolted up in bed, my heart pounding, the memory of his expression still clear in my mind. How disappointed he'd looked. Like I was his biggest failure.

Mama was asleep, but she was burning with a fever. I took a cool, damp cloth from the kitchen and wiped her forehead, praying for guidance. For mercy. God couldn't do this to me. Not both of them.

Eventually my eyes began to droop again, but I forced myself to stay up. The thought of going back to that nightmare was enough to make me never want to fall asleep again. I must have drifted off while I was attending to Mama, because the next thing I knew, I was striding through a burning church, axe held in a two-handed grip, screaming for the devil to come fight me. I knew he was somewhere just out of view, and I kept whirling to catch him, but, no matter which way I turned, I couldn't find him.

I stepped through the door of the church and found myself in Signora Caravaggio's parlor, the roots from the tree in the roof writhing this way and that, reaching out for me. I still had the axe, and I hacked back at them. They sent tendrils snaking around my arms and legs faster than I could move, and then they began to pull, lifting me off the ground and coming close to wrenching my joints from their sockets. Enzo came in and laughed at me.

And then I was lying in my bed again, panting from fear.

Once again, I checked on Mama and told myself none of those dreams were real. Which would I prefer? A regular nightmare, or another nighttime vision from the Axeman? These were just a symptom of the stress I was under. Mama was still sweating, but she seemed less restless than she'd been before. Like, this time, the sleep was actually doing her some good.

I lay back down and stared at the ceiling, waiting for sleep to take me away again, if it ever came.

It must have eventually, since, one moment, I was contemplating the different bills we had coming due for the store, and, the next, I was walking down the streets of New Orleans. It was night. The sky was clear above, with just a few stars, though the partially full moon scared many of the others off. My footsteps were light. I was excited, as if I were on my way to hear a great jazz band.

I recognized the street after a moment. Just a block away from my house, though the shadows had made it seem foreign at first. But there was the butcher's and the bookstore, just down from Mr. Broussard's, who always yelled at people for kicking up dirt on his flower pots.

No one was out tonight. Black ribbons hung in some of the windows, but even the sight of them wasn't enough to discourage me. I was walking toward my house, not away from it. That was the first detail that felt off, though I wasn't sure why.

I saw my parents' store with fresh eyes. The tired paint, the frayed awning. A hundred little details that added up to say the place was struggling, though Papa had done his best to keep it repaired. What would we do now that he was gone? Who would mend the shutters when the hinges broke again? How could we afford to hire anyone to do everything Papa had watched over?

As I put a hand on our back fence, my legs tensed up as if I were planning to vault over the obstacle. Then someone came around the corner: two men walking side by side. I let go of the fence and continued walking, tipping my hat to the men as they passed. I realized I was taller than I should have been. The fence normally loomed over me by a good foot, but it had been almost level with my eyes this time. And why would I have been jumping over it when I could have just gone in through the front door?

The other details followed in a flood: the way my body felt larger. Longer arms and legs. More strength than I was used to. The rapid beat of my heart. I was excited to the point I was surprised I wasn't shouting out in anticipation. The clothes I was wearing: trousers and a collared shirt and jacket. A hat I pulled lower to shadow my face.

I turned right at the corner and continued on my way, patting at my left jacket pocket and feeling a tool there: a chisel.

No matter how much I didn't want to believe it, I wasn't just in the Axeman's head right now. He was circling my house, and I knew all too well what happened when he visited.

I wanted to jump out of the vision and run for help. Or I could grab Mama and hurry her to safety. At the very least, I could have time to get something to defend myself. If I could surprise him, maybe I could turn this to my advantage.

But I was locked in the dream, the same way I'd been frozen in place during the Cortimiglia attack. I might as well have made a rock walk down the street as broken free of that vision. I turned the next corner, circling around the block to come at my backyard fresh again.

I could just picture what came next. Would I have to watch as I came inside and attacked Mama and my body in my sleep? I didn't have an axe yet, but there was a hatchet by the wood stove in the kitchen that would serve very well. Why had I been so stupid as to confront him? Why hadn't I just kept my head down and ignored him? It felt like my entire life had been leading to nothing but this from the moment he first attacked us seven years ago.

No! I wasn't going to let this happen. I couldn't just sit back and not do anything to fight him. If I could get back to my body in real life, then I'd have the advantage. All it would take was breaking out of this nightmare.

But how?

I'd turned the corner and come back to my backyard. This time, there was no one around, and I vaulted the fence with ease. *Come on, Gianna! Wake up!* I took the backsteps in a single leap, then crouched by the door with a practiced motion. The panels on the door were large—four giant rectangles that took up the whole of the face. I took out my chisel and set to work on the lower left one, scraping against the wood in long smooth strokes.

I tried to picture myself in my bedroom, imagining the feel of the sheets on my skin. Mama's breathing just across the way. I had to wake up! Why had I been foolish enough to fall asleep in the first place when I knew this demon was out there? He was out of sight, making almost no noise, on a deserted street in the middle of the night. Nothing was going to come that would get him to leave unless someone showed up to call for help.

This couldn't be happening. How could I know I was about to be attacked and yet be forced to do nothing other than try to slow down the murderer's hand? What else could I do? *Wake up, Gianna. Wake up!* But, if yelling at myself to wake up would have done the trick, I would have been out of this nightmare a long time ago.

Was it possible it was just a nightmare? I'd had the others in quick succession: Papa yelling at me. The burning church. But this had all the details of the other visions I'd had through the Axeman's eyes. I could feel the rough fabric of his shirt against my wrists. The way my palm was sweating around the handle of the chisel. The pressure of the boards on my knees. The sound of the chisel scraping against the wood in a slow steady beat.

It wasn't a normal nightmare.

Out of the depths of memory, a conversation came back to me: Mama talking with Signora Caravaggio about dreams. There was a trick to waking yourself. What had it been? I'd thought it was so ridiculous at the time. Sneezing? Hiccups?

Blinking. That had to have been it. I seized on the idea like a man drowning at sea goes for a piece of wreckage. *Blink blink blink blink—*

My eyes began to water. I blinked three times in quick succession, then rubbed at my face with my other hand.

This was working!

I kept at it, focused on nothing else, even as I made my way through one whole side of the panel, then another, and then a third. I pushed against the wood, and it splintered inward with a single crack.

I had less than a minute.

Blink blink blink blink—

My vision swirled, and then I was fluttering my eyes open, confused about where I was and what I'd just been doing.

The back door. The chisel!

The memory of the vision came rushing back. I leapt out of bed and ran into the main room to the front door, convinced the Axeman was right behind me. I didn't have time to fight back or protect myself. I unlocked the front door and threw it open in a quick motion. "Help!" I screamed out into the night air as loud as I could. "Murder! Help!" My voice was raw and crackling still from sleep. The sound echoed down the street. No lights came on. No one magically materialized to come rushing to my aid.

"Fire!" I shouted. The Axeman had to be hearing every word. Was he already inside with Mama? Would it be enough to scare him away, or would he just wait, hidden? What if no one came? "Fire!" I called out again.

A light turned on at the Hebert's Café, followed by one at the Boudreaux's and the Fontenot's in quick succession. And then people were running out of their houses to come see what was happening.

I'd never felt such relief. I went from panicked for my life to full anticipation in a matter of instants. With all these people here, maybe I could bring them all around to the back of the house. Catch the Axeman and overwhelm him with numbers.

"This way," I said, "He broke into my house through the back door." I darted around to the wooden fence behind our house. It was locked, but I wasn't going to let that stop me. I slammed into it at full speed, knowing just how flimsy the latch on the back was. It splintered with a single hit and barged open, revealing our backyard.

And no one else.

No fire. No murderer. No Axeman hunched over, leering at his job.

And no gaping hole where the door panel had been chiseled out. The door was normal. Solid. I stumbled up to it, pushing at it. It held firm. There were no signs of chisel marks. My eyes darted around the rest of the scene, wondering if I might catch a glimpse of a racing figure. Nothing. "He was right here," I said. "I just—"

My neighbors went from alarm to irritation as quickly as I'd changed emotions just before. They all seemed to remember the epidemic at once. You could see them all look at each other and notice how closely they'd packed together for a moment. The group spread out like drops of oil floating on water. My family wasn't the most popular on the block, and they knew we'd just had a death to influenza. There were some grumbles about false alarms and a couple of nasty looks and mutters about "idiot girls."

"No," I said, running up to Mr. Hebert and pulling at his arm. "Please, just come inside. He's in there."

He hesitated, looking down the street at his house but followed me in, grudgingly. I turned on the lights. There was no evidence of a struggle. No one there other than Mama, still fitfully sleeping. Mr. Hebert scowled at me and left through the front door, leaving me bewildered in the middle of my store.

So it had all been my imagination? I couldn't believe it. I had *been* there. If that was make-believe, then I might as well think I'd been making everything else up as well. Etta had said something about magical bags that made people invisible, hadn't she? Was something supernatural at work?

Or a premonition. It had to have been. I'd seen what the Axeman was going to do, not what he had already done.

I spent the next hour hammering boards across the doors and windows. The noise irritated the neighbors even more, but I didn't care.

The Axeman had been intent on coming here, and I'd been helpless. I had to do what I could to stay safe. I'd stay awake the whole night if I had to, and, when the morning came, I'd do whatever I had to in order to finish this. If he was coming after me, I had to think he might come after Enzo, too.

We were out of time. Whatever we were going to do to fight back had to happen tomorrow, or who knew when the next one of us would be killed.

CHAPTER SEVENTEEN

Whether or not you agree with the theory that all the recent
ax murders were the work of the same criminal, you must
acknowledge the crimes constitute a remarkable series.
Read the latest chapter in the Times-Picayune. FIFTEEN
CENTS A WEEK, DELIVERED TO YOUR HOME.
PHONE MAIN 4100.

═══════════

S OMEONE WAS POUNDING ON THE door.

I woke, startled, staring around me wildly as I tried to remember what had happened. Was it the Axeman, come back to finish the job?

Then I noticed the early morning sunlight streaming through the kitchen shutters, blocked somewhat by the crooked boards that had been nailed up in my hurry. I was huddled next to the back door in the kitchen. The hammer from last night was still next to me: I'd fallen asleep with it in my hands as I sat there, waiting just in case that demon returned.

The pounding came again, but it wasn't here in the kitchen. It was out front. What day was today? What time was it?

The produce delivery!

We should have been up and getting things ready for the day. I scrambled to my feet, trying to wrap my head around what was supposed to be happening. The store wasn't cleaned up, the kitchen was a disaster, I didn't have any of the displays out to take the produce in the first place, and it was just me.

I couldn't be running a store like this. Not today of all days. As I hurried to move the display case out of the way of the front door, I tried to compose what I would say. We were still sick with influenza. We'd open again in a few days. They would understand, wouldn't they? And I'd just tell the same thing to the newspaper deliveryman, and any dry goods that showed up, and the customers who would come by. The world could get by without the Crutti General Store.

But then I froze with my hand on the doorknob. The world could get by without us, but could we get by without the world?

Mama had been forcing herself to keep the store open while I was sick, despite the fact that she clearly hadn't been feeling well. I didn't know what our finances were exactly, but I knew she wouldn't do something like that without a very good reason. What sort of daughter would I be if I let my mother push herself that hard, only to fold and do nothing when it was my turn?

So I pulled my hair back and prayed it looked somewhat

presentable, then straightened my back, opened the door, and
started to apologize.

Once I was committed to it, there was no going back. I had
watched my parents do all of this for years, and I'd been tasked with
taking care of each of the jobs at one point or another, but we'd
always had three of us there to handle it, and I'd always been able to
just follow my parents' lead.

Today it was all me, and never mind that my head still spun
from time to time if I turned too quickly, or if my muscles didn't
seem to quite have the same strength I was used to. Should I
have been inviting people into the store when I had been sick
and Mama was in our bedroom, feverish and sweating? I wasn't
sure, but it felt like I had no choice. So I wore my face mask and
pushed forward.

The deliveries continued to come in as I was still setting everything up. I closed the door to the kitchen and tried to forget about
what I left behind there: the hastily boarded shutters. The cabinet
in front of the back door. Signs of my panic when the Axeman had
attacked. Reminders of what might happen again tonight. For now,
I had to focus on keeping the store going for the day.

Somehow, I pushed through it. That's the best that could be
said about everything I did. The store opened. People came in
and made purchases, and I didn't think any of them had been too
alarmed by what they saw. Some of them made comments about
Papa, and a few of them asked about Mama, and there were plenty

of glances to the boards on the windows, but this wasn't the only house in the city taking extreme precautions, after all. Most people these days were so focused on what was happening with themselves and their family that they didn't have the time or attention to think about others.

If it had been a normal day at the store, I might have been overwhelmed. The more I worked, the more I realized just how far from fully well I was. I had to take frequent breaks if the room started swimming too much, and I learned to avoid sudden movements. But the number of people we had coming into the store was less than half of what we might typically see. No one seemed concerned by how I acted or spoke, though having half my face covered by a cloth mask the whole time helped. It was strange how much that one change affected everything else. I had a harder time understanding what people were saying, and several times I didn't recognize long-term customers until they started to speak.

The whole day, I kept an eye on the clock, counting down the hours until five. If I could just make it until then, I thought I'd be justified in closing the store a bit earlier than usual. Sometimes the time seemed to speed by: it went from 11 to 12:30 in the space of a few seconds. But that was counterbalanced by other times. From 2:00 to 3:00, I must have looked at the clock thirty times. I was thirsty, my head was worse than it had been, and I'd made the mistake of checking on Mama. She was lost in a fever and thrashing

DON'T GO TO SLEEP

on her bed. I tried to fix her up as best I could, and I would have sent for a doctor if we could have afforded it, but instead I had to just hope she would turn the corner again.

And then it was 5:00. I was turning the sign on the door to *Closed*, bringing in the fruit and vegetable stands, and thanking God I'd somehow made it this far. Papa would have been proud. True, I'd turned down the two requests for haircuts that came in, but I'd sold twelve drinks over the course of the day. I reasoned people wouldn't mind so much if I did something wrong with their drink, but a bad haircut or shave would be a sign to everyone who saw that person that they should avoid the Cruttis'.

Mama hadn't eaten anything all day, and she'd only managed a few sips of weak tea. "I'm going to have leave for a bit," I told her as I put on my jacket and tried to pretend I didn't have butterflies. I was exhausted and had a hard time standing straight, but I needed to get help. The Axeman might come again tonight: for me or for Enzo. My friend needed to be warned, and, if things went well, I could convince his family to come back to my house. I worried about moving Mama in her condition, but, if we were all in the same place, we could take turns keeping watch at night.

I'd certainly feel better with more people under my roof.

But I couldn't leave Mama alone for as long as it would take to get to Enzo's, and I wasn't up to carrying her there myself. I might not have been comfortable with telephones, but there was one in the cafe across the street. I had enough money to make the call.

Mama would be okay for five minutes, and I could keep an eye on the store through the window.

"I'll be back before you know it," I told her. She was still feverish, her eyes closed, forehead covered in sweat, and her breath coming in little gasps. "Then Enzo will be here. His parents might have to come later, but at least they can spare him until their store closes, sì?"

The sky outside was dark and overcast, the clouds lower than I'd remembered seeing them before. As if God Himself were coming down, preparing to level the entire city. It was the sort of sky that made me think of arks and forty days of rain, but it was still dry as I rushed into the cafe, feeling like an idiot as I asked Mr. Hebert how to use the telephone. He was still irritated at me from last night, so his directions were little more than a point and a grunt.

I closed myself into the booth, feeling like I was stepping into a coffin. The telephone stared back at me. How could Enzo's family be comfortable with one of these in their house? I might have eyed it suspiciously before—what sort of a device let you talk like that to people who weren't even there, and who might be listening in between?—but now wasn't the time to let suspicion stop me. It was a telephone. How hard could it be?

I hesitated before picking up the speaker, then chided myself for being such a fraidy-cat. If I couldn't even face down a contraption like this, what right did I have to go against the Axeman?

When I put the speaker to my ear, it was quiet and muffled,

like I was listening to a seashell. I waited for someone to talk to me, until I remembered I had to ring it first. There was a metal crank on the front of the box. I turned it twice, and a bell sounded within.

"Number please," a woman's voice came from the tiny speaker.

"Um. The Rissetto store?" I cleared my throat, and then forced my voice to stop being so high pitched and questioning. "I need to speak Vincenzo Rissetto."

"What extension?"

"Extension?"

"What's the number?"

"I don't know," I said. "It's a brown building over on the corner of—"

"Unless it's public, I need a number. Use the telephone directory. It's usually right next to you."

It took some fumbling, but I found the book: a series of last names with addresses and numbers listed next to them. The Rissettos' address was listed. "UP 7842?" I said.

"Uptown 7842. That'll be five cents."

I put a nickel into the slot. That was followed by silence. "Hello?"

"I'm ringing the number now," the woman said. Another pause. "There's no answer."

I scrambled to think what to do next. I needed help now, no matter where it came from. Mama would want to kill me, but better for the two of us to be alive for her to yell at me later. "Then can I call the police?" I asked.

"Which precinct?"

"Downtown."

"One moment."

The speaker fed crackling noises into my ear. "District 8," came a man's voice. Uninterested. Tired.

"Yes," I said, suddenly hating my Italian accent and furious with myself for feeling that way. It was almost enough to make me want to slam the speaker back down on the hook and forget about this.

"What is it?" the voice asked, an edge of irritation already there.

"I want to report an attack," I said. "By the Axeman."

The voice sighed and it sounded more muffled for a moment. "Got another one," he said, before the muffling went away. "Where and when did the attack happen?" By his tone, he might as well have been asking about how long it took paint to dry.

"It didn't happen yet. I mean, I stopped him, and he ran away. But I'm worried he's going to—"

"It didn't happen yet?"

"No," I said. "He's after me and my family, though. I know he's going to—"

"Listen, lady. We don't have time to be coming by every Guappo's house just because they saw something fishy. Did he attack you or not?"

"What do you care?" I asked, the fear and anger bubbling over all at once. *Guappo*. He turned me into a word and used that word to ignore every trouble I might have. I wasn't one of *them*, so he didn't have to pay attention to me. "All you police are all the same. Too busy sitting on your fat—"

The line clicked, pulling me up short. "Hello?" I asked, still frustrated I didn't understand enough about the technology to know what had just happened. "Hello?"

There was no response. I grunted in frustration, but I didn't slam the speaker back down as hard as I could have. If Mr. Hebert saw me abusing his telephone, I'd be in even bigger trouble.

I glanced out the window at my store. The rain had begun to come down in torrents, thundering onto the street outside. No one had tried to go in, but what if the Axeman was creeping around the back? I had to *do* something, and, instead, I'd done nothing more than make myself angry and remind myself just how frustrated I could get with the police. They were probably taking calls from across the city, and it wasn't like they knew my call was the one that really mattered. But they still could have been polite about it. They were paid to serve us, after all. They still took our taxes, the same as any other person in this city.

"Are you about done?" Mr. Hebert asked me. "Someone else might need to use it."

"One second," I said, inspiration coming to me. The police didn't know to listen to me because they didn't know me. But I knew someone they knew. Etta had gotten them to turn out in force a few nights ago. If I were to tell her about this, she could do something right away.

I patted myself down, wondering if I still had the card she had left for me when I'd yelled her out of our store. It was deep in my pocket, crumpled and looking pretty sorry, but I could still read the number she had written. Hemlock 1138. I picked up the speaker on the telephone again.

"Number please?"

"Hemlock 1138," I said, feeding another nickel into the slot.

"One moment."

This time wasn't as bewildering. I knew what to expect. And I had to admit it saved a lot of time. Imagine just having to talk into a microphone to go around the city instead of having to walk. If we could afford something like this in our store, we could—

"St. Charles Hotel. How can I help you?"

Of course it wouldn't be the phone number straight to her. I cleared my throat. "I need to speak with Etta Palmer."

There was a pause, and then, "One moment."

Another wait before a different voice came over the speaker. "Palmer."

"Etta?" I asked.

"Gianna," she said. "Where are you? I thought your store didn't—"

I explained hurriedly what had happened and what I was worried about. She heard me through without interruption. "I called the police," I said at last, "but they didn't even listen to me. I thought if you called them…"

"Stay at the store," she said. "Close all the windows and shutters, lock the door, and get something to defend yourself with. A shovel or a crowbar. Anything you have at hand. I'll be there in twenty minutes."

She hung up without saying another word, leaving me staring at the phone, wondering what had just happened. I was wasting time. If Etta was taking it this seriously, that meant I had good cause to worry. I ran out of the cafe, leaving the telephone's speaker dangling in place and ignoring Mr. Hebert's protests. Even the short dash across the street was enough to get my shoulders drenched, but I arrived in our store to find Mama still where I had left her. The boards were still across the back door and windows.

Nothing had changed.

I picked up the hand axe we used to chop kindling, and I stayed in the middle of the storeroom, listening to the rain hammer on the roof until I realized it wasn't just the rain anymore.

Someone was at the door.

From there, Etta took over. She had three policemen with her, and they swept into the store as if President Wilson himself were in danger. For the last seven years, I'd dreamed what it would have been like if the police had really taken the Axeman seriously the first time. With Etta there to boss them around, I didn't have to dream anymore.

She left two of the men at our store, and she and the other one bundled Mama and me into a police van. We were driven straight to the Rissettos', which seemed like a beehive of activity in comparison to what I'd left behind. There were two officers at the front and two at the back, watching the area as if they expected a maniac to jump out at them at any moment. Inside, a doctor was waiting for Mama, and Enzo's family was watching all of this go on with wide eyes.

I'd worried Mama would have taken the ride poorly, but she didn't seem much changed as I made sure she was as comfortable as possible in Enzo's bed. She only muttered a few stray phrases in Italian, but she was still feverish. The doctor inspected her as I towel-dried her hair. Her skin was like fire to the touch. This was a nicer bed than she had at home, and the doctor had to make a difference, didn't he?

Would Papa still be alive if we could have had a doctor see to him right away? Or did it not even make a difference? Sometimes it felt like the doctors were guessing at cures right along with the rest of us. Could anyone find a cure for death?

I stared at Mama for a moment once she was situated. If she died as well, I wasn't sure what I'd do. For my entire life, Mama had been this unstoppable force. She was a constant, and I'd never thought what it would be like to lose her. Even back when the Axeman first attacked us, I'd been angry that he'd hurt my family and frightened by the general concept of losing my parents, and I'd thought I'd been frightened when I'd seen what the influenza had done to Signora Caravaggio.

It had taken Papa's passing for me to face what death was actually like.

Mama seemed much smaller, lying in a huddle on Enzo's bed. The disease might go either way, and it was infuriating to think there was nothing I could do about all of it. I might protect her from the Axeman, but, in the end, it still wouldn't matter.

These days, it was much too easy to get discouraged in a matter of moments. Better to not let my mind dwell on such things.

I left the bedroom and went out to find Enzo sitting to the side, watching as Etta and the Rissettos talked over plans with the other police.

"What happened?" he asked me. "The last I knew, you were in bed sick."

"Mama came down with it yesterday," I said. "Or at least, she succumbed to it. I think she was pushing herself for much longer than she should have, and she finally collapsed. Then last night *he* came for us."

Enzo stated at me for a moment before recognition dawned on his face. "The Axeman?"

"It wasn't Babbo Natale," I said, trying to recapture some of my normal energy. At the moment, all I really wanted to do was find a hole in the ground I could disappear into and never come out of again. Seeing how easily the two of us had been shunted aside only helped me see that much more clearly that this is what we should have been doing all along. Who were Enzo and I to think we could have brought down a villain like this murderer? I should have stayed home and tended to my family.

"How did he find you?" Enzo asked.

"How should I know?" I asked. "I don't think he'd need a map and directions. He attacked us in the same house seven years ago. He probably just remembered from back then. I was the idiota who bragged to him in person that I would finally get revenge on him. I might as well have invited him back for tea and cookies."

I went into the kitchen and made a fresh pot of tea. I might have realized I shouldn't have been trying to lead this fight against the Axeman, but I still felt the need to do *something*. By the time the tea was ready, the activity in the main room had died down. The police were gone, the Rissettos had retreated to their bedroom, and Enzo was spreading out two sets of blankets on the floor while Etta looked over a checklist. She glanced up when I entered, and took the cup of tea I offered her.

"What's the plan?" I asked.

"We've got a team over at your house right now. They'll stay the night there. With any luck, the Axeman will try to break in, and they'll take care of him. We also have guards in plainclothes around the block of the store here. They're on shifts, just in case he tries to switch up his attack and come for you here tonight."

"He doesn't come when there are people around," Enzo said. "Won't all this scare him off?"

"Just because you think you know what someone's going to do

doesn't mean you should only plan for them to do that," Etta said, sipping her tea. She talked about all of this as if she were chatting about the weather. "The sooner you start realizing whoever you're up against has a plan of their own and is going to adjust it accordingly, the better your odds of coming out alive."

I wondered what she'd gone through to give her this sort of familiarity with facing situations like this. "What happens if he doesn't show up tonight?"

"I have his description from you. We know what he looks like and how he normally behaves. The police are scouring through the city even as we speak. With any luck, we'll have him well before he even has a chance to try attacking you."

"How did you convince all of them to do all...this?" I asked. "Don't the police think you're overreacting?"

"We're facing a man who wants to kill every one of you. A man who has experience with it, and who knows how not to get caught. Do you really think there's such a thing as being too prepared? I'd much rather he come here and be overwhelmed than we go easy on him. It's not as if we win any awards for making do with less."

"He disappeared for years before," I said. "He could do it again."

"Last time the police had mixed descriptions, and they didn't have me. The good news for us is that we know how this man thinks. He's been using the same approach time after time. He'll circle to the back of the house, and he'll spend time chiseling his way through the door. We'll let him think the coast is clear, and then when he's crouched there chiseling, I'll nab him. If I have to, I'll shoot. I won't miss."

"How do we even know he'll come?" Enzo asked.

"He attacked Gianna's house not once, but twice. He knows she's on his trail, and he's smart enough to do what needs doing to keep himself safe. In the end, he'll come to where Gianna is. When you want to catch a predator, you keep track of its prey."

Was that all I'd been reduced to now? Some monster's *prey*? Maybe that's all I'd been good for in the first place. It was all I could do to present an upbeat front to Enzo and Etta. Inside, I was already dead. The sooner this was over, the sooner I could sink into obscurity.

Right where I belonged.

CHAPTER EIGHTEEN

Authorities Holding Son of Cortimiglia's Rival in Business:
Despite the fact that a formal charge of murder Saturday was placed against 17-year-old Frank Giodano,...as a result of the attack of an axman upon the Cortimiglia family while they slept,...New Orleans police in no degree relaxed the vigilance they have maintained in an effort to run down the murderer.

———

E NZO AND I WERE TO sleep on the floor in the main room of the store. We checked on our parents, and Etta went outside to make sure all the other preparations were in order. Then Enzo and I settled in for the wait to come. We were in place by 10 o'clock.

The first half hour went by quickly. There was still enough excitement from the preparations that I was partly convinced the Axeman would spring from the shadows any moment. But all that came was silence and more waiting. I felt like a guitar string wound too tight: under high pressure, anchored in place, with nothing to do but wait. If I could only be *doing* something—putting all that energy to use—then everything would be better.

But I couldn't. And the more I sat there in the darkness, the more I began to think. There were plenty of thoughts waiting to barge into my mind. The influenza. Mama lying in the room not thirty feet away from me. The Great War. If the Axeman might come. *When* the Axeman might come.

Papa.

I didn't want to be left alone with my thoughts. The more I dwelt on them, the more I thought I might go mad. Except the time just kept creeping forward. What was Etta doing outside? Would we just know the plan had worked when we heard her call out, or when a gun went off? He might be crouched by the door this instant, with the police taking careful aim, ready to come out of hiding. Should we even give him the chance to surrender? After what he'd done to my family, wouldn't it just be easier to kill him before he had the chance to try anything else?

Over the years, I'd thought about what it would be like to have his life in my hands. To be able to take some revenge for what I'd been through. But that had been before the Great War and all this sickness. Before Papa. Tonight, I found my appetite for more death wasn't as sharp as it had been during peace time.

And, still, nothing had changed. The floor was cold and hard, and I hadn't slept well last night, and I'd had a terrible nonstop day. Not that I wanted to fall asleep now. As long as *he* was out there,

I never wanted to sleep again, no matter what that meant for the next day.

Tomorrow! The thought washed over me like cold water. I'd pushed myself to get through one day at the store, as if that one time would be all I had to worry about. Except the same difficulties I faced this morning would be there tomorrow morning again. Yes, I had Mama situated now, but the store itself still needed tending.

"Enzo," I whispered, not wanting to be too loud to disturb Mama in the next room, but no longer ready to be alone with my thoughts.

"What?" he hissed back.

"Have you heard anything?"

"I can't tell. I don't know what I'm listening for. At first I kept thinking someone was on the back porch, the way it was creaking, but I think I just never paid attention to how the house sounds at night before."

Silence again for a while. It felt foolish to talk, as if, by doing that, we might not be ready for the Axeman. But, if he came, we'd hear him working on the door, wouldn't we? "Are you scared?" I asked.

"No," Enzo said. Ten seconds later, he added, "Yes. I don't know. I can't tell anymore. Are you?"

"The same," I said. I couldn't pretend anymore. Not after everything I'd been through.

"I don't know how long I can do this," I continued. "What are you going to do about the store?"

"Oh," he said, sounding like he hadn't considered that yet. Maybe he hadn't. He hesitated before he answered. "It'll be up to my parents, but I'll bet they'll want to stay closed until this is over with. We've got enough savings. What about you?"

"I have to go back in the morning. We don't have any savings at all. If the store folds, it won't matter what the Axeman does to us."

"Don't say that. We'd figure something out."

In my experience, it was always easier to think you'd figure something out when you had enough money to buy yourself time to figure, but I didn't tell Enzo that. "I hardly slept last night," I said. "Today was hard enough. Tomorrow's going to be terrible."

"Sleep now. I'll wake you up if anything happens."

"I can't," I said. "Every time I close my eyes, I'm terrified I'm going to be inside his head again. It feels like the connection is getting stronger each time. What if the next time I can't get out at all? I'd be trapped inside that devil's head, never to come out again, while my body just rotted away to nothing."

"You can't be thinking like that," Enzo started. "If you—"

"I have to be," I cut in. "This is real to me, Enzo. Everyone else can treat it like I'm making it up, and, after what happened to me last night, I guess I don't blame them. But it feels real to me. And I wonder if he can see out through my eyes as well. What if he's in there right now, seeing what I'm seeing. Hearing what I'm thinking? He could know every part of our plan. What if he's come up with a way around it?"

Enzo was silent, considering. "If he knows what we're doing, I think he'd run. This many police? He'd be insane to try anything."

"And that's just what he is."

"No," Enzo said. "Insane people don't get away with it for this long. He's planning these killings. He knows where he wants to attack, and he knows how to get in and out without anyone catching him. There have been at least what—ten attacks now?"

He was right, wasn't he? Why did I feel disappointed when I considered that the Axeman might run away, and then terrified when I thought he might actually attack? I was a mess, no matter what happened.

"Wake me up if I fall asleep," I said. "Promise?"

"Promise. And, in the morning, I'll come with you?"

"With me?"

"To help at your store. My parents can take care of your mother, and you'll need all the help you can get."

"Thank you," I said, wishing the promise made me feel better. I wondered if I'd ever feel better again.

I tried to remind myself I wasn't in this alone. I felt responsible. I was the one with the visions. I was the one who kept seeing the Axeman kill again and again. I was the one who hadn't done anything to stop him. I was the one who hadn't been there for my parents. I was the one who was letting everyone down, no matter what I did.

The reasonable side of me clamored that this couldn't all be on me. I was part of a team, and the only way this would work is if we all came together to make it happen. The plan Etta had put in place was solid. I just had to sit back and let it happen, now.

I settled back down on the floor, shifting my weight to find a comfortable angle on the floorboards. Patience. I could do that. But the time didn't get any shorter, and the floor didn't get any softer. Time continued to crawl by, and I drifted in and out of sleep, dozing against my will at first, then startling awake and swearing to myself I wouldn't fall asleep again.

But there's only so long I could stay on high alert. My eyes drooped once more, and I entered this sort of in-between state, where I wasn't quite asleep and wasn't fully awake. I could sense time dragging on, and I knew I should be more with it, but I couldn't pull myself together enough to stick with it.

Sleep came on me, layer by layer. My mind shut down until it was almost at rest, but, before I could lose myself, a noise caught my ear. Faint and distant, but steady and getting louder. At first I thought it was footsteps: someone walking through the kitchen or on the porch outside. But the footfalls were too heavy. Was someone jumping? And why were they taking such pauses in between each jump?

Except the sound was too sharp for footfalls. Too abrupt for a jump. It kept repeating, growing louder until it registered.

The axe.

Just like that, I was back in my nightmare, shut inside the coffin as Mama screamed outside. I tried to tell myself it wasn't real, but the wood was rough on my fists. I could smell the pine boards. Taste the salt of my tears.

The knothole from my earlier struggles was still free, and I scrabbled to my toes, trying to see what was happening. "Mama!" I shouted. "I'm coming!" Another axe blow. And another. Mama shrieked, her feet scrambling for purchase on the floor.

I tried rocking the coffin back and forth, hoping to tip it over. It bobbled on the first few attempts, and then hung in the air for an eternity before it came crashing down face-first.

Covering the knothole completely.

My nose smashed against the wood. If this were a dream, that should have woken me up.

The axe was louder, now. Mama's screams had turned into muffled sobs. I slammed my shoulder into the side of the coffin, hoping the fall had knocked some of the nails loose. On the third blow, light leaked in through a small gap between the back of the coffin and its side. If I arched my neck just right, I could glimpse a portion of the room.

A ring of smoldering embers circled a crude chopping block. Mama had been dragged through the circle, flames tickling the edges of her dress. Her hands were bound behind her back. A rag had been shoved inside her mouth, then tied in place. She was on her knees, her head lying on the block, tears streaming down her cheek.

"Mama!" I cried out again. I barreled against the wood twice more, but it didn't have any effect.

I shoved myself up as far as I could, pressing my face against the side to try and see more. There must be someone around who would help. Some way to break free. No one was there. No sign of the Axeman or any other captor. We had time, if I could just *see*.

My eyelashes fluttered against the wood. If I could get a better angle, I could—

A face appeared right outside my box. One green eye staring straight into mine, inches away.

I bolted upright, the nightmare gone but still leaving me shaking. I was falling apart. Wearing down layer by layer until there was nothing left of me. If this didn't end, I didn't know how much longer I could go on.

Someone shook my shoulder. I screamed and lashed out with my hand. It was caught at once in a vice grip. "Save it for the Axeman," Etta said. "I was just checking everything was okay in here. Go back to sleep."

"No," I said. "No sleep." I blinked my eyes several times—they didn't want to focus at first, and then I realized it was still dark, and I couldn't see anything, anyway. I struggled to remember where I was and why I was on the floor. The memory of that coffin was still too strong.

Etta unshuttered a light briefly to cast the room in uncertain shadows. My heart pounded in my ears. Why had I let myself fall asleep again?

And Enzo was snoring a few feet away. So much for him being ready for anything that came.

She smiled at me. "The two of you were out cold. It sounded like you were saying something in your sleep. Any dreams?"

I sat up, my head pounding from resting against the floor. "Not that I can remember," I lied. I didn't want to have explain what I'd just experienced. Didn't want to remember any more of it than I had to. "What time is it?"

"Three-thirty. Halfway through."

I put my hands over my eyes and pressed back against my eyeballs, praying it would clear somewhat. It only got worse. "How do you do it?" I asked.

"Keep going? Practice. It also helps to remind yourself there will be time to sleep when this is over."

I sat there in a ball on the floor, wishing my headache would go away. "What if it's never over?"

Etta came to sit down next to me, breathing a long sigh as she did so. "You can't think that way. All problems have an end. All of them can be solved."

"Sure," I said. "He kills us."

She cocked her head to the side. "Well, then it won't be your problem anymore."

I scowled at her. "Oh. So funny. I'm glad this is amusing to you. Like you can come in here and—"

She held up her hand to stop me. "So you still have some fight left in you after all. That's good. You're going to need it. But I'll tell you one thing that definitely *won't* help you. Self-pity. The more you think about how hard your life is, the less you'll be ready for when you can actually do something to change it."

Which might have been intended to make me feel better, but only served to make me feel guilty. Just another instance of me trying to do something and failing.

"I was your age when I went up against my first murderer," Etta said. "He killed my sister, and I swore I'd find him and make him pay. Then it turned out I'd been living with him for months, without a clue of what he'd done."

"Did he give you that scar on your face?" I asked.

She shook her head. "Sometimes you don't learn a lesson the first time, but my scar doesn't enter into this. What does is the fact you need to focus on what you have, not what you don't. Your father's dead, but your mother's alive. You have a young man who's absolutely devoted to you. There are worse positions to be in, believe me."

"It won't matter if we can't beat the demon."

"No," Etta said, her voice firm and confident. "It always matters. Those connections are what makes life worth it, and, if you let yourself dismiss them, you lose a part of who you are. You're not alone. So stop focusing on how bad you have it, and start pushing yourself to get through the night. If there's one thing I know about people like this Axeman, it's that they're compelled to do what they do. They're like a cat that's found a mouse. Sooner or later, they just can't help trying to kill it. Time's not on his side. The longer he waits, the better your mother gets, and the more options we have."

At least someone could feel optimistic, even if I couldn't believe her. She stood soon after, heading to see what was happening at my store across town. I refused to lie down again, still convinced if I did I might never open my own eyes again.

Somehow the time passed. I didn't think I'd drifted off again, but, the next thing I really knew, I was staring at the clock and realizing it was light enough for me to tell the time more easily. It took a bit for that to sink in—I was so exhausted, and my back was seizing up from the angle I'd been sitting, and my head was spinning from fatigue—but then I realized that must mean it was morning.

We'd gone the whole night, and there hadn't been any sign of the Axeman. Not inside the house, at least.

I got up, and I almost stumbled over Enzo, who was slumped in a heap by the kitchen door. It took a couple of shakes before he was close to awake. When he came to, he wiped at his face and blinked his eyes. "What time is it?"

"Time for me to be getting to the store. Did you hear anything from outside during the night?"

He shook his head. "I was so out of it, I don't think I would have heard a military parade."

He wasn't lying. I rapped three times against the back door, then opened it a crack, calling out, "Are we okay to come out?"

"Fine," Etta's voice answered right back. When I was outside, she walked over to meet me. Her eyes were bright, her hair was in order, and you never would have known she'd stayed the whole night on watch.

"Any sign of him last night?" I asked.

"None. A few people passed by on the street, but no one even paused. Your place was clear as well, last time I heard anything."

I explained about the need to go take care of the store, half worried she'd tell me it wasn't safe to leave. Instead, she replied, "The cows need milking, no matter the weather." As if that made sense.

"We'll come back here tonight?"

"Yes," she said. "I'll have men watching both stores throughout the day, just in case, and we'll continue the hunt for him while we've got daylight. If we're lucky, we'll catch him before nightfall."

"Watching during the day?" I repeated. "He's never attacked then."

"He's never been so close to getting caught, either," Etta said. "If he realizes how in danger he is, there's a chance he'll do something extreme. We have to be ready for it."

I nodded. My eyelids felt heavy, but I did my best to ignore that and move forward with my day.

Enzo and I didn't speak on our way over to my home. I still felt like my head was stuffed in a pillowcase, and Enzo was nursing his back in a way that told me he'd definitely slept on it wrong just like I had. The city was empty, the streets dry. I tried to remember it the way I'd always loved it: filled with people at all hours, with constant music. Street buskers during the day, and jazz groups taking over at night into the small hours.

"Do you think it'll ever be back the way it was?" I asked Enzo a few blocks from my house. My voice was slightly muffled by my face mask, but it was something we were all quickly getting used to.

"Our lives?" he asked.

I laughed, a single bark of derision. "I don't have much hope for that," I said, trying not to think of Papa. "I mean the city. The world. They're always going on in church about the end days. Do you think this is it? Between the War and this disease, maybe God's getting ready to kill us all off, the same way He did with the flood."

A year ago, Enzo would have assured me it was all going to be fine. We would win the war. We would beat the Axeman. The epidemic would go away. This morning, he only shrugged, apparently not trusting himself to answer.

As we drew nearer to my store, the low buzzing at the back of my head picked up again. Distant and intermittent at first, so that I thought I must have been imagining it, but it grew stronger and more persistent as we kept going. The same feeling I'd had a few nights ago when Enzo and I had been on the hunt for the Axeman. I stopped, putting my hand on Enzo's arm. "He's close," I said.

"The Axeman?"

I nodded. "I can *feel* him. I think he might be at the store."

We broke into a sprint, our footfalls echoing off the buildings around us. Anything might have happened since Etta had been there. Had that demon tried to attack and been caught? Had he butchered the policemen? The thrumming inside my head got more intense until it felt was never going to end. As we turned the final corner to bring my home into sight, I expected to find the entire block on fire. All exhaustion had vanished from me. I was ready for anything. Ready for this to be done at last, one way or the other.

But my store looked unchanged. No police outside, but the door was closed, the area around it orderly. He must have come in through the back and taken them by surprise. I put out a hand to slow Enzo, then whispered to him, "We can come in when he's not expecting it. Let's not alert him if we don't need to."

Enzo nodded, and the two of us ducked close next to the side of the street my house was on, out of sight of anyone who might be watching out the windows. We padded down the sidewalk, crouching beneath my windows as we passed. No noise came from inside. If the police were still there, they were unconscious or dead.

A rage built up inside me, along with the sense that this was the way it should be. I didn't need all these other people to stand between me and the Axeman. It was Enzo and I against the monster. I'd be able to feel the life go out of that demon as I throttled him with my bare hands, if I could.

No! Another thought came immediately. Wanting to kill him and take pleasure from it? That wasn't me. Those were the Axeman's thoughts bleeding into my own. I wouldn't flinch back from killing him if there were no other choice, but it would be better to capture him and turn him over to the police.

Wouldn't it?

I peeked over the fence at my back door. It was open, an empty hole into a dark abyss. Anything might wait inside. I rubbed my eyes, trying to clear the last bit of fuzz from my head. If I could just be fully aware for the next fifteen minutes, I might be able to never have to worry about this again. For a moment, I could see the end. Picture a world where the Axeman wasn't a problem anymore. A place where the epidemic was past us, and the war was over, and Enzo and I...

Now wasn't the time to daydream. "I'll rush in and surprise him, then run out to try and get him into the open," I told Enzo. "You come and wait by the door. When he comes out, hit him from behind. Don't hold back."

He nodded once to me. The bass note was still inside my head, as strong as ever. There was no doubt in my mind of what I was going to find when I ran into my house. I felt bad for the policemen, but I couldn't let myself dwell on what had already happened. The Axeman was here to find me, and I could somehow sense that he wanted this to last longer than a single slice of a blade. He'd chase after me as long as he knew I was this close.

And he had to, didn't he? If I could feel him like this, he must know I was nearby. He'd be preparing for me just as much as I was for him. Worse, he would have had time to lay whatever trap he was thinking of. Part of me was yelling for me to slow down. Wait for Etta to come so we could attack him with a larger force.

But I'd waited seven years for this. Maybe it was because the Axeman was already in my head. Maybe I was just too tired to think straight. Either way I was convinced, if we didn't strike now, it would be too late.

I pushed open the gate and dashed for the back door, leaping inside—

And startling two very confused-looking policemen who were sharing a loaf of bread and jam at the kitchen table.

CHAPTER NINETEEN

[T]he frequency of ax murder in the past warranted the continuation of an investigation here upon the theory that the ax murders in New Orleans were the work of a degenerate madman. Police are watching carefully corner groceries here, for it is in establishments of this kind that most of the ax murders have taken place.

―――――――

T HERE WAS NO AXEMAN. No chaos inside. No bodies dripping with blood. I practically fell over in surprise, then rushed past them, grabbing for the same hand axe I'd had two nights ago. So the police were clueless. That only meant the Axeman had managed to hide somewhere else inside the store. It was a trap, then. He'd been hoping to catch me unaware in the middle of the day. But I wasn't going to go down like that.

The main storeroom was empty. No one crouched behind the counter. The area back in the corner by the barber chair was clear. I tiptoed to the bathroom door, which stood ajar. The policemen followed me in, clearly confused by what was going on. I signaled them to be quiet, then slammed the bathroom door open. It ricocheted off the wall behind it. The room was empty.

That left only the bedroom.

I steeled myself for what I might find there. With the police behind me, we had the advantage. By now, even Enzo had come in. The three of them stared at me with varying degrees of confusion, but I still had the sense the Axeman was close. I crept over to the bedroom door and eased it open.

It looked much the same way I'd left it: Mama and Papa's bed unmade, the dresser partially open from when I'd ransacked it to bring what she'd need at the Rissettos'. The sheet that separated my part of the room from my parents' was still up, billowing slightly in the air current from the opening door. There was no sign of anyone. He *had* to be behind that sheet. It made no sense, but why else would I feel like this?

I raised the axe up behind my head and inched over to the spot where I'd slept every night for my entire life. With a quick motion, I swept the sheet aside and brought the axe whipping down through the air.

Where it passed through without hitting anything else.

The space was empty.

"Gia?" Enzo asked behind me.

I turned to stare at him, confused. "I can feel it," I told him again. "I know I can."

He signaled to the police for them to give us some privacy. When they'd left, he said, "You haven't slept well since before you were sick. Why don't I take care of the store today, and you stay here and rest? You're no good to anyone if you can't keep upright."

The thought of lying here doing nothing the entire day was enough to make my stomach turn. I shook my head. "I'll be okay. I need to be working to take my mind off this. If I just sit here on my thumbs, I'll be even worse."

"Fair enough. Let's get the displays set up. The newspapers and deliveries should be here soon."

I let myself be ushered out, and I kept busy dealing with the different deliveries for the next forty-five minutes while Enzo worked on unloading and arranging. As I worked, I took time to go through the house more carefully. I knew every hiding place better than anyone could, and I still felt sure the Axeman had to be somewhere. That note at the back of my head was so constant it almost didn't register with me anymore.

But the cabinets with the bedding in them didn't have anyone crouched inside them. The panel that led to the attic didn't appear to have been moved, and, when I took the ladder over there to double-check, it rained dust and rat droppings onto my face. I sputtered and ran to the bathroom to clean myself off, thankful Enzo had been out dealing with a customer when that particular incident happened.

There was the crawlspace underneath the house, but the lattice work that Papa had put in place to cover the openings was all still solidly attached, and any fool knew better than to go into a crawl space in New Orleans, anyway. Not unless they wanted a personal meeting with a brown recluse or cottonmouth.

It was enough to make me think of Etta and her story of the Church of Sacrifice again. The Axeman couldn't be able to turn himself invisible, could he? At this point, I was willing to believe anything. I began searching not just with my eyes, but with my hands, feeling my way through each space to be absolutely sure it was empty.

He was nowhere to be found.

In the end, I had to acknowledge that "feeling" had to be nothing other than pure exhaustion. Tonight I'd have to sleep no matter what, or I'd be worthless on another day. I tried to set any premonitions aside and focus on the things that had to be done running the store. In some ways, I was grateful for the work. Doing the same things I'd done day after day, year after year, let me turn off my mind and let habit carry me through. Enzo helped me with all of it with the same practiced ease. We might have grown up working in different locations, but we each knew what was required without the need to be directed.

But that only really worked for the first part of the day, when there were all the chores that needed doing to get the store in order. Once those were squared away, I faced the same long stretches of time that came with the territory of running a store. They were worse during the epidemic, of course. Fewer people were out and about, and so the rushes were shorter, with more time in between.

The day was a slog from start to finish. Every little detail was enough to throw me into a tiny rage. If too many people showed up at once, I got flustered. When no one was around, I was anxious, wondering every few minutes how Mama was doing. I was angry people weren't wearing masks when they came into the store. Didn't they know how serious this was? But then I caught myself also being angry at people for wearing masks in the first place. I wanted things to be normal again, without everyone looking like a surgeon or a bandit.

Interactions like that reminded me the world wasn't completely falling apart, but they also made me miss what we'd lost that much more acutely. Just a month ago, my biggest worries were around which concerts I'd be able to go to, and how unfair it was that my favorite bands never got to make Victrola recordings. Papa had been alive, the city had been normal, and life had been…life. And then it was all gone in the blink of an eye.

It made me think of the nightmares I'd had of the Axeman. Seeing the world through his eyes. Knowing how easily any one of us could be changed forever with a single stroke of a blade. Each of us was like a balloon, floating around on the wind, with branches waiting to pop us if a single gust threw us the wrong way.

I knew my thoughts were too dark, but, with the amount of sleep I was running on and the things I'd been through, I couldn't find the energy to get them to go anywhere lighter. I was a person who liked meeting new people. Normally I loved being in the store and interacting with everyone who came in. They all had a story: the man who was running late for his date and so wanted to be out as quickly as possible. The grandmother who had nothing to do at home, so she'd love to spend as much time talking as she could. Tourists from faraway places. Sailors on leave for one day in the city.

Maybe it was the masks that made me stop caring. Maybe it was the lack of sleep. Maybe it was the worries. Maybe it was Papa. It was probably a mixture of all of them, but, whatever the cause, the love for the job wasn't with me today. I didn't enjoy the work—I endured it. And no matter how hard I tried, I still caught myself glancing over my shoulder now and then, convinced I was being watched. It wasn't just the low note playing in the back of my head. It was the hairs standing up on my neck. The itch between my shoulder blades.

The police stayed throughout the day, switching off in shifts every few hours. Etta came by to check on us and let me know how Mama was doing. More of the same, but at least she hadn't gotten worse. That had to mean something good, didn't it?

The policemen told Etta about my behavior in the morning, and she insisted I explain to her all about the feeling I had experienced. Instead of dismissing me as everyone else had done, she accompanied me around the house again, asking if the sound was still there, and if it got stronger or weaker in any place. She had a powerful flashlight, and she used it to inspect the attic and the crawlspace alike.

"I'm just too tired," I told her after all of that.

"Justifiably so," she said, taking one last look under the back porch, running her finger along the line where the latticework was screwed into the house. "But feelings matter, even when you're tired. When something feels off, it's usually because it is. Stay sharp. Maybe he's at one of the neighbors' houses."

With that in mind, she sent patrolmen up and down the block, knocking on doors and asking if anyone had seen anything suspicious. Other than some grumbles about a certain young woman who had screamed bloody murder in the middle of the night, no one had seen anything.

Somehow we made it to the Closed sign again.

At that point, it was time to check through the house once more. The locks were set, the shutters tight. The boards I'd hammered across all the windows were still in place. No one could have gotten in by any way other than the front or back door, and those had been watched the entire time. Everything was ready for another night of absence.

A woman's shriek cut through the air fifty feet south of us, in the direction of the Fontenot's. At first I stared dully in that direction, wondering what all the commotion was. But then Etta called out to the police, and an army of men were swarming toward where the cries were coming from. Someone pulled me into my house. I got a glimpse of a policeman's dirt-covered jacket sleeve and heard the man yell at Enzo to come inside with us.

Then I was standing in the main room of my store, listening as the policeman dragged my table in front of the kitchen door even as Enzo did the same for the front door. My head spun with confusion. "Is it him?" I asked, not sure anyone would answer.

"I don't know," Enzo said. "But it's better to be safe, isn't it?"

That didn't feel right. I didn't want to be cowering inside while everyone else was out fighting the devil. But I was so worn down, it was all I could do to keep standing. In fact, as soon as I thought that, I gave up even that much will, sliding to the floor and just hoping it would be over soon.

I stared over at the kitchen, watching the policeman as he peered out through the slats in the window shutters. It was dark without the lights on, but, even from here, his uniform looked wrinkled and ill-fitting. Etta had been pushing everyone hard, it seemed.

"What's going on?" I asked.

"Something at the neighbors'," he answered. "Somebody found something or someone. I can't tell. You stay there."

My head was pounding, that low note even stronger now. Maybe the Axeman had finally snapped and attacked before he could get to me. Or maybe I was hallucinating everything. Enzo went into the kitchen and stood next to the policeman, doing his best to look out as well. "They're pulling out a body."

In the distance, sirens began to wail. "Is it him?" I asked.

"From what I can see, the person is naked," Enzo said. "A man, though."

The policeman reached over onto the kitchen table and picked up the hand axe that had been lying there. Had I put it there after I explored the house this morning? Just another example of me being useless. At least Etta had come on the scene to show me how a real manhunt was done. I'd wasted my time playing psychic, instead.

I never wanted to move again in my life. If I could have had the earth swallow me up that instant, I would have jumped at the chance.

The policeman stepped behind Enzo and raised the axe into the air, revealing, for a moment, a large scar on his right wrist. I gasped when I saw it, and Enzo turned just in time to see the blow coming down. He dodged to the left, and the axe sunk into the space between his neck and shoulder.

Enzo barreled forward into his attacker, slamming the two of them into the kitchen floor.

I scrambled to my feet, my head spinning from excitement and exhaustion, but eager to do what I could to help.

Enzo was using every ounce of his weight and fury to fight back. The two of them thrashed on the ground, trading punches as I looked for a way to join in without hurting Enzo. I couldn't see the wound the Axeman had already landed on Enzo with the first blow, but plenty of blood was pouring out of it, painting the floor and their clothes a bright red. Enzo managed to grab the Axeman by the face and slammed it into the floor. The demon bit back, but Enzo's hands were gone before his teeth found purchase.

I lunged out with my foot, landing two kicks on the Axeman's back before the two of them rolled into my legs, sweeping my feet out from under me. I fell on top of them, and for a few seconds it was impossible to tell who was who. I tried to punch back with my left hand, but it got tangled in a chair leg and the blow fell short. Enzo, meanwhile, was above me and almost punched my face before he realized who he was aiming at.

The Axeman didn't have to worry about those distractions. Anyone he could hit was an enemy. I put my left hand down to give myself a better angle to fight back, and something bright and glinting flashed before my eyes, *thunking* heavily into the wooden floorboards by my hand. It was only when I spared it a quick glance that I realized it had met my hand first.

When the Axeman pulled the blade free, my left pinkie rolled across the floor, blood flowing from my hand.

I gasped in shock, everything else disappearing from around me as I stared at that finger lying on the floor. My hands were my world. I'd never even imagined they might be taken from me. That playing the piano would—

The Axeman punched me in the face with his free hand, sending me tumbling. When I had my wits about me—what ones I could quickly gather—Enzo was back on top of the Axeman, holding his arm across the demon's neck to cut off his air.

The Axeman thrust upward with his left hand, his fingers digging into Enzo's face and rooting toward his eyes. Enzo screamed in pain and thrashed his head back and forth, the action losing him purchase on the Axeman, who wriggled out of the chokehold.

Enzo managed to get the fiend's hand off his face, but it only dropped down to his shoulder where it probed at the wound the Axeman had made earlier, finding it and digging into the flesh, opening it and tearing at the skin.

Enzo cried in pain and horror and moved back. The Axeman used the opportunity to shove him backward, trying to flip the situation so he was in control. They ended up struggling back and forth again, but it did give me what I thought was another opening to strike at the demon's unprotected head. One hard club over his ear, and he wouldn't be doing anything anymore.

As I moved in for the blow, the Axeman twisted over so he was looming over Enzo, then swung the axe down in two quick chops. The first hit my friend, a glancing blow on the right side of his face, slicing into his scalp and running through to cut off part of his cheek and his ear. The second one missed with the edge but hit Enzo full-on with the flat of the blade, right on his forehead.

Enzo's eyes rolled up, and his body went limp. He was unconscious... or dead.

CHAPTER TWENTY

My opinion is based on experience and a study of criminology. Students of crime have established that a criminal of the dual personality type may be a respectable, law-abiding citizen when his normal self. Then suddenly the impulse to kill comes upon him, and he must obey it. It has been further proved that such unfortunates remain normal for months, even years, without being seized with the affliction. The axman of [seven] years ago, after being normal all these years, might have broken out again.

———

I STOOD MOTIONLESS, NOT WANTING TO believe what I'd just seen. The Axeman glanced up at me, his eyes wide with excitement, a trace of a smile peeking out the edges of his mouth.

Enzo was going to wake up any second. He was just knocked out, right? Why hadn't I done something more to help? Why had I just *stood there*?

And why was I still standing there staring at him?

"Just you and me," the Axeman said as he stood.

I turned and ran from the kitchen, my mind racing for someplace I could go that would be safe. I'd already nailed all the windows shut, and there was the huge display case in front of the door. There was no way I'd be able to move it in time. I could hear him behind me, straightening and stretching. It wasn't as if I could dart behind the counter—he'd know right where I was.

So I hurried around the corner and over to my bedroom. At least I'd be out of his sight for a moment. I slammed the door behind me, then glanced around the room for something I could block it with. Light streamed in through the slats in the shutters, casting the room half in shadow.

Nothing would work. The door didn't even have a lock on it, and, even if it did, he had an axe to break it down. When I'd put boards on the windows, I'd nailed them to the shutters. There was no way those were opening, and outside still brought in the noise of sirens and shouts. A manhunt was on for the monster chasing me, but no one would think to find him here.

There had to be something I could do. Anything.

I lunged for my parents' bed and hauled it backward, the legs groaning against the floor in protest. It wouldn't hold him more than a few seconds, but a few seconds were better than nothing. I rushed to the sheet that divided the room and straightened it out. When I'd come in here the first time to search earlier in the day, my eyes had gone straight for the sheet. It was the only place anyone could hope to hide.

He'd slam the door open hard enough to move the bed, and then he'd go right for my sleeping area.

I ducked under my parents bed, praying he wouldn't think I'd hide beneath the very thing I was using to bar the door. When he rushed past me, I could roll out into the hallway and then…at least be alive for a few more seconds. Maybe Etta would send someone to check on us. Maybe I could get a weapon. Maybe I could—

His voice came from outside, muffled by the door. "It took me a while to figure out what was happening. I worried I was going mad, at first, even though I'd always prided myself on my mind. The papers, the police, they all wanted to think I was some madman, and I would have hated to prove them right."

He sounded so relaxed, as if we were chatting over drinks in the park. The floorboards were cool against my chin and palms. Did I have enough time to try something else? If I moved now, he might hear me and guess what I was trying. I stayed silent.

"It was the dreams that gave you away. Silly dreams about things I never cared about. Jazz, and your family, and that idiot of a friend. I've never liked you people before, so why would my brain imagine I was one of you, night after night? I would dread falling asleep. It felt like I had to take a bath after each dream. Anything to take the stink off. But then I *felt* you in the middle of the attack that night, and you even came after me. I always knew there was more to the world than he'd told me, but I never thought I'd get a chance to..."

He trailed off, and something hard banged into the door. The axe? Not hard enough to split wood. What was he doing?

"I walked home that night, stunned. We were connected, but how? Why? Did you make a deal with him as well? Were you given powers, too? But that didn't make sense. I was at a loss until it hit me. Creatures like you don't get access to those sort of gifts, but you could steal them. I've dropped more than a few coins over the years. If you'd picked one of those up, then you and I might be linked."

The *coin*? All of this was because I'd picked up that silver coin all those years ago? I didn't want to believe it, except the visions had gotten stronger when I'd found the second coin. Could it be true? It didn't matter. I couldn't let myself be distracted by him. He kept talking.

"Once I knew they weren't just dreams, but a window into your life, I wanted to see more. I wondered what it would be like to see an attack through your eyes. My mind filled with possibilities, and then you got sick, and I discovered it wasn't just the thoughts that transferred over. I experienced some of the same symptoms as you. The fever. The cough. The sleepless nights. For a while, I forgot who I was and what I was doing.

"This made things even more complicated, of course. Because, if that's what the influenza does to me when you catch it, what would killing you do? Would I feel it right up until your soul was his, and then I'd snap back to myself? Or would I die with you? I'm still not sure, and I don't know which excites me more. One way or the other, I'm going to find out."

Running in here had been a mistake. The store had tools I could have used as weapons. A pickaxe. A maul. Even a shovel would have been better than the nothing I had right now. Was that all I was when I was in real trouble? A brainless girl who flitted away to hide under a bed?

My muscles were sore, my shoulders bruised, and my breathing sporadic. My head felt like I'd been on a merry go round for an hour. My hand throbbed from where he'd chopped into it. How fast was I bleeding? Would I faint?

"If I could," he continued, "I'd let this go on for an hour. This close, it's almost as if I can feel what you're thinking. Do you hear it? The thrum in the air when we're together like this? I think we probably have at least ten more minutes before they settle down enough to realize whose body it was they found out there. I did a number on his face, but, eventually, it'll dawn on them that they're down a policeman. But, in this uniform, I'll be able to run away in the confusion, and you'll be dead, just like your friend."

He turned the doorknob, trying to open it. The door stopped on the bed, and he laughed. He took a step back, then lunged forward, slamming the door into the bed more strongly than I thought possible. The whole thing slid two feet across the floor, and I had to roll twice to stay beneath it. Had he glimpsed me? I could picture him leaning down, peering under the bed and smiling at me as he lunged in to pull me out by my hair.

But he didn't. He walked in. "I like it like this, even if it's different. It's like unwrapping a present. But, sooner or later, you need to see the surprise." He whisked the curtain back, and I used that moment to hurry out from beneath the bed. It made more noise than I'd planned. As I ran through the door, I caught him turning out of the corner of my eye. Something whipped through the air and *thunked* into the doorframe I'd just left.

It wasn't until I was in the middle of the store that I realized that must have been his axe. He'd missed, and I could have taken it from him right then.

No time to keep second-guessing myself. I went straight to the tools and picked up the shovel, my hand throbbing and my grip awkward. The shovel had a long enough handle to give me some reach, and it was lighter than the maul and pickaxe. My one hope was being able to hit him in the head while he was still too far away to do any real damage to me. Maybe he'd throw the axe again, and I could bat it out of the air and fight back.

And maybe la Fata Turchina would grant me superpowers while I was at it.

The Axeman strode into the room, head high, eyes bright. The shutters let in enough light to cast the room in the same dusky aura that had been in the bedroom, as if I was already halfway to the grave. The walls of the store pressed in around me, the shelves feeling like they were about to fall in, the baskets overhead waiting to catch in my hair. I had huddled against the canned beans section, furious at my situation, and ashamed for being caught in it. Was this a game to him? If he wanted me screaming and crying and running in fear, I could at least deny him that. Though I still scrambled to think of a way I could turn this to my advantage. I already knew he was stronger than me from my earlier struggle with him.

"Who would have thought, all these years later, you and I would be back together like this?" The axe hung loose in his hand, and he cracked his neck.

"Why are you doing this?" I asked him, taking a firmer grip on my shovel. Every second I kept him talking instead of attacking was another chance of something else happening. Etta coming back. Enzo miraculously waking up. God striking this devil dead.

He grinned. "No time to chat about it, I'm afraid." He stepped forward, and I lost my patience, moving in to swing at his head with the shovel. He leaned back, and the blow fell short by a foot, leaving me exposed. The Axeman feinted with his weapon, and I shrieked. His smile grew wider.

All at once, I realized what I was doing was completely backward. What was I thinking, standing here trying to take on this man on his own terms? Enzo had done the same thing only minutes before, and what good had that done for him? It was foolish to think I might have better luck than my friend.

But something else clicked in my head as well. As the Axeman taunted me, I saw the one advantage I did have. We were in my home. The store I'd stocked and tended for as long as I could remember. Yes, there were shovels and mauls and pickaxes, but there were also cans and baskets and razors and any number of things I might use against him. Each of them noted, counted, and double-checked they were in their proper place.

Thank you, Papa.

I backed up three steps and swung the shovel up and to my right. The Axeman darted clear again, thinking I was going to aim for him once more. But I didn't need to hit a moving target. I just had to snap through the line we hung the baskets from. The shovel snagged on it for a moment, then ripped its end from the wall, sending seven baskets tumbling down around the Axeman.

It startled him, and I used the distraction to head back to the cans, throwing one after the other at the Axeman's head. I might not have had the best aim, but I knew I had a good arm. How couldn't I, after moving produce and shipments around day after day?

The Axeman held up his hands to shield his head. One can hit his right forearm, and another sailed past him to crash into a candy jar, sending peppermints and glass shattering to the floor.

I sidled along the wall, knowing, without looking, I was in the spice section. Fourth shelf up, two to the right: ground red pepper. I hurled the shovel at the demon. It was the wrong weapon for me anyway, but at least it could serve as another distraction. As he dodged to the side, I grabbed one of the tins of pepper and ripped it open. When I was five, I'd gotten a few grains of it in my eyes by accident. I'd cried for almost a half hour.

While the Axeman was still recovering from the shovel, I rushed in, grabbed as much of the pepper in my right hand as I could, and threw it into the air at his head. It flew out in a wide spray, and I backed up as soon as I'd let go. He looked up to see what was coming, and the pepper hit him squarely in the face. The Axeman cried out, rubbing at his eyes, all thoughts of his prey forgotten for the moment. He would have been hard-pressed to remember a charging bull was after him right then.

So I took another handful of the powder, stepped in again, and shoved it right in his face, aiming for his eyes and then grinding it in as best I could before I darted back again.

He couldn't hit me with the axe if he couldn't see me.

But, in my haste, I must have gotten some in my own eyes as well. They burned and teared, not enough to blind me, but enough to make things difficult. I rubbed at them with my left hand—the one that hadn't held the pepper—but it was still hard to see. Then again, some things you didn't need to see to be able to know.

I felt behind me for the shelves, then held on to one of the cans I found there. Square sardine tins: ten feet from the door. That was all I needed to see the room in my mind. In front of me the Axeman thrashed from side to side, cursing and screaming in pain. I threw a few more cans in his direction, just in case, then kept moving along the wall, using my hands to guide me. Two more shelves, and then it was the corner. Turn to the right, and another four shelves would bring me to the register area.

If we still had any from the afternoon's shipment, milk bottles would be right... *There!*

Three of them held empties, but the fourth was full. I picked it up and poured it into my face, blinking my eyes rapidly to clear them, just as Mama had tried to make me do all those years ago.

It worked, reducing the pain and letting me see a bit more easily.

Just in time for the Axeman to barrel into me from my left.

I hadn't realized he'd grown quiet, listening for my movement and then rushing toward me. He careened into the counter, but he hit it at an angle, which let him slide forward after he'd slammed into it. He lunged, swiping at the air with his axe as I backed away from each blow, thankful I could see better. Something caught at my feet, and I tripped, sliding into the counter myself. That brief blunder was all it took for the Axeman to catch up to me.

He threw his arms around me, crushing me and landing blows into my back. I tried to knee him between the legs, and I connected on the second effort. He howled and bowled over, inadvertently slamming his forehead into my nose on his way down. My entire face erupted in pain, and the room swam in front of me.

Then his hand was around my throat, the axe swinging back for a clear strike at my face. I groped around on the counter for anything I could use as a weapon. My hand hit the register, and then the spindle we kept for the bills. For a moment, my heart leapt as I grabbed it and tried to pull it free and jab it into the Axeman's face, but Papa had done too good of a job fixing it to the counter-top. I might as well have tried to pick up the register one-handed.

If I did nothing, I was dead. Finished.

He'd said we were connected. He'd gotten sick when I'd gotten sick. I'd felt the pepper in my eyes when he'd gotten it in his eyes.

When all you have is one last chance, you take whatever you can get. Even if it felt like I was sacrificing the piano forever.

I let go of the spindle, spread my hand wide, and slammed it down onto the spike as hard as I could. My hand slapped against the table, and for a moment I thought I'd missed. Then the Axeman hissed in pain, and I saw the spindle sticking straight up through the back of my hand.

But he hadn't dropped the axe like I'd hoped he might, and he brought it slashing up over his head and forward, straight for my shoulder. I twisted out of the way and pulled back against my pierced hand. The spindle ripped a jagged path through my hand, running between the bones and coming free in the space of my middle and ring finger.

I gasped in shock, frozen by the sight of my hand torn apart, blood flowing from the open wound, spilling onto the counter faster than I would have thought possible.

But through my shock came the unmistakable sound of an axehead hitting the floor.

I turned off the rest of my mind. Ignored the pain and the blood, and rushed straight at the Axeman, barreling into him as hard as I could. He brought an elbow down on my back again, but my momentum carried me forward and bowled him over. We fell to the floor with me on top of him.

I kicked and punched and bit and scratched at anything I could hit. But my right hand was useless, and his was only hurting mentally, not physically. It wouldn't take long before he'd be able to regain control of the situation. I had to do something now, before my one window closed forever.

He struck me in the side of my head. My vision went blurry, and the room spun. I was going to lose. After all of this, I'd become another bloodstain on the floor, and he'd move on to the next family and the next.

With my left hand, I fumbled around for where I thought I'd heard the axe fall to the floor. If I could get that, I might at least do some damage before I fainted. The thought flashed through my mind: if our minds were really connected, what would a killing blow to him do to me? But I was beyond caring at this point. I would die if I did nothing, so, if I could kill him on my way out, that would be worth anything.

My hand hit something smooth and heavy, sending it skittering off farther across the floor. I lunged after it, giving away any potential advantage I'd had in positioning. None of it had been helping anyway. The Axeman clubbed at my back with his fists again, then grabbed me by my hair, pulling back hard on my head and twisting my neck around.

But not before I'd gotten hold of the axe handle.

I leaned into the pull, using the extra momentum to crash into his face and stun him for a moment. The light through the shutters cast crooked shadows in the store, and I caught a glimpse of the Axeman's face twisted in fury.

Right before I swung the axe as hard as I could into his left temple. As soon as it connected, my head exploded in agony, and the world went dark.

CHAPTER TWENTY-ONE

No civilized community can afford to tolerate such crimes,
and the officials will be derelict in their duty and warrant
some fears as to their detective ability if they fail to unravel
the mystery surrounding these cases.

———————

SOUND WAS THE FIRST THING that returned to me. Voices as if
someone was talking to me while I was underwater. Footsteps
echoing down a tiled corridor. A door opening and closing. For the
first long while, it felt like I was nothing more than a pair of ears. I
couldn't sense my body, couldn't open my eyes, couldn't even smell
anything around me.

The voices gradually became clearer, and, as they did, I began
to sense the passing of time itself. Somehow I went from being
content to do nothing but exist and listen to the world around me,
to wanting to somehow be a part of it again. That sense grew slowly,
however, and it really only became focused when I began to recognize who the voices belonged to.

The first few were women. American. French. Talking about patients and schedules and conditions. *Nurses*, the thought came to me after the fifth time listening, though even then it was nothing more than a hazy picture of a woman all in white, with some sort of a white hat on her head. Wasn't that something they wore in churches? It was all too fuzzy.

Then another woman's voice came in. Lower than the others, and more assertive. She was arguing with a man. *Doctor* came the thought, and I would have been pleased with myself for making the new connection, but I was more focused on trying to remember where I'd heard that voice before.

"—leave her here forever, as far as I'm concerned," the woman was saying. "Or is Pinkerton money worth less in New Orleans than everywhere else?"

The doctor answered something about influenza and cases, but my mind was still on one word: Pinkerton. As I focused on it, two things happened. First, I came up with a name. *Etta*. But, second, I had my first sense of something other than noise. My head hurt—a sharp piercing sensation that jolted straight through my right temple. I passed out.

Time went by, and at some point I was listening to voices again. Two women's, though, this time, I didn't need to focus until it hurt, because I'd have recognized those voices anywhere. Mama, yelling at the staff that they wouldn't let her stay, and Signora Caravaggio sounding healthy again, backing her up. I wanted to call out, to tell them I was fine, and to ask for a hug, but my body wouldn't move. The argument broke off all at once.

"You see that?" Mama asked. "Her hand twitched. You saw that, didn't you?"

My attention swirled away again, but, this time, it felt more like I was falling asleep than losing total consciousness. A dreamless sleep for which I was more grateful than words could express. When I came back, my memories came with me. The fight in my store. The Axeman's wide eyes the moment before the blow connected. Mama. Etta.

When my eyes fluttered open, the first thing I saw was a white ceiling. My throat was dry, and my head still hurt. I wanted to spring out of bed and run to find someone—anyone—to tell me what was going on. But moving was beyond me. My joints felt stiff, as if they'd rusted shut sometime in the past. It was all I could do to blink and try to look around the room as best I could without moving my head.

There were flowers on a table to my left, and a window to my right. It was bright outside. Blue sky with fluffy white clouds floating over a sea of buildings. As I stared at them, I began to recognize the skyline. I was facing south, which meant the Mississippi would be in view if I were higher up. Off to my left would be my parents' store. Mama's store now, the thought came immediately. I steered myself away from Papa and the bundle of emotions still there. I couldn't face those yet.

To my right would be Enzo's store. How were his parents? How was he? Was he sorry I'd asked him back into my life?

Actually, this meant that right ahead of me must be the back of the Orpheum Theater. It seemed like a year ago now that Enzo and I had gone there. How long had I been unconscious? Had it been days? Months? I had no way of knowing.

My hand was wrapped in bandages. The memory of my severed pinky flashed through my head again. The wreckage of my right hand, torn apart, along with my ability to play the piano…

Footsteps came behind me, and only then did I realize sometime during my window gaze, I'd managed to move my head so I could look out the window more easily. I turned the other way, my muscles protesting but making the movement without. I wasn't sure who I expected: a nurse, a doctor, Mama, Enzo, the police? But, instead, it was Etta, smiling at me through that jagged scar on her cheek.

"You're still here," I said, stating the obvious but still surprised. "I thought for sure you'd…"

"After abandoning you in the middle of everything? I had to stay to make sure everything that could be done *was* done for you."

"What happened?"

"Shoddy detective work is what. The Axeman was at your store the entire day, it seems. He'd found a space to hide underneath the back steps. At some point he killed one of the officers and changed clothes, then tossed the body over the fence into the neighbor's yard. They didn't go out back until you were closing the store for the night, and, when they saw it, things became chaotic. The Axeman used the distraction to go inside and, well, you know the rest. When I broke through the door, I found Enzo in the kitchen and you in the main room the floor next to the body of a man in uniform, dead. We rushed you here as fast as we could."

"Is Enzo okay?" I asked.

She nodded. "More or less. He's not as pretty as he once was. He's been in and out of here each evening to check on you, jumping back and forth between his parents' store and yours to make sure everything keeps running as smoothly as possible."

A knot of tension that had been with me for as long as I could remember—probably going back to the first night when the Axeman attacked my family—suddenly disappeared. It was as if I'd been carrying a huge stone in my arms for years, and then someone came along and made that stone vanish.

"He's dead?" I asked. "The Axeman?"

"Dead and buried."

"Who was he?"

"That's a more complicated question. The police aren't exactly eager to shout what happened from the rooftops. They failed the same families twice over a decade, they were unable to protect the Italian American community, and, even at the end, we dropped the ball. So some of it comes down to you. If you want me to push to identify the body, I can. The police are paying more attention to me now than ever. It helps that solving the case makes my superiors at headquarters happier with me. The Pinkertons care more about their image than anything else."

"Why *wouldn't* I want to know who he was?"

Etta licked her lips, then sat down on a chair next to my bed. "Sure. You could push to find it out. If you did that, though, more of the story would get out. Maybe that sounds appealing right now. You'd be able to get some credit for killing a monster of a human being. But, once word like that is out there, you can't get it back. You can't control where it will go, or what people will think about it."

She touched the scar on her cheek for a moment, her eyes focused on something far outside the window. Before I could ask her what she was thinking about, she continued. "Everything has a consequence. It was in self-defense, and we both know that, but you'd be surprised how people change how they approach you once they know you've killed someone. Some people will blame you. Some will say God hates you for what you did. With how so many in this city view Italians on a good day? You'll have some problems that come from people knowing your story.

"So you need to decide now how you want your life to go. If you always want to be the girl who took down the Axeman, or if you'd rather just keep being Gianna Crutti. I can't tell you which one is better or worse, and you don't need to decide right away, but it should be in the next bit, or the choice will be taken from you."

I nodded, thinking over what she'd said. "Do you think it would help?"

"Would what help?"

"Knowing who he was and why he did it?"

She pursed her lips. "Those are two different things. Knowing who he was might give you some idea of why he did it, but I don't think you'll ever really know. Even when they're still alive and you can ask them to their face, you can't make them tell the truth. I'm not sure they all know why they do what they do in the first place. So does it help? No, I don't think it does. There will always be questions, and the answers you get will just send you further down the rabbit hole. Sooner or later, you have to decide for yourself that you won't keep looking. He's already stolen enough from you. The more you focus on him and what he did, the more he gets to steal."

"But we were connected," I said. "How did that happen? He said it was from some coins he had dropped, but that can't be right. Coins?"

Etta considered the question for a moment. "I've been around long enough to know I can't always explain why things happen the way they do. No one can deny there's more to this world than we understand. People like the Axeman come up with reasons to make sense out of what they do. Spend too long listening to them, and you're liable to end up as lost and confused as they are. How were you connected? He attacked your family at a young age. Maybe something happened that night that linked the two of you together in a way we'll never understand. But, again, knowing *how* it started doesn't do anything for *what* you're going to do now."

My head was beginning to hurt again from all the conversation, and Etta must have noticed it. She stood and excused herself, explaining that she had to call Chicago to see what she might be doing next. I let her go, relieved to be alone again, my mind swirling with questions.

I closed my eyes to rest, doing my best to ignore things, for the moment, that I couldn't do anything about. Somehow I fell asleep again, because the next thing I knew, someone was knocking lightly at the door, and it was dark outside.

"Come in," I said.

Enzo ducked in, carrying a small bouquet of pink and purple dahlias. "You're awake?" he asked. "How are you feeling?"

I forced a smile. "Like I'm probably going to get tired of that question soon enough."

He stutter-stepped forward, clearly uncertain about what he was supposed to do. Seeing him so out of sorts was enough to earn a real smile from me.

"Just come in and sit down, would you?" I asked. "This isn't a dance competition."

He sat down without another word, his eyes on the bouquet in his lap. His ear had been wrapped in fresh bandages.

I closed my eyes, doing my best not to sigh or seem impatient. "Enzo," I said.

"Yes?" His eyes stayed glued to the flowers.

"You're not looking at me."

He didn't respond.

"Are you worried those flowers are going to jump out of your hands?"

"It's my fault," he said.

"What?"

He looked at me then, and his eyes were full of worry. Little lines across his forehead. His shoulders tense. "It's my fault he got to you. I was there by the door, and I was supposed to stop him, and I couldn't even—"

"Enzo," I cut him off.

"What?"

"Don't take all the credit. I was the one who hammered all the windows shut and made my own death trap. We both missed it. He attacked you first because he knew you were the bigger threat. He had the whole thing set up to use everything we'd gotten ready against us. So go easy on yourself, okay?"

But the thing with Enzo was, when he thought something hard enough, you had to work four times as hard to convince him differently.

"Look," I said, trying a different approach. "Let's just agree there's plenty of guilt to go around, okay?"

"That's not everything."

I cocked my head to the side, wishing he were making more sense. "What?"

He set the flowers down and walked over to the window, staring out across the city. "I think your fortune-teller was right about me."

It was all I could do not to roll my eyes. Enzo could get so—

"My parents were sick, and I had you work in the store anyway." He turned around, his eyes intense, shoulders squared back, jaw clenched. Classic "Enzo doing something he didn't want to do" behavior.

"What are you talking about?"

"I should have just sent you out to keep you safe, but I…wanted you to be there. I like spending time around you, and I thought, if they just stayed in their room, then you couldn't get sick, even though I knew how much you don't like being around sick people. But then you did get sick, didn't you? And your father died. And Signora Caravaggio said I'd bring your family heartache, and it all clicked together. I ran into her, here in the hospital. She was furious with me, and she was right. It's not just my fault the Axeman got in and attacked us. It's my fault your father died."

A year ago, I might have believed him for half a second. I'd always been so focused on getting readings from Signora and making sure I was living my life just right. She'd been harping on me for over a year before Enzo and I stopped seeing each other. And, with all I'd just experienced, you might have thought I'd be more ready than ever to believe in the supernatural.

But what had all that preparation and concern really gotten me?

DON'T GO TO SLEEP

Had I felt any more prepared than I would have been otherwise? Did it do anything other than take up my time? Signora had still gotten sick. The Axeman had still attacked me. Papa had still died.

There was a chance the Gianna from a year ago would have yelled at Enzo right then. Gone off like a grenade and dumped all her problems in his lap, even though he already clearly felt terrible about what had happened and even though the thought of that now was preposterous.

But that was me then, and this was me now. There'd been evil inside me, and I saw that now. I'd felt it when I was in the head of that demon. I wasn't a perfect person, but I wanted to be better, and I'd want people to give me the benefit of the doubt just like I gave it to myself.

Enzo had stood there watching me, and I'd let his words hang in between us for too long. He nodded once and started to head out of the room.

"Stop," I said. "Come back."

He turned and faced me, still clearly prepared for the tongue-lashing he expected.

I held out my bandaged left hand to him—my right hurt too much to move—and opened and closed it a couple of times. He eyed it like he thought it might sink fangs into him.

"Would you just come take my hand before I have to snap at you?" I asked at last.

He stumbled forward, tentatively putting his hand in mine. I pulled him toward me as best I could, though I still was far from at my full strength.

"Vincenzo Rissetto, I'm sorry." I looked up into his eyes and tried to show with my expression how serious I was. "I took you for granted for too long. Treated you like—like—like a carpet. A nice rug, maybe, but still something there for me to walk on and to make me comfortable. When I said we were through, I tried to pretend it didn't matter, but it did. I missed you more than I wanted to admit. These last few weeks, with you back in my life, it's felt...*right* again. Even with all the terrible things that have happened. You didn't kill Papa. I wandered all over this city in the middle of an influenza. We ran a public store with hundreds of customers every day. I tended to Signora Caravaggio when she looked like death itself."

I gripped his hand tighter, the wound from my pinky protesting. "And as for Signora...Maybe I need to have a talk to her. I always thought it was important to know what the future might bring so I could avoid the worst of it, but, after what we've just been through, I'm not sure you can avoid anything. Knowing the evil was coming didn't let us duck around it, did it? If anything, you could say we walked right into it because of what we knew."

He began to grip my hands back, maybe finally believing I wasn't just leading him up to a last second knife in the back. "I can help, Gia," he said. "With your father gone, and your store, and—I can help."

I squeezed his hand three times in quick succession. "I know. And I intend to hold you to that for a long time."

AUTHOR'S NOTE

The murders and attacks described in this book are based on real life events, though, once again, I took some liberties with the exact details. In real life, the Axeman's attacks were spread out over the course of a year and a half. There's some debate about whether the first round of attacks (1910–1911) were connected to the later ones (1918–1919), but both groups of victims were the same: Italian grocery store owners and their families. No real reason for the attacks was ever discovered, and the culprit remains a mystery. Eyewitnesses gave conflicting descriptions of him, though his MO was typically the same: sneaking in through a hole he'd chisel in the back door, and then using an axe he'd find in the house to do the attack. (Back in the days of wood stoves for cooking, axes were much more common.)

I tried to be as true to history when I could as possible. Many of the murders happened exactly where they happened in the book, and the victims were also true to life. The Maggios, Romanos, and Cortmiglias were all victims in the second round of attacks, and the Cruttis and Rissettos were victims in the first. When the Cortimiglias were attacked, Frank and Iorlando Giodano became the prime suspects, and they were even found guilty of the crime. Iorlando was sentenced to life in prison, and Frank was to hang. A year later (before the hanging took place), Mrs. Cortimiglia admitted she had accused the two out of spite, and they were released from jail.

While the timeline of the attacks was compressed, the timeline of the Spanish Influenza in New Orleans is portrayed as accurately as possible, right down to the specific dates and the responses of the city to the disease. The first wave of influenza hit New Orleans at the end of September 1918, came to a quick peak, and then subsided by the mid-November. (A second round of the disease hit in December and lasted another two months.) All told, the city had 54,089 cases, with 3,489 people dying. New Orleans had the third worst death rate in the nation: 734 out of every 100,000 people there died. (As of November 2021, the worst hit state affected by COVID-19 has been Mississippi, with 343 out of every 100,000 people dying.)

The excerpts at the beginning of each chapter are direct quotes about the case and various events in the city, taken from the New Orleans *Times-Picayune*. The letter from the Axeman is also taken verbatim from a letter that was published on March 13, 1919. Its exact author is disputed; some believe it was nothing more than an advertising gimmick for a new jazz song that was released shortly thereafter.

As I was researching this book, I was surprised by just how many axe murders were happening in that portion of the country around the early 1900s. The Barnabet case and others mentioned by Etta in the text all really happened.

For further reading, I recommend *The Axeman of New Orleans: The True Story* by Miriam C. Davis. She does an excellent job compiling the facts and placing them all in their historical context, from the attitudes of the police at the time to the way Italians were largely viewed in the city.

ACKNOWLEDGMENTS

Writing a novel isn't the easiest thing to do under normal circumstances, and this past year and a half has been anything but normal. In some ways it was therapeutic to be writing about an earlier pandemic, just to remind myself that all pandemics have an end. In any case, I first wanted to thank my wife and children for their support. Sometimes it's been a slog, being stuck at home and balancing life, and I'm very grateful to them for keeping me motivated and moving forward.

Thanks as well to my agent, Eddie Schneider, and all the JABberwocks. Annie Berger, my editor for this book, offered great input and suggestions and really helped me get started off on the right foot. The folks at Sourcebooks have been so supportive, and I really appreciate all their hard work in getting my books out into the wild. My writing group (Courtney Alameda and Brian McClellan) did a fantastic job with critiquing my first draft, which (as usual) was much much worse than the ones to follow. And a big thanks to Joel Cundick, for stepping in with his Italian skillz at the last minute.

A big shout-out to my patrons, because they're awesome: Kevin Angell, Gwen Coltrin, Samantha Cote, Merle Embleton, Phil Hilton, Karol Maybury, Katie O'Donnell, and Theresa Overall.

A tip of the hat goes out to Rachel Cundick, who won my March Madness tournament this past year and got naming rights for a main character. She went with Enzo, and I thought it was a fantastic choice.

And finally, a thanks to all my other family and friends. If there's one thing the last year and a half has taught me, it's that I rely much more on other people than I suspected. I liked to think of myself as an introvert. COVID called my bluff. I'm very grateful for all the listening ears and words of support people have given me. It may not seem like much to you, but it means the world to me.

Think of the list that follows: men and women, young girls and innocent children, blotted out by one monster's hand, and you, my reader, of a tender and delicate nature, will do well to read no further.

———

I WAS SEVENTEEN AND OLD ENOUGH for boys to come calling, even though none of them had, and nothing Mother said could fool me into thinking there was a reason other than the length of my nose and the size of my chin. "Handsome" is about as good a compliment any boy paid me, and that was only when his parents were listening. But I was a hard worker and I knew my way around a farmyard and in a workshop. Father didn't have sons, and Ruby wasn't worth a thing when it came time for work to be done.

The boys hadn't come calling for me, but they more than made up for that by lining up for my younger sister Ruby. She never had a moment's rest at the dance hall, and she'd have been out nightly if Father had permitted her. As it was, she still went out twice as often as she should have.

Father would scream at Ruby each morning, and I imagine she thought she had it pretty rough the way he handled her. However, he was careful to keep his blows to places where no one would notice the bruises—and she was careful to keep those bruises from getting noticed. I wasn't as lucky, but I made sure Ruby never had a chance to see what he did to me.

It's amazing what a family will do to make other families think everything is normal and fine.

But one evening Ruby came into the room when I would have sworn she was already on her way into town. I was in the middle of changing for the night, and there was Ruby barging in through the door, all breathless and hurried as she searched for a missing earring she just had to have for the dance.

"Zuretta," she said, breathless from running. "Have you seen my—"

I tried to turn fast enough, but the way she cut off told me I'd failed. Her eyes widened and the blood drained out of her face faster than if her throat had been cut. The two of us stared at each other, neither of us speaking, for a full minute and maybe longer.

"That was Father?" she asked me at last.

"It wasn't Mother."

She nodded. Once, then twice. "There's a lot there," she said. "On your back. How long has he been doing this to you?"

"Long enough," is all I said. I could take the blows, and I wanted things to stay the same between Ruby and me.

Ruby had never been the sort of person who let things be, though. She'd march straight to the store and elbow her way into the front of the line if she thought it was necessary. She didn't wait then, either.

"Come on, Zuretta," she said.

"What?"

"We're going, you and I."

"Where are we going?"

She headed to her dresser. "East. North. West. I don't care. Anywhere but Manti, Utah."

"But Mother—"

"Mother knew what she was getting when she married that man. You and I didn't ask for it."

"But what should we do?"

She rushed over to her dresser and took out a bag and began throwing clothes into it, almost at random. "Anything we want," she said, and then looked up at me as an idea struck her. "Chicago." Her eyes were bright.

"Chicago?" I scrunched a little tighter into my bed.

"The Columbian Exposition. Remember? People have been talking about that for months. We'll go to Chicago. We might even see the Pinkertons!"

"We can't afford a ticket," I said, hoping some reasoning would work with her. "And it'll cost so much to live there."

But Ruby was already packing again. "I'll take some money out of the jar on Father's shelf when we leave, That'll pay for the ticket and when we get to the city, we'll get jobs. Real jobs. Maybe as maids in a fancy hotel. Meet people from around the world. Come on, Zuretta! We'll be free!"

I could see the future with Ruby there, just for a moment. Expensive rooms and swaying train cars. *Free.*

But Mother cried out in the room next to ours, and it all came crashing down. "I can't," I told Ruby. "She needs my help. *Our* help."

Ruby licked her lips, thinking. Then she shook her head. "Not from me, Zuretta. I'm sorry, but no more. We all have our agency. God gave it to us to make our minds up. I'm getting out of here now. Tonight. You can come with me, or you can stay here and get beaten whenever Father pleases. I know the choice I'm making."

And I could see that she did. But I knew my choice as well. I thought it was the right one. The sensible one. I said goodbye to Ruby that night.

I never saw her at home again.

ABOUT THE AUTHOR

Bryce Moore is a librarian in western Maine. When he's not up to his nose in library work, he's watching movies, playing board games, and paying ridiculous amounts of money feeding his Magic the Gathering addiction. Visit him online at brycemoore.com.

#getbooklit

Your hub for the hottest young adult books!

Visit us online and sign up for our
newsletter at FIREreads.com

 @sourcebooksfire

 sourcebooksfire

 firereads.tumblr.com